Heads & Tales

The Other Side of the Story

Edited by Chapel Orahamm

Cover Art by David Simon
Illustrations by Chapel Orahamm

First International Paperback Printing: July 2021
First United States Paperback Printing: July 2021

Paperback: ISBN: 978-1-7374002-0-2

For those who need fairy tales to grow on, and want to see the other side of every story.

CONTENTS

1 **Asterion and Theseus**   1

Musings   2

Peter Linton

The Minotaur   4

D.S. Levey

Theseus   14

Peter Linton

2 **Sigurd and the Dragon**   28

C. VanDyke & C.D. Storiz

3 **Sleeping Beauty**   54

Once Bitten   56

Debbie Iancu-Haddad

Twice Shy of Truth, Once in Love   64

also known as Rose's Thorn –

Sarah Parker

4 **Goose Bastardly**   76

Wild Fortune   78

Darius Bearguard

Intrepid Hero   90

Mara Lynn Johnstone

5   **The Daughter's Toll**   98

The Tale of the Troll's Heart   100

Imelda Taylor

A Wickedly Powerful Love   108

Sarah Parker

6   **The Herdsman and the Herbalist**   116

The Herdsman   118

Dewi Hargreave

The Herbalist   130

Alex Woodroe

7   **The Giant Battle of the Little Mermaid**   142

Perseus Greenman & Nikki Mitchell

8   **The Wild Hunt**   170

A New Start   172

Renée Gendron

The Wild Hunt   186

David Simon

9 **The Little Peasant of Cransley Manor Boys School** 198

Archie's Story 200

Sean Southerland-Kirby

The Prefect's Story 216

Mickey Hadick

10 **Footprints** 234

Turnabout 236

Rudy Alleyne

The Photo 242

Pan D. MacCauley

11 **Hansel & Gretel** 248

The Kids 250

C. Rathbone

The Witch 264

A.R.K. Horton

12 **Little Red Riding Hood** 276

Craig Vachon & A.Poland

13 **Stardust** 304

Anna Klapdor & Danai Christopoulou

14 **The Depths of Albion**   332

The Right Hand of the King   334

Chris Durston

Cautionary Tales of a Server Closet   346

Chapel Orahamm

The Authors   362

*The purpose of a good education is to show you that
there are three sides to a two-sided story.*

- Stanley Fish

Preface from the Editor

This wild ride came about after quite a few events. First and foremost was being invited to write in a set of three anthologies run by Chris VanDyke, Renée Gendron, and Nikki Mitchell back in 2020. I'm blaming this all on them. Yep. Can't tell me otherwise.

Well, okay, I have to accept some of the blame. I got it in my head that I wanted to see the other side of the story. Someone was mentioning how they liked the concept of reading the villain's point of view. At which point, out of sheer boredom after staring at yet another of my manuscripts, I reached out to Twitter and asked if anyone would want to read two-sided stories. There was actual interest. Which sort of surprised me for some odd reason.

That got me thinking, maybe some people would get together and write an anthology on it. I was hoping someone else would nominate themselves to host it. I let myself get ahead of myself though, and somehow volunteered to do the thing. I just wanted to write a shared story with someone and explore a few different viewpoints. I promise. That was all I had intentions of doing.

Then I invited people to come in and do

this. And people came in. I'm still blown away by that fact. The contributions to the stories have been marvellous. Some have been outrageously funny. Some are deep and thoughtful. Some are the openers to a possibly longer adventure.

The authors have been wonderful to work with, and I'm glad they've helped so much in getting this whole thing off the ground by not only providing the text to fill it with, but also help in editing, formatting, getting people information, cover art, everything.

Special thanks to Nikki Mitchell, the co-editor, for helping get the emails and polls up and running and helping me keep this whole ship afloat when I started floundering.

Chapel Orahamm

Foreword

I've been a fantasy nerd for as long as I can remember. I read *The Hobbit* on my own when I was five (my dad was reading it to me at bedtime but not reading fast enough), and I was the kid that came home from Walden Books with a "book that was really a game" and a handful of weird dice to introduce my friends to *Advanced Dungeons & Dragons*. I've spent my entire life steeped in wizards and warriors, in wicked dragons and brave elven warriors. But from a very young age, one aspect of these classic, high-fantasy worlds bothered me, and that was the Goblin Problem. The Goblin Problem is this: in *The Lord of the Rings* (and thus in *D&D* and the countless intellectual heirs Tolkien has spawned), goblins (and their slightly more bad-ass cousins, orcs) are simply and unreservedly evil. When gobins show up, the heroes kill them, no questions asked, because if not the goblins will kill them. In the Battle of Helm's Deep, Legolas and Gimli have a lighthearted, friendly competition as to how many orcs they can kill while defending the Hornburg, joking and teasing one another as the body count rises into the dozens.

We are asked to believe that goblins and orcs forge weapons, wear clothes, build subterranean cities, speak their own language, and do everything the humans, elves, and dwarves do -- yet somehow we don't expect them to have any role other than "to be killed." As if they don't have families somewhere. As if goblin mothers don't nurse their infants or weep when their loved ones fail to return from battle. In countless D&D campaigns, intelligent, sentient creatures -- people, really, by any definition -- populate caves and dungeons, but it seems all they do is hang out in dusty rooms without food or water, without hopes or dreams, and merely wait for some group of heroes to come along and murder them. Our boundless imaginations can picture a necromancer commanding an army of undead to ravage an elvish kingdom, yet we are never asked to imagine a bugbear working on her newest poem. Or an etinn whose deepest desire is to travel and see the sites on the Dragon Coast.

Of course, this myopic view of whose side of the story gets told did not start with Gary Gygax or J.R.R. Tolkien; it reaches at least as far back as the *Epic of Gilgamesh* or *The Iliad* and *The Odyssey*. Odysseus blinds Polyphemus and abandons Circe, yet we root for *him*, as we are reading *his* eponymous tale. They say that history is written by the victors, and for centuries the history of these imaginary realms have been written by warriors and rangers, by the poor farm boys and lost princesses who serve the role of "the heroes." By Beowulf and Sigurd, by Little Red Riding Hood and Snow White. By Sleeping Beauty and Hansel and Gretel and Perseus.

In recent years, however, there has been a growing audience for retellings of well-known stories that flip the classic narrative on its head. *Wicked* and *Maleficent* may be the most well-known, but back in 1983 Marion Zimmer Bradley's now classic *The Mists of Avalon* revisited the masculine Arthur mythos from a female point of view. More recently Tad William's *Calliban's Hour* and Madeline Miller's *The Song of Achilles* and *Circe* both revisited staples of the Western canon to give voice to characters who had long been relegated to voicelessness.

As we all know, there are two sides to every story. The tales in this book set out to make sure that, at long last, both sides are told. Some of these tales are dark, others lightly humorous, but all of them retell a classic story that you most likely know… or thought you did.

C. Vandyke
Founder and President of Skullgate Media
Editor-in-Chief of Tales From the Year Between

Memorandum

To: Lance Eliote
From: Arthur Pendragon
Date: March 7, 3208
Subject: A New Development in Parallel
Universe/Time Travel

I have been absent from board duties for
some time now with good reason.

See me next week in the basement labora
tory. Ask Larry at security for access.

This is going to revolutionize Albion Corp
and make the Grail Key a speck compared
to what we are going to offer the world.

*Plutarch, Mozino, Great - grab everyone
from the office. Londinium is about to get
the best scoop of the millenium!!!*

THE LONDINIUM TRIBUNE

THE FASTEST NEWS ON THE CYBERLINK

VOLUME 5.   CAMELOT, WEDNESDAY MARCH 19, 3208   NO. 1

CARNIVOROUS CREATURE CONTINUES CARNAGE

BY JOSE MARIANO MOZINO

More body parts have been turning up in the Piney Woods. Forest rangers have had to double staff to deal with the number of hunters that have disappeared as well as try to find any human remains that have turned up. Local hunters are saying they're too afraid to camp overnight lately and there are rumors that the woods are being stalked by one of North America's most infamous legends: Bigfoot.

TREASURE OR MENACE?

BY GRIMM

A young man discovers a goose with golden feathers, but is the goose what he seems? Luck, shenanigans, and feathery scheming are afoot.

DRAGON SIGHTED IN CAVE, MAY HAVE STOLEN DWARVEN TREASURE

BY WILLIAM MORRIS

THE END OF ALBION CORP.?

BY GEOFFREY MONMOUTH

With Elaine Corbenic suing against Albion Corp and Arthur Pendragon for infringement of Rights of Personhood in the creation of Gyndroid Gwen, will the corporation be able to remain standing after reporters found a teleportation device called Arthur's Chair last week? Regardless, it has made for some great coverage this week.

WAR IS HELL - LITERALLY!

BY THEODORIC GREAT

Fort Detroit, August 16, 1812. American soldiers, Canadian irregulars, and British forces clash over Detroit and the Devil comes to call, unleashing the Hounds of Hell.

WAS THE MINOTAUR A MONSTER?

BY PLUTARCH

Demigod or Monster? Three newly found scrolls might hold the key to th Bull-man. What became of Ariadne'

It appears a reporter and their cohorts have gotten it in their heads to use Arthur's Seat to parallel universe and time travel jump for a bit of interesting news to help out their newspaper. What follows is their chaos.

Heads and Tales

based on

Theseus

Plutarch

Asterion and Theseus

Peter J. Linton & D.S. Levey

1

Asterion and Theseus

Peter J. Linton & D.S. Levey

Musings

Peter Linton

Why when this span might be fleeting as a laurel, tawny before luscious grass bordered by sheer and clean stone brindled and streaked by stains and clinging ivy, smile in a breeze or sting from a rain? It's as vines seek to reclaim all land, eager to expand their own dominion, demanding fate. Oh, why have I, thought bound, shun destiny and at once yearn for it? Thus I sit, contemplating my home.

Pathways between the marble slabs beckon one to explore further these virgin wanderers to lost and fruitless ends. How many have I rescued? How many fled?

Rows of flowers aside the boundaries. Some call them weeds, but to me they are the purest yellow rosette and globular heads of downy tufts. One blow and they drift free, but they remain and pepper the floor of my prison.

The pond centers this pathway of walls, built no doubt for me, not the paradise for frogs and fish it truly is. A pond!

The biggest eye catch of the labyrinthian garden. Flowers I love, as are the walls and climbing green, but nothing routs the majesty of the pond.

My tiered bower stands beside, offering a tranquil rest. For indeed, inside lay another slab, topped by rough bolsters and weathered rugs. On clear nights I lie, listening to sounds, thinking of my namesake: the starry sky. Who is more patient, they or I, waiting here. For chance or fate has me the impossible hope.

So say I, Asterion, Minotaur, Monster of Minos.

Perspective 1: The Minotaur

D.S. Levey

The world is vast.

Being "raised" on a little island, I had no knowledge of just how immense, however. And yet, ironically, my own existence was well known to so many. Or at least as much of my existence as some dared to whisper. They have even named me; in an epitaph as inaccurate as it is unimaginative: "Minotaur." "Minos' Bull" they call me. I am as much "his" as the throne of Atlantis. Yet, such is the moniker the world bestowed upon me. Now, the opportunity to tell the world my own story is here; if they are curious enough to listen.

My first memories are of my beautiful sister, Ariadne, and the love in her eyes as we would play, whether with her handmade clay dolls, or, as I got older, the ball game episkyros, or tug of war, or any of a number of others. One thing was always there: the light of love in my sister's eyes.

She was four summers older than me, and took a motherly joy in assisting with my upbringing in as much as she could. The eternal love that shone from her was the only love I knew. Without that light to guide me, I would doubtless become the monster that the world believes me to be.

I saw the fear and loathing on the faces of all others who came near. I had done nothing to deserve this, and yet, my mere existence frightened them. In hindsight, I am surprised it took as long as it did for that wretch Minos to conceive of the doom he planned for me. I was eight years old when it happened.

In his hatred of me, Minos refused to treat me as a boy to become a man, but rather a pest he could not be rid of. This may be understandable due to my unique heritage, but as a child, I only knew I was devoid of love except for my sister. Even my own mother, the queen, had little affection for me.

The queen, Minos' wife, was seduced by Poseidon, a coupling where I was the result. In my mother's womb, Minos held out hope that I was his own, even after he learned of her infidelity. Needless to say, when I emerged with the head of a bull, all doubt was removed. I believe I was born with this unusual feature specifically so Minos could not claim me when I came into my manhood.

To make matters worse, Minos' father Zeus, my uncle, held a contentious relationship with my father. Yet, I was the son of a god, what could Minos do? He forbade my learning, and ensured that anyone who might take pity upon me was never allowed near. That wasn't difficult, I'm sure, as I was seen across the Island as a monstrous bastard. Thus, a lie! A story, which slightly salvaged his reputation, representing my own conception in as undignified a way as possible.

My beloved sister, and those she bullied into joining her, were the only ones to spend time with me. When I was eight years old, Ariadne was caught by a tutor teaching me arithmetic. He seized her. An anger rose in me I had never felt before. I grabbed the tutor, and threw him bodily across the room. I meant only to protect my sister, but Clotho, the Fate who spins our destinies, intervened. The man hit the parapet of our balcony and tumbled over. His neck shattered when he hit the ground, and the fate of myself, and the island, was inexorably changed.

Minos heard the news of the accident with glee. He ordered me kept under guard and bade the greatest inventor of all time build a giant labyrinth to be my eternal prison. While he dared not kill me, he had been given the opportunity to imprison me with "righteous" justice.

The king ordered that I have a place to sleep, water to drink, and even a view of the heavens within my confines. Let it not be said he was inconsiderate. It took the master craftsman two years to complete my subterranean demesne.

Those two years I continued to grow, physically and mentally. I had been afraid the outburst which led to my incarceration would scare my sister away from me. But no, she knew why I had acted and that it was an accident. She even pleaded with her father against my sentence until he threatened her.

Nonetheless, she never gave up on me. She found a secret way into my chamber wherein she taught me all that she herself was learning. When lessons were complete, we would gaze out at the stars and look up at Orion with his faithful hounds; the scorpion that had killed him forever chasing him throughout the night sky.

Those days were too few. One evening, whilst pondering the heavens and my future, she begged me to run. I told her I could never leave the island without her.

The next day, when Aurora rose to signal the morn, a platoon of guards entered my room. It was time. My prison was ready. I was barely able to grab the only personal thing near at hand: a small leather doll Ariadne had made. I hid it in my breeches before being hauled out by the guard captain and his many men. (I was ten years old, but physically akin to the guards in height, and already surpassing all but the most muscular of them in strength.)

I begged them to let me say goodbye to Ariadne, but their cruel laughter showed neither mercy nor understanding. And so, realizing the futility, I decided that no good would come by fighting and I went silently with them to my new "home."

The king stood near the entrance, a sneer on his face. More guards stood by. He was afraid that I would not go quietly. I was determined to prove him wrong.

"You are a disgrace," he shouted, spittle running down his chin. "Notice that when MY father, almighty Zeus breeds sons, they are iroikós, HEROES! You, on the other hand, you are a MONSTER! I won't kill you. That is for the gods to declare. I am merely an instrument. They deal justly with murder, as do I. But I am not a monster. At the center Daedalus has constructed a pool and a gazebo for you to live out your days. I have already ordered a large number of rats to be thrown in with you. If you are as smart as your sister seems to think, then you will not be lacking in sustenance."

He laughed, but I knew his purpose: monster I was in their eyes, and so as a monster I would live. I made my way towards the entrance, determined to get this disgusting scene behind me. As I squeezed through the narrow entrance, Minos gloated. "You should know that if you ever come through this entryway again you will be executed, after I cut the hands off your sister. That should be enough to keep you from trying something foolish."

I growled, but kept my composure.

"I know you are trying to be brave. I assure you, you are impressing no one." He spat this out like so many words before. I saw through him though. His hate was as palpable as his fear.

"No matter your actions," he continued, his grin growing more sinister. "Ariadne will hear a full account of your blubbering like a baby and asking to be killed instead. She will believe that

8

my mercy alone stayed your death and she will be grateful I spared your life. Then perhaps she will become the obedient daughter she should be."

I knew he was goading me, but something had to be done. They had already decided I would live as an animal. I obliged them. Instead of attacking him head on I sank to my knees, feigning despair. His guard was down, goading me, but I suddenly bit him on the calf. Before any retaliation, I leapt up, and raced down into the maze. His howl still fills me with warmth.

I gave no thought to which way I went. It was a maze after all. To try and keep my bearings would be madness; and would lead to such quickly enough. There was neither rhyme nor reason to any of this impenetrable construct. Tunnels made of beautiful marble gave way to plain stone. Other walls were filled with whorls and geometric designs that tantalized the eye. Torches there were, but few. Most tunnels had something like a torch, yet no flame emanated. Pathways of rough dirt gave way to cobbled stone and then back to dirt. The walls were ever changing from mirrors to dull or colored slabs. All of this with never a clue as to which way to go. I could not keep count of the days before I discovered the smell of water. My bovine senses honed in on it. A few more turns and I discovered the center of the maze.

As promised, a small gazebo lay near one edge of a large pool. Water lilies and hyacinths ringed the edge of the pondlike structure. To see the sun again was a joy I could not describe; and to realize I had a few amenities gave me hope. I settled into a routine. I discovered more than rats lived here. Birds made nests at the top of hedges, and I let them be so I could enjoy their company through my exile.

Despite the king's wishes, I did not spend my days hunting for rats to sustain myself. For a time anyway, I was able to live as a normal bull: upon the grass that grew upon the sunlit bit of land that was my new home

My loneliness soon ended in the most surprising way.

Dozing one afternoon, I heard cries and voices coming from a variety of directions. Eventually, two young men found their way to the eye of what I had come to consider *my* maze.

I tried to speak with them, but they screamed and raced back into the labyrinth below.

Then, three girls came upon me from a different exit. I kept my distance from them--I didn't wish to scare them. They huddled in a corner until one approached tentatively.

"If I give myself up willingly, would you spare my two friends? I cannot bear to think of my friends, who are as sisters to me, being eaten."

What did they think I would do? A meal? Amazed at her words and loyalty, not to mention bravery, I recovered.

"I have no intention of eating you," I stated. "Let alone harming one such as you--so long as you do not strike first. Now, tell me how you have come to this place."

Then another of Minos' lies came through. He had decided to use me as a sort of ogre against Athens-- ever a thorn in his side. His depravity led him to gather their youths and send them to me for sacrifice. And I would cannibalize them! Whether true or not, he knew they would die in the Labyrinth, even if I did nothing, and thus the myth he had created would remain intact.

Five youths made it to the center and stayed. Others came and fled as the first had done. We heard screaming at times and I believe the hordes of rats found those who had not stayed with me. Together, we mourned and wept.

Though they stayed, this was no idyllic life. I taught them to hunt the rodents, but with no fire, some sickened and died. All we could do was watch. We took their bodies into the maze so we would not have to look upon them.

One day, one of the youths wandered close to the depth of the pool and asked about it. I told him that other than a shallow area near one end, the other side seemed to have no bottom.

"Too deep to swim in?" he asked.

"I am the son of Poseidon," I replied. "I can hold my breath longer than any mortal."

It was then decided I would explore the depth. To my astonishment, I discovered a flat bottom of packed earth. There was, however, a large stone right in the center. I pulled this stone over and found a passage of darkness which Erebus himself would approve of. Feeling my way through, and after what seemed longer than possible to hold my breath, I discovered myself on the shore of a deserted beach. A small lagoon and virgin woods lay nearby. As I walked this new landscape, I thought it could be a much better place for the youths to live.

I made my way back through the underground stream, fighting the current pushing me towards the sea. I emerged into my subterranean prison to the amazement of the three I had befriended. I explained what I had found and that it would be possible for them to eke out a living in that deserted wood if they would dare the swim, and survive. Although they were children of the Mediterranean, none could remain underwater that far on their own. Trusting my divine heritage, we hoped I could pull them through. But they had to trust me.

The venture succeeded and they began making a small camp. When they were settled, I bid them farewell and went back to the Labyrinth. Until I knew how I would get my revenge on Minos, I did not want to be accounted as missing. I feared he would send a hunting party that might find my new companions. I was not yet ready to take on his guard, so I waited, I grew, and I trained.

At times, a new group of youths would enter the maze. Some would trust me as those first few did. Others suffered a terrible demise, succumbing to the true monsters of the maze, the rat hordes. Occasionally, a trio of soldiers would be thrown into the maze as well; whether for punishment or to confirm my continued residence I don't know. They typically tried to fight me and their deaths are the only ones I have truly been responsible for while incarcerated.

This went on for some years until one day something new happened. Instead of a group of youths, only one was sent into the maze. The man's name was Theseus.

Perspective 2: Theseus

Peter Linton

Here, let it be told the true tale of the first Minotaur. Some have called him Moraga, but this was a falsehood, set forth by his Cretan enemies. For he was told to be a monster and they named him as one. His true name I did not know at first, for none of the subjects of Minos spoke it, but I came to know him as Asterion. It means 'The Starry One." That was fitting, for he had a gleam in his eye. Thus says I, Theseus, son of Poseidon, brother to the Minotaur.

He was the offspring of Pasiphae, the wife of King Minos, and a snow-white sea-bull sent to Minos by Poseidon for sacrifice. But instead of sacrificing it, Minos kept it. As punishment, Poseidon had Pasiphae fall in love with the bull.

The Minotaur was the resulting child, deemed a monster to be shut away in a great

14

maze: the Labyrinth. King Minos had Athenian youths sent into the maze to be killed and devoured, yet this too was a lie. The truth came out when I journeyed to Crete to end the travesty. I did so with the help of Ariadne, daughter of Minos and Pasiphae, but that is the last falsehood, one turned to good. I know this, because I am the one who invented the end of the story.

To know why, I must take myself back to the beginning when I set sail for Knossos, city of the King. That morning Zephuros, The West Wind, offered a brisk breeze for our journey. We had just departed Athens with fourteen youths as our passengers, all fearful of failure and death.

I demanded to see the King upon handing over the youths. With customary greetings, I met him in his private audience where he walked with a limp. 'An old battle wound,' he said of it. He was regal, charismatic, holding himself with pride. Clean robes of red and beige draped over his shoulder, partially covering his hairy chest. Late in his prime, he had not the joy of youth, nor the gravelly voice of old men. I respected him, he shared his wine freely. Only when I broached the subject of my visit did his hostly demeanor change.

"So you brought the youths, Hero Theseus?" the King asked.

"I seek a barter," I replied.

"A barter? What haggle could you possibly offer me?"

"What do you lack?" I said. "Yet, you demand fourteen of Athens' most vibrant. I seek to barter for their lives."

"I am merely the go between," the King said. "They are demanded not by me, but as security for my Kingdom, lest it fall."

I blanched at that. I believed him to be an honorable King, one whose power was granted and earned. What was he telling me? My doubts were put to rest with his savage words.

"The true tyrant-ruler lives in a maze that drives giddy those who venture inside. Eventually, they welcome their horrible sacrifice even as their bodies are eaten alive."

"The Minotaur," I said, my eyes narrowing, my anger kindling at the tale.

"I have sent in my troupe, but no reply, no survivor, no one has ever returned to speak. Now none shall enter in save by force for the monster bellows: "Food and sacrifice! Lest I venture out!""

The King paused in his story, eyeing me through his glass of wine. He must have seen my anger, for my hands shook. I was ready to put an end to this creature.

"Surely you understand the position I'm in. Wouldn't you, strong as you are, sacrifice the weak. That is the design of the world."

I stood, hazy. "How do I find this *cattle*?"

"Go. Prepare yourself. He is immense, standing two feet above you. Matched by his build, he possesses such strength as to lift ten times your weight and hurl you just as far.

"I wager he is naked," I said whimsically.

16

He laughed at that. "Hah! Theseus, I will have the Labyrinth creator meet you. If any will know the way, it will be him."

I turned to face him. "Then you will release the youths to me, and never again them again."

He squinted and the grin left his face. "Do not seek to intimidate a son of Zeus, Athenian. Bring me proof he is dead and I will free the children."

Looking back, I should have seen through his facade.

The next morning I would dare the maze. Armed with a piercing xiphos and round buckler, I met the Labyrinth's designer— Daedalus, a cackling scorpion of a man. Thin scraggly hair was unevenly pulled behind his oversized ears. An imposing set of glassware sat on his nose and over his eyes, making them seem bigger than they really were. 'A creation of my own,' he said. 'Brings focus to this messy world.' Now I wonder, for his Labyrinth has no copy in the natural world.

"There is a simple solution to finding your way out and here it is," he said. From a side bag he pulled out a ball of twine about the size of a head. "Unravel as you go in, then follow back. There is no more than you need, but have a caution," he said with a wily laugh. "Mind your twine."

The walls at first were plain, then they took on patterns: triangles, squares, oblong quadrilaterals going into circles and swirls, Ever moving and never-ending snail-shells and blobs of color. The maze became a tunnel. Darkness

17

ensued, the air becoming damp as a warm fog. By touch alone, I found the tunnels branching left and right, up and down.

After wandering thus in the dark, light emanated far ahead. I followed, but it was not the light of the sun or moon. It came from torches without fire. I could not observe for long--they stung my eyes even as they drew me in like an illusionist's trick.

More than once did I thank Daedalus for the twine, for I would have surely perished seeking my way through countless corners. Bodies I found: some eaten down to their bones, others with the madness of their death scarring their face. How many hours I wandered I do not know, but it must not have been too long before I found a gently sloping tunnel upwards. Emerging, I found the high sun shining upon plain walls, the pathway fresh with green grass. I heard the hushed sounds of a pond. Then, I spied him inside an unadorned gazebo, leisurely prone on a blanketed stone bench chewing. Intelligent eyes I did not expect looked upon me.

Swallowing his wad, he spoke. "Athenian, you don't look like a sacrifice with that sword. Do you propose a battle or should we talk?"

"So, you have a tongue, bull-shitter. You must know the pleas of those you slay. Talk? I have nothing to say to you."

"Bull-shitter? Indeed. You should not say so to a son of Poseidon."

"Do not blaspheme before me, ox-head. Now up, or I shall slay you where you lie!"

18

"You think you could get close enough to stab me?" he asked and from behind his bench he produced a long, stout staff. Then the creature stood as a tall, powerfully muscled human male. The King lacked adulation for his majesty. His skin was bronzed as any native of the Aegean. He would have been anyone's coveted lover except for the apparent proof of his bull parentage. Brown fur covered his snouted head from which two sharply pointed horns projected straight out and up in equipoise.

I taunted him. "You think you intimidate me with a stick, Gorgon?" I called. "The sword is the true weapon of the Greek."

"Gorgon? They're hardly bovine," he replied, swinging.

Prepared and intent on finding an opening, I leapt aside.

"Perhaps some malinformed imagination will depict a Gorgon as a bull, but it belies a basic knowledge," he said, blocking my sword.

He jabbed. I deflected. I knew he was gauging me as well. I worked my way, edging in. His reach was longer and he was quick. Thus, did we go round and round, but I began to see his pattern. "Truly, I did not expect to find you so worthy," I said.

"Do you mean to make peace?"

"What I mean is I expected a cowbell and nose ring!"

"Your insults are pointless," he shouted. "Now, at you!"

He swung at me as I charged in, but I ducked low and jabbed upward, slicing into his arm. He took the scratch and twirled with an upward blow on my groin. I stumbled back. He did not let up. Seeing me struggle, he continued to jab, forcing me back. Gaining some balance, I deflected once, twice, but his subsequent blows were straight and forceful. He hit me below my sternum knocking the wind out of me. I fell into the wall. Then he weighed in, grabbing hold and lifting me high. I thrust my sword. He hurled me far into the pond. I emerged drenched. Again he was upon me swinging his staff down hard on my sword arm. The xiphos dropped into the water and I was forced further in by another blow. Truly, I was beaten.

I broke the surface of the pond, standing chest deep in the water.

He relented, but stooped to recover my sword. Standing at the edge, bleeding from my small scores on his arm and shoulder, he spoke. "The sword for blood, the staff for deep water," he said. "Which shall it be, Athenian?"

"I yield," I replied. Indeed, I did not ever expect to be asked such a question. "The battle is yours, but do I wonder at mercy from the monster of Minos, even if only for a few short breaths?"

"Who knows the monster?" he responded with a growing firmness. "The son of Poseidon did not enter your house with killing intent."

I paused at those words. A second time he named my father, he whose spirit became one with my mother Aethra at my conception. Though I looked upon one whom I thought a monster, at my very death it seemed, I had to know the truth. "By what you say, the son of Poseidon is indeed a monster," I said, risking it all. "And he stands before you."

He paused and bent his deep brown eyes upon me. "It is not for the victor to prove himself. You plead your life with a lie. Yet, if you dare, dive to the bottom. There you will find a slab of stone, lift it and swim beyond. The stone will close behind you and you will be trapped to your death, but a son of Poseidon will not fear. Onward, he will be met with answers. Know that I will follow. Finding You dead, I will feed your body to the crabs."

"You will not find a dead man," I replied. I dove to the bottom. Locating the stone, I raised it and passed through just as he said. Darkness enveloped me. I could only feel my way. Too soon I felt the tightening of my chest, my lungs demanding air, but I thought of what he said, 'a son of Poseidon.' I crawled more than swam, I felt my blindness give way to sight, my lungs rewarded with breath. A current carried me, warmed me, healed me. The surface appeared and I swam up and out.

I emerged near the sunny beach of a small lagoon. At the shore's edge crouched a youngster working on a net.

"Who are you?" she asked.

"I am--"

"THESEUS!" someone called. "Captain!" Running up came a young man. "By all the gods, I would have never guessed to see you here."

Before me stood a fresh face, yet also familiar. "I see a man before, where there was a boy I once knew.

"It has been a long time," he answered. "You knew my father Karalides."

"Now I recall, Miron," I replied. "Where are we?" Before I got an answer, there was a loud splash behind us. The Minotaur had surfaced.

"Asterion!" Miron called. "Look who it is," he continued. But upon seeing his wounds he cried out, "What happened to you?"

Asterion walked straight up to us. Standing tall he said, "I am healing, Miron. It was a misunderstanding between brothers." We clasped hands and arms, each feeling the warmth of a newly found friendship.

"Tell me your tale, brother, and I will tell you mine."

In due time I learned of the truth--that it was not the bull that impregnated Pasiphae, but Poseidon himself. This he did in anger to the King's defiance. Pasiphae had other children, but one of them, Ariadne, took to the young 'calfling' as she called him, before Minos tossed him into the Labyrinth. The King was fearful, and jealous. It was he who created the myth that the bull-child of Poseidon was a monster.

By this time, a collection of faces surrounded us and started a fire.

"It was a hopeful guess," he said. "That I could bring them here to safety."

"For me," one answered. "It was like a watery dream where fish danced."

"They were all brave," Asterion replied. "Taking me at my word that there was safety and freedom beyond. I have never slain any of the Athenian youths, I brought them here. Some, impatient with rescue, now have children of their own."

I stood. The beach fire had been rekindled. "I am sorry for my part in this," I said. "But by Poseidon, it will end. I have the means to come here by boat and take you all anywhere you wish. And you, Asterion, I will not leave you in that Labyrinth. Come! Together we will see the world."

There were many cheers. They had been torn away from their families, but Asterion replied, "No, I cannot. I do not wish to leave my sister. Our final words to each other were vows to leave Crete together. I will not leave if there is any hope for that."

"Then I will have to convince her to come. I will return to Minos, tell him you are slain, but find some way to reveal the truth to her."

Then Asterion stood before me. "You will need some proof. Take this." He reached up with both hands and grabbed onto the horn on his left side. With a horrible rip-snap, the horn pulled off with remnants of fur and flesh. He merely smiled. "They grow back."

After a second magic swim, I slept that night on the Minotaur's bench. Upon waking, I took his staff. I placed my sword on a rock and shattered it in half with a thrust. At the feet of the King's throne, I threw my token down. Ariadne was there.

"He is dead."

Ariadne shook at the news and had to hold herself up on a pillar. Both the King and I eyed her. He had a smile on his face.

"Tell me," he said through his grin. "Tell me why you only brought one horn? Why not his whole head."

I smiled in return "The Minotaur broke my sword," I said, tossing the useless handle before him. "Then I leapt upon his back and strangled him, killing him with my bare hands. His head lies submerged beneath pond water."

With that, Ariadne let out a shriek. "You *monster*!" she called. From within her robes she pulled out a dagger and hurled herself at me.

She did not catch me by surprise. I was able to grab onto her wrists and restrain her. "You don't want to kill me," I whispered to her.

Ariadne continued to struggle for a few seconds before the King commanded, "Seize her! Seize her and hang her naked above the Labyrinth. Her rotting flesh shall serve as a warning to what befalls those who betray me!"

Little did he know that he gave me the very chance I needed. "No, King, no," I said. "Such a beauty, her life is mine. Let me take her. If she fails to please me and my crew, we shall toss her to the waves."

"Hah!" he laughed. "So shall it be! Take her and let me know no more of her."

"And the youths," I reminded him. "Release them and we shall depart."

He stopped laughing, but still regarded me with an evil-looking smile. "That was our deal, and I shall honor it. Remember that the next time you are in Knossos."

"I pray it shall be soon," I said, playing on his vanity. We departed before he could discern my true meaning.

Before the King's guards, I tied Ariadne by her neck and hands and pulled her along. I waited until we cast off before I took her to my quarters. She ran into a corner shaking with rage and fear. Wide-eyed, she glared at me expecting the worst. I waited for her to settle.

"Princess Ariadne," I began. "I have one thing to say to you, then I will leave you here as my guest."

"There is nothing you could say that I want to hear," she replied half speaking, half crying. "And I would rather die than be your whore!"

"Asterion lives, Princess, and he awaits you on a hidden shore."

She paused, though still fearful. "What you're doing may seem honorable, but you simply seek to gain my trust, which you will never have."

"Here is the key," I said, holding up the only one for the door to my quarters. "On my honor as a son of Poseidon and brother to Asterion, he lives and I promise to take you to him. I leave this with you. When you need food, I will send the Athenian maidens to serve you. And when you hear their voices, you will know you are safe." I placed the key on a small table and departed the cabin. I heard the slock-sound of the bolt driving into the cabin wall.

I did not wait for her to call. After a short time, I sent the youths to her door where they were let in for a time. Yet she was ever fearful. Even when we came into the lagoon, she would not open the door. It finally took Asterion himself, on board the ship, speaking through my cabin window, when she trusted her fate and beheld the great Minotaur.

"Have any wheat-grass, sister?" he asked.

Ariadne came up to him slowly, as if still unbelieving.

"No longer your calfling, but my love for you has also grown."

Then she hugged him and there was much cheering from those on board and ashore.

Now my tale reaches an end. Not all the talk and planning needs to be retold. Some joined me on a return to Athens. There we would be living witnesses of Minos' duplicity, his fear and his vulnerability, that we of Athens should rise against him, that he may die a wanderer suffering a thousand boils till he finds his place in Hades. Athens would become the new kingdom of the Aegean, the powerful and just Kingdom for which it was destined.

Others chose a different path and joined Asterion and Ariadne, brother and sister, on Naxos. There they wished to build a home of their own. It has been said that once I escaped with Ariadne, I treacherously abandoned her on the isle. I care not. Dionysus, God of the Isle will take care of her.

27

based on

The Völsunga Saga

Sigurd and the Dragon

C. VanDyke & C.D. Storiz

Sigurd and the Dragon
C. VanDyke & C.D. Storiz

The young man stood in the middle of the trail and peered into the thick underbrush. It was not a full-fledged footpath, merely the suggestion of a path where the spindly grass and pine-needles had been beaten flat by the regular passage of white-tailed deer.

The young man was not a full-fledged man, either, but much closer to a boy, with the gangly awkwardness the adolescent body adopts in that liminal stage between childhood and adulthood. There was an air about him, a confidence bordering on recklessness, that is only borne by great heroes. Or great fools.

"Are you *sure* it's this way, Regin?" He shoved his mass of tangled hair out of his eyes and turned doubtfully to his companion.

Regin nodded emphatically. "Yes, yes, quite sure! Straight ahead to the large oak, right to the cliff's face and behind the boulder. Do you really think I wouldn't know where that blasted wyrm's lair is?" Regin was the boy's antithesis: short where he was tall, stocky where he was slender, thickly bearded where his cheeks were soft with youth.

"Blasted wyrm?" The boy chuckled ruefully. "You mean your *brother*?"

Regin growled and spat on the ground. "That... monster is not my brother!" He clenched his fists as his eyes flashed fire. "It hasn't been my brother since it killed my father and ran off with Otr's wergild! After Loki measured out our brother's weight in gold, I trusted that snake! I should have insisted I take my share there on the spot, but no! I... I thought—"

"A brother's love meant something." The phrase rolled off the boy's tongue from rote, a snippet from a well-worn, thread-bare rant he had long since memorized. He sighed, rolled his shoulders, then drew the sword hung from a scabbard at his waist. "Well, if I'm going to fight him, I guess I might as well get on with it."

The dwarf rested a gnarled hand on his arm. "You remembered to sharpen Gram?"

The boy rolled his eyes. "Yes, Regin, I remembered to sharpen Gram." The keen edge of the blade caught the sunlight piercing the thin canopy of leaves, glinting as if to confirm that it had, indeed, been honed to a killing edge. The boy took a step forward, then hesitated. "Are you sure this is the right thing to do? Killing him, I mean? I know he killed your dad and stole your gold, but maybe if you talk to him, Fafnir would—"

31

"Don't say that name!" Regin's face darkened. "The time for talk passed years ago; now is the time for vengeance! Am I sure? Does the sun rise in the east? Did Odin hang for nine days from Yggdrasil? Of course I'm sure. Why do you think I've raised you all these years?"

The boy, face blank as he nodded, turned to walk down the path. "I don't know," he muttered under his breath, not loud enough for the dwarf to hear. "Maybe because you loved me?"

"And Sigurd?"

The boy paused at the sound of Regin's raspy voice. "No mercy. Make me proud."

The sound of flapping wings echoed in the valley below as Fafnir increased his speed. When the wind slapped his face, he turned towards the heavens in a beautiful arc and glided through the air. As he passed the highest cloud, he dipped. Pulling his wings tight to his side and narrowing his snout, he let the aerodynamics of his body do the rest as gravity plummeted him downwards. The exhilarating rush of air over his scales gave him a sense of freedom. He closed his eyes and let the sensation wash over him. It wasn't often Fafnir chanced leaving his home unprotected, but when he did—he made the most of it.

Fafnir fell faster and faster. When he opened his eyes, the jagged edge of his mountain home approached more quickly than he expected. For a heartbeat, as he always did, he considered not pulling up. Letting his body crash into the rocks at full speed. But he knew from experience a dragon was made of sterner stuff than that. Oh, it would hurt, but he'd live. Pushing out his clawed feet, he spread his wings, shifted his weight, and then slowed his body.

With his destination in his sights, he twisted his snout and opened his jaws revealing large, razor like teeth. He roared above the tree line before spewing his poison along the face of the cliff. A precaution to keep unwanted souls at bay. Fearful someone might attempt to enter his domain, and steal his treasure, he laid out his plan. Scour the land and trespassers be damned. Satisfied his gold was safe, it was time to go home. Clipping the tips of evergreen trees, he brought himself to a running halt. Bits of dirt and pebbles kicked up as he landed in a swirl of dust.

The glint of gold and sparkling gems gave off a yellowish luminescence that greeted Fafnir. He sighed as his front claw touched a pile of coins.

Without Regin as audience, the young man felt ever more a boy; gone was the swagger he donned like a coat of mail when with his foster-father.

Regin was right, of course—it's what he'd been raised for. His entire life led him to this day, and when the moment arrived, it threatened to buckle his knees. Gripping Gram tighter, he forced himself to continue walking. He would not waver; he was a Volsung. Raised less by a parent than by that name, nursed on myth and swaddled in family legends; he was Sigurd. Son of Sigmund, son of Volsung, son of Rerir, son of Sigi, whose father was Odin himself. Sigurd spent his life in the shadow of that family tree, a tree whose many branches had been hacked off and whose roots were watered with familial blood. Regin had told him the histories as bedtime stories, sung to him ballads of his ancestors' glorious deaths. Tales of betrayal. And of revenge.

Revenge was the fiber tying them all together. The crimson thread woven through the tapestry of the Volsungs. It had consumed his grandfather and father. And Regin, of course. Sigurd had heard the tale a thousand times. How Regin and Fafnir's brother donned the magic skin of an otter to swim in the icy stream tumbling down Mount Esja. That Loki had killed the otter with a stone, only to find it was not an animal, but an enchanted dwarf. How Regin and Fafnir and their father, Hreidmar, had gone to Odin to demand justice for their brother's death. How Odin forced Loki to pay wergild—Otr's weight in gold. Stories that Fafnir claimed all the gold for himself, killing their father and driving Regin from their home. And Fafnir's avarice transformed him into a scaled dragon, a mighty wyrm that terrorized the country and kept Regin from his rightful inheritance.

Sigurd paused to catch his breath. Up ahead, a massive oak towered over the rest of the trees. He wiped the sweat from his brow with his sleeve. Revenge. He wondered, as he often did, what his life would have been like without revenge. Had Signy and his father merely fled Norway without spending years plotting King Siggeir's death. Had Regin mourned his brother and told Fafnir that gold wasn't the point.

But, of course, it was the point. Gold and blood were all heroes cared about. That and honor, and honor said, Regin could not forgive. Honor said Sigurd had a legacy to uphold. After all, was he not a Volsung?

His thoughts were interrupted as a deafening roar split the still noon sky and shook the earth. Through the branches of the forest and higher up the mountain flickered the red-glow of flame.

Dragon fire. Fafnir had returned home.

Sigurd straightened his shoulders and continued up the slope.

After a meal of half a dozen goats, charred to perfection, and a barrel of wine... What's that you say? Dragons don't drink wine? Of course they do! Especially shape shifting dragons who are really dwarfs in disguise. After Fafnir was sated and his thoughts dulled by wine, he wobbled through the cavernous room. Perhaps he shouldn't have drank that extra barrel... but he needed it tonight. To forget.

Or was it to remember? Earlier, while on his flight, he'd seen something—or rather someone—he'd not thought of in years. Fafnir would recognize that plump belly and 'waddle as he walked' anywhere. How dare Regin come so close? Come to his forest. *What are you up to, dear brother? Hoping to steal back the gold? If so, you'll need more than a scrappy lad with you.* Fafnir wondered aloud who it was with Regin. He didn't recognize him. The boy was at least a foot and a half taller than Regin, but scrawny as a birch among oaks. Probably just another villager Regin had roped into being his patsy with a promise of a share of Fafnir's hoard... with the lies that it was Fafnir who stole his inheritance. Hadn't Regin done enough already without occasionally sending some fool to try to kill him?

'Tis bad enough Fafnir would live out the rest of his days as a dragon. Was bad enough he had no company to keep. No friend to entertain, to drink and be merry with. No woman to warm his bed. Who dared befriends a dragon, let alone bed one? 'Tis a lonely life, that of a dragon. What was it the old poets said? *A man should keep faith with his friends always, returning gift for gift; laughter should be the reward of laughter.* He had no friends. No laughter. No one to trade snippets of poetry with. Not like back when she used to... no! That's exactly what he needed the wine to forget.

Fafnir slithered along the cold, hard ground towards the far end of his domain. It was a cavernous room that echoed when he called out. The echo's reply made him feel less alone. He swayed as he moved. His tail possessed a mind of its own, as his body went one direction and his tail the other. It knocked a pile of coins and gold trinkets stacked near to the ceiling. The deafening din of crashing coins made bile burn at the back of his throat. He thrust his claws over his ears and when the last gold piece settled, Fafnir noticed something he hadn't seen in ages.

A painting of a beautiful maiden encased in a delicate gold frame. The frame itself was like a twisted vine with interlocking leaves, but it was the picture itself that gave Fafnir pause. He remembered the day he buried it beneath the pile of gold. The agony today on its recovery was as the day he pushed it inside the mound of gold, hopefully to never be seen again. But here she was. Uncovered. And just as beautiful.

Gods, dammit. He should have had more wine.

At the base of the cliff, Sigurd came across a wide track where the dragon had dragged its enormous bulk along the ground. Regin told him the dragon would be large, "but nothing you can't handle. Like an angry bull, or a mid-sized bear." But this path was wider than an ox, wider than a wagon. The claw marks on either side of the scratched soil were deep furrows, and Sigurd's heart beat faster as his mind conjured up an image of a creature capable of leaving such scars. After a few hundred yards, the boulder that Regin told him marked the entrance to Fafnir's cave jutted on the horizon. He crouched toward the large rock on tip-toe, careful not to step on a stick or loose stone. When he reached the boulder, he pressed his back against the cool granite and took a series of deep breaths to calm himself. He was ready to be Sigurd, the dragon slayer. His father and grandfather had been heroes. It was in his blood.

With several calming breaths, he slowly eased around the edge of the boulder. The mouth of the cave was wide. Inside was dark. Even in the darkness there was no mistaking the massive bulk of the dragon.

It was not like a bull or a bear, but like a small house made of bone and sinew and scales. Fafnir lay curled on a pile of gold and jewels, his neck and tail wrapped around his massive bulk, his wings folded like the sails that topped the warriors' longships.

Sigurd hesitated. He knew what his father and grandfather would have done—rush in without thinking, slaughter the beast with one or two mighty blows, chop off its head, then waltz back to Regin whistling a jaunty tune. Or they may have died, charred to cinder and bone, but either way they wouldn't have paused. Wouldn't have flinched in the face of death. Sigurd reflected as he crouched behind the boulder. He didn't *want* to die. And from where

Sigurd stood, the dragon looked like death incarnate.

"Come on out, little boy." The dragon's voice rumbled like Thor's own chariot during a thunderstorm. "I can smell you, so there's no point in hiding."

Sigurd stood and stepped into the mouth of the cave. "I wasn't hiding," he said. "I was… biding my time."

"Sure you were, kid." The dragon yawned, showing off a mouthful of gleaming, dagger-sharp teeth.

Sigurd set his jaw and gripped Gram's hilt. "Don't you want to kill me?"

"Kill you?" The dragon laughed and a small gout of flame shot from his mouth. "Why would I want to kill you? I don't even know you."

Sigurd frowned. "But Regin said—"

"Regin?" Another gout of flame, this one larger. Sigurd ducked, but felt the scorching heat of the dragon-fire. "So you're the newest of my no-good-brother's flunkies." He chuckled, a sound like landfall tumbling down a mountain.

"I'm not his flunky!" Now Sigurd's voice was the one with fire in it. "I am no man's slave. I am a Volsung!"

"Wait—you're Sigmund and Hljold's kid?" The dragon's head swiveled until his eyes were level with Sigurd's. "That explains a lot."

"What's that supposed to mean?"

But the dragon didn't answer, merely held Sigurd with his deep, unblinking gaze. The boy tried to force himself to stare back into the deep, bottomless pits of the wyrm's eyes, but it left him lightheaded. *It must be some kind of dragon magic!* he thought. His desire to appear fearless briefly clashed with his common sense, and Sigurd looked away.

"So, what will it be?" Fafnir said after a bout of silence from both parties. "You're here to slay a dragon, aren't you? That's why Regin's spent the last decade or so pumping you full of lies and family history. Piss and vinegar, as my father may have said. But if you're going to do it, do it now while the wine still dulls my senses. Come on, dragonslayer—slay a dragon."

Sigurd raised his sword. "Aren't you going to fight back? Defend yourself?" he said, taking a striking stance.

The dragon rolled his eyes and sighed. "What would be the point to that?"

Sigurd thought it over. What glory is there without earning it? With taking a life so easily? "I'll not fall for your trickery. Stand now, beast, before I strike!"

Fafnir yawned and closed his eyes. He'd grown weary over the years and tired of his lot. Sigurd's arrival couldn't have come at a better time. Fafnir had thought to do the deed himself, but that would be the coward's way out. No, let this boy do it for him.

"Come on, boy. What are you waiting for? Get it done and be on with it. Or leave me

to my misery. Makes no difference to me."
Fafnir opened one eye a crack. The boy mulled
it over. Perhaps he needed to push him. "Are ye
a coward? Do you hang by your mother's teats
and have her spoon feed you?"

Certainly the boy would be cross at
Fafnir's harsh words and teasing. "Do the other
children call you names and curse you because
you are so scrawny?"

Redness blossomed on the boy's cheeks.
He continued to tease and probe the boy further
and finally his hell would be over.

The boy raised his blade and advanced,
but the toe of his boot caught on part of Fafnir's
pile of gold. Sigurd tripped and stumbled to the
ground. The sword tumbled from his hands and
slid against the rocky floor. On his stomach,
Sigurd's mouth hung agape, stunned; this is
where Fafnir would normally let out an angry
puff of smoke and charred the offender.

Something stopped Fafnir. He tilted his
head to one side and examined the boy. "Are you
hurt?"

The boy pushed his palms against the
cold, stone floor. Rising, he stared at what he
tripped over. A gilded frame of twisted vine and
interlocked leaves. The boy studied the painting
inside the frame, then glared up at the dragon.

"Why do you have a picture of my
mother?"

The cave rumbled with Fafnir's shifting
weight. Specks of dust swirled about as he
circled around and came to a resting position.
Much like a dog does before it beds down. The

dragon stared into the middle-distance. "Leave me be, boy. Sigurd, son of Sigmund and son of the beautiful Hljod. Either strike me dead or leave me be."

Sigurd did not make as if to leave, nor did he raise his sword to fight. Instead, he continued to stare at the dragon. "Why do you have a painting of my mother?" he asked again. The boy narrowed his eyes as he flared his nostrils. "I shall ask you only once, beast. Did you bring her to a fiery death as you've done to others before you?"

Gods dammit, Fafnir thought. *He has her eyes.* Fafnir chuckled. "I see we're gaining our strength and confidence once more."

"You mock me, dragon? For this alone, you shall die." He scrambled for his blades, picking Gram from the ground, and took his stance once more. "Prepare to die, Fafnir. For I, Sigurd, son of Sigmund and Hljod avenge my family."

"Good," Fafnir replied before Sigurd could strike. "It is good that you have anger in your heart when you pierce mine. You will need your heart to harden if you truly want to be the slayer." The dragon snarled, "Now do it, boy, before I lose my patience!" The dragon released spiraling puffs of smoke.

Sigurd didn't move. When the smoke cleared, he noticed something about the dragon. It wasn't malice as Regin would have wanted him to believe, but... sadness.

The boy leaned Gram against the wall and held the frame out to Fafnir, who let out a drawn out breath with no flame. "Who was she to you?" the boy asked, taking a hesitant step closer to the sleeping dragon. He brushed his mop of hair out of his face with his left hand as he stared down at the painting in his right.

The dragon met the boy's eyes. Again, he spoke, in a voice heavy with the ages:

> *Like a star among stones, the King's heart-spring!*
> *Her word-horde held poems and promises*
> *Proud she stood, like a war-banners in battle*
> *Fairer than all others was Harrold's sweet Hljod.*

"What—?"

"Skaldic verse," grumbled Fafnir. "What, did my brother only teach you to wave a sword? A true hero must be able to fight, but also know his kennings. All the warriors once were poets as well as killers." The dragon shifted his heavy limbs, then sighed, steam seeping from the edges of his mouth. "Since you've come all this way, I shall tell you the truth. Whether it is a tale you believe shall be up to you. But no, I did not cause her demise, nor ever would I. For what's in one's heart, one can not kill. But I feel responsible all the same. And why not take the blame for her death, too? So many have been charged in my name, caused by my hand, so why not claim hers, also?" Fafnir said, nodding towards the weapon. "So be on with it. Put an end to my misery once and for all."

"One's heart? You knew my mother."

"Yes. Now let's get this over with."

The boy drew in a breath but did not reach for his sword. No, in fact he did something that surprised Fafnir—and Fafnir was rarely surprised. The boy sat on the ground and crossed his legs.

"Did you... love her?"

Fafnir blinked through a pool of salty tears. "Yes."

"But—you—you're a dragon!" His eyes widened.

"Are you daft, boy? You think I was always like this?" He let out a sulphury puff of smoke. "You think a dwarf can't be tricked into becoming a beast everyone hates? You sit around your fire pits and listen to those who weave tales of lies." Fafnir bellowed so loudly the walls in the cave shook, sprinkling a fresh layer of dust over the boy from head to toe.

Sigurd shook the dust from his hair. "I'm waiting," he said with an expression much like that of a child ready for a bedtime story.

Fafnir nodded and filled his lungs with stale air. The boy listened with an intenseness on his face but didn't seem to judge. Fafnir shared the events as best as he could recall. "Our real mistake was trusting Loki. A trickster God earns that appellation for a reason," the dragon said. "When Loki paid Otr's wergild, he included a ring. A ring, cursed by Andvari, which led my father to his ultimate death."

"I sensed the evil," Fafnir said. "I urged my brother and father to throw it away, to melt it in the fire of our forge. And they agreed. But when I came to help them do the deed, I noticed my father was… different. He was unkempt, his hair disheveled and wild eyed, a foaming at his lips. No, this wasn't Hreidmar, King of the Dwarfs. Something evil had taken him." Fafnir paused. The boy hung on his every word.

"That's when I noticed the ring on father's finger," Fafnir said morosely. "Regin saw it too, though he quaked in his boots and shit himself. Did he tell you that?"

The boy smiled. "He left that part out."

"Father promised us he'd leave the ring be and let me destroy it, but it called to him. When we were out of his sight, he'd put the ring on and it possessed his soul. He was crazed with rage. We did all we could to control him, but his strength was tenfold with that ring. I had to transform myself into the dragon. I had no choice." The dragon turned away and lay down his head.

"What did you do?" the boy asked, inching closer.

"Boy, there is something you should know. Out of my brothers, I was gifted with strength, but it was my brothers who were gifted with cleverness. Regin didn't have the strength to stop our father, but he tried to trick him into surrendering the ring. Father saw through his ploy and was wringing the life from Regin's neck. He accused Regin of wanting the ring for himself. Perhaps he was right; perhaps the curse of the ring was already eating at Regin's heart."

Like a cat on a windowsill, Fafnir's tail pounced gently up and down, causing the ground to tremble. He continued his tale, "I still remember how Regin's feet dangled above the floor and the look in my brother's eyes as our father squeezed the life from him. It was then that I transformed into my dragon shell and ripped our father from my brother's throat. Regin choked and gasped for breath, writhing on the floor in pain. With the strike of my claw, my father bled. I still remember the stench. The acrid smell of death," he said with a snarl.

"Regin crawled to our father on his hands and knees shouting at me, 'what did you do?' 'What did I do?' I replied. 'I saved your scrawny arse from a madman.' I huffed and puffed to calm myself down. I looked down at my hands, which weren't hands at all, but scaled claws with my father's blood. When I looked up, I saw Regin remove the ring from father's hand, but before he could put it on his own, I swiped it from his grasp!"

The boy's mouth hung open as if he were to say something but then closed it and nodded. Sigurd blinked. His Adam's apple bounced up and down with each hard swallow.

"Say something, boy. Go on. Spit it out," Fafnir said.

"But… what about my mother?"

"I'm getting to that. It's all the same story. This gold was how I lost my father, my brother." The dragon's eyes fell once again on the painting. "How I lost Hljod. Not that I ever had her, mind you." In the pools of Fafnir's eyes existed the dwarf, buried deep within the beast. The dragon took a deep breath, like a wind blowing through the tree-tops, then continued. "I loved your mother."

"Did she… did she love you?"

"No." Fafnir's voice sighed with steam. "For a time, I thought she did. Or I convinced myself she did. But what I mistook for love was even more precious and harder to come by— kindness. The other maidens scorned me. Gudrun, Borgir, Oddrun. They grimaced whenever I approached, laughed at my short stature, recoiled whenever I tried to speak to them, as if I were not merely a dwarf but a leper. Hljold was different. She spoke to me without malice and made me laugh with her soft humor. I loved her, but she was already promised to your father. Even then, Sigmund was known far and wide. The mighty son of King Volsung, breaker of rings, wrecker of mead-halls, Siggier's Bane. 'That was a good King!' as the poet said of the half Dane, Shield Sheafson. Sigmund was strong and handsome and ruled a kingdom. What could a dwarf offer compared to that? What princess could resist such a betrothal?"

"My dad was an asshole," Sigurd said.

Fafnir laughed. "Ah, but when did *that* ever stop a king from wedding the maiden of his choice? For a while I could lie to myself about Hljold's affections, but after I took on this form…" He extended one long claw and gently stroked the gilded frame. "I kept this to remind me. Of her kindness. Of what never could have been, even had I not become a monster."

Sigurd shook his head. "But didn't you even *try*? Sure, you were a dragon, but you can

47

speak! Didn't you even try to talk to her, to tell her what had happened? If she was as kind as you say, wouldn't the fact you were sacrificing yourself to save your family have meant something to her?"

"Perhaps. But not as much as marrying a king."

"I don't believe you."

The dragon's eyes flashed dangerously.

Sigurd continued. "Maybe if you would have told her, maybe if you'd have said—"

"Said what? I'd already become a great and ferocious monster. I already had my *Ægishjálmur*, my helm of terror. Armies fled before my visage!"

"She wouldn't have feared you," insisted Sigurd. "She would have—"

"You are right. She would not have fled," agreed Fafnir. "She would have pitied me, which would have been even worse. No, I made my choice, as she made hers."

"But you never really gave her a choice! What if she—"

"I made my choice and I regret nothing!" Fafnir's voice rose to a thunderous rumble. Sigurd fell quiet once more as the dragon's voice shook the mountain. A puff of steam escaped Fafnir's nostrils. "No, that is a lie. I have regret. A man who says he has no regrets is a man who has not truly lived."

"Do you regret killing your father?" the boy asked hesitantly.

"I regret *everything*. And yet I would make the same choices again if I had to. I did what had to be done. No man can outrun Fate, little boy. Or dwarf, for that matter. Speaking of which…"

Fafnir raised his mighty head from the cave floor. He sat back on his haunches, his massive back rising until it nearly brushed the rough stalagmites hanging far overhead. Sigurd snatched up his sword as reflex and took a step back. The sheer size of the dragon awed the boy as Fafnir now rose to his full and terrifying height.

"Well?" asked Fafnir. "Let's get on with it."

The boy didn't move.

The corners of Fafnir's mouth crept up in a smile. He nodded to the boy. "It also says, 'love turns to loathing if you sit too long / on someone else's bench.' So, let's wrap up this little chat and get on to the epic battle. You didn't come here to learn ancient history from a tired old man; you came here to slay a dragon!"

"What if I don't *want* to slay you?" Sigurd lowered the tip of his sword. "What if we just… don't?"

"What are you going to do?" asked Fafnir with a sneer. "Go back down the mountain and be Sigurd the Not-Dragon-slayer? Sigurd, Who-Had-Tea with Fafnir? You can't tell Regin you didn't go through with it."

"I could lie," Sigurd said. "I could say I killed you."

"He wants my heart." Fafnir gestured to the wide expanse of his scaled chest. "Didn't he tell you to cut out and roast my heart?"

Sigurd nodded.

"Sick bastard," Fafnir muttered, "but not a crazy one. A dragon's heart bestows great powers on any who eat it. I suggest a little fennel and a generous pinch of sea-salt."

"I could say you weren't here."

"He saw my flame and heard my roar, same as you."

"I could just tell the truth!" Sigurd was getting desperate now. "I could tell Regin I decided not to do it. That you told me the truth."

Fafnir settled his forelegs back on the cave floor and lowered his head. "You could do this; you could do that. How about I save us some time?" He dug his claw through the glittering pile of gold until he drew out a gilt torque. The dragon slipped it onto his finger. Although the torque would have been too large if placed on Sigurd's neck, it fit neatly onto Fafnir's claw as if it were a ring. "I haven't used this in a long, long time," he said. "The ring wasn't the only enchanted doodad Loki slipped into my brother's wergild. This is cursed as well."

"What... what is the curse?" asked Sigurd.

"It lets you know the future," said Fafnir.

"How is *that* a curse?"

Fafnir laughed. "Trust me, boy, it's a curse. It's better just to be surprised. But it seems you'll stay here dithering all day. Now, this won't tell the entire future, not everything, but it can tell the outcome from a given act." He gestured to Sigurd. "In this case, what happens if you fight me." Fafnir closed his eyes and stroked the

50

torque with a claw. When his eyes opened, they were deeper than before.

"Well?" Sigurd's voice was a whisper.

Fafnir shook his head. "This is magic. There're rules, kid. You have to actually ask the question." Sigurd opened his mouth, but Fafnir continued. "Just know there's also a cost. With magic, there's always a cost."

Sigurd paused. He gripped Gram tighter. "What is the cost?"

"The same as the reward: you'll know the future."

"That's it?" Sigurd started to laugh, but something in Fafnir's voice brought him up short.

"That's more than enough." Fafnir blew a jet of steam from his nostrils. "Alright, are you going to ask or not?"

Sigurd took a deep breath. "What happens if I fight you?"

"You'll win." said the dragon flatly. "And go on to great glory and fame. You'll kill me and roast my heart and gain the power to speak to birds. You'll kill my brother, reclaim your father's kingdom, rescue Brunhilde from the tower of flame. You'll become the most famous of all the Volsungs. More famous than your father or grandfather. They will write sagas about your adventures. Ballads. Operas, one day, when those become a thing. Your death will come early and be painful, but it will be glorious. The stuff of legends."

"And if I don't fight you? If I walk away?"

"Perhaps, you'll be happy." The dragon's voice was a soft rumbling purr.

"That's it? Will I still be a famous hero?"

The dragon chuckled, but without mirth. "Aw, kid. You know you won't. No one remembers the happy heroes. Only the tragic ones."

"But I don't want to kill you."

"And I don't want to live!" bellowed the dragon. "But I cannot kill myself, and all the other heroes flee before me! Even your father! I bet he never told you that, did he?" Sigurd shook his head. "The mighty Sigmund came to slay me, years ago, when I first took on this form. But he trembled and fled. Pissed himself, in fact. The sagas conveniently leave out that episode from his life." Fafnir's voice grew soft as his eyes widened and his shoulders drooped. "Sorry, kid, but it's got to be you."

"But *why* me? If all the brave heroes couldn't stand before you, why me? I'm not brave!"

"No, but you're kind. You're just like your mother. They all saw a monster; you see a man." Fafnir's great eyes drifted to Gram's keen edge. "So do the kind thing. Kill me."

Sigurd shivered at Fafnir's words as he mulled over what he had learned today. "I won't kill Regin. I will grant you your wish, but I can't..."

"But you must. Without doing the deed fully, Regin may get the ring and it will be his ultimate demise. You'd be doing him a favor and saving him from the greed that will follow if he gets his hands on these treasures. He has neither the strength nor the ability to fight Andavari's curse. Do you wish to see him like me? A bitter old dwarf with loneliness and despair?"

Sigurd shook his head as he bit down on his lower lip. He didn't want that for Regin. Nor did he want Fafnir to die by his hand. But when he examined the dragon sitting across from him, he empathized with the dragon's pain. Not just any pain, but deep hearted pain. The kind of agony that hides in the depths of one's soul, and in the marrow of one's bones.

He drew in several calming breaths, sniffed back the snot running from his nose, and wiped the pooled tears with the back of hands. He trembled as he gripped Gram. With a shaky step, he approached Fafnir.

"Below the chin and with one clean swipe, aye?" Fafnir instructed, basking in reflected light as the sun set with deep crimson hues that bled to an orangish golden glow and filled the cave.

The rays of light glinted off the steel of the blade. Sigurd was in position. "Fafnir?"

"Yes, boy?"

"I'm sorry," said Sigurd.

"Me, too, kid. Me too."

The End

based on

Dornröschen

collected by

Jacob & Wilhelm Grimm

Sleeping Beauty

Debbie Iancu-Haddad & Sarah Parker

Sleeping Beauty
Debbie Iancu-Haddad & Sarah Parker

Once Bitten

Debbie Iancu-Haddad

Thorns tear my flesh. Again and again, they rip into my skin, cruel and unforgiving. A standing ovation to my persistence. The malicious vines wind around my wrists, cutting and rending in silent abuse, but I push on until my clothes are in tatters and covered in blood.

The forest of thorns shifts and weaves, soundlessly dancing its deadly jig.

I pause, tearing off the remains of my shirt, waiting for my flesh to mend. Slowly, like a fist closing, the ragged tears of my rough wounds knit back into smooth skin. There are advantages to my condition, though nothing can be done for my clothes. I throw away the useless shirt, the thorns catching it midair, gleefully ripping it to shreds. No mind. My only regret is this is no way to see my beloved for the first time in one hundred years. I smile. Maybe she will not mind my unclothed state.

That thought gives me strength to push forward once more.

That witch is a fool if she thinks she can keep me away with something as meaningless as pain. For my beloved, I would swim any ocean, climb any mountain, or brave any forest of thorns enchanted to keep me out.

Not far now. From here the weather vane on the highest turret is visible. The flags lying motionless. *Even the wind does not blow upon these walls.*

Dawn is rising when I force my way through the last vines of the endless thicket. The leaves curl away, black and thick, sated after tasting so much of my blood. Wisps of mist drift around my legs, pooling in my footprints. The brittle grass crackles under my boots. Even the lawn sleeps. The air holds its breath. My footsteps split the heavy silence.

I must hurry. I don't have long, yet my feet still upon the path, rooted in memory. These grounds I used to guard remained untouched for a century, but it feels like yesterday.

I pass by the tree where I waited for her, the night we made a pact to flee together from her father's home. We were young and naive. All we wanted was to be together forever. *Was it too much to ask?*

I come upon the first body in the courtyard. A maid, curled up, her head resting on a pile of mildewed laundry. Her eyelids flutter as if in a dream, her pulse beating strong in her neck.

Tempting, but I don't have time for a snack.

My beloved awaits.

At the entrance to the castle, sentries slump at their posts. I know them both. Yosef, who initiated me into the guard when I turned fifteen, and Finbar, the happiest man in the king's guard. He used to sing as we patrolled the grounds.

"We are the luckiest men alive," he'd nudge me with his elbow, almost knocking me off my feet, with a wink and a jocular tone, "to witness such beauty."

All I could do was smile and nod as the princess passed. Her maids, giggling and whispering behind their palms. Her eyes, blue as the midnight sky, found mine, a shy smile tilting her rosy lips, and I was lost. From the first time I saw her, I loved her. Not because of her beauty, but because of her kindness. It's easy to believe a lowly guard fell in love with a princess. Inconceivable for the princess to love him back. I truly am the luckiest man alive... well, not exactly alive, but... in existence.

I push open the wide, wooden doors of the palace, their intricate carvings dusty and covered in cobwebs. Turning my back on my old friend and my mentor, I hurry across the courtyard. Stepping over napping dogs and around standing horses, their riders slumbering uncomfortably in the saddle in full armor. *That will be a sore awakening.*

The great hall is unchanged. Courtiers sprawl on the dusty carpets, oblivious to the accumulated dirt. Spiders spin webs from nose to chin, the generations of trapped flies a silent testimony to time passing. The king and queen rest side by side on their thrones, her head on his shoulder. They look younger than I remember and peaceful. The last time I saw this room, I was being carried away for my heinous crime. I recall the fury in the king's eyes as he had me cast into the deepest dungeon in the furthest prison.

After an unsuccessful attempt to take my life.

Hanging wasn't the way to go.

My crime? Love. If not for the creature waiting in the forest that night I would have paid with my life. Only, by the time the king's men caught us together, I no longer had a life to take.

My fist clenches. I could take my revenge now, while they lie dormant, but no. I will let my sweet Rose decide their fate.

My feet move faster now. I push through silent halls and echoing rooms.

I check her chambers, finding them empty but for the memories. Her silk sheets lie untouched, reminding me of whispered words and sweet kisses. Stolen nights when I was supposed to stand sentry outside her room, protecting the princess from those who would steal her virtue, while she was busy stealing mine. I'll admit, I didn't put up much of a fight. How could I refuse lips that tasted like honey and words as soft as *love*?

Finding her here would have been too easy. Now I'm close enough to sense her. My Rose calls to me from the tallest tower. The sun shines over the treetops now, casting pools of molten fire through the windows of the lengthy corridor connecting the main hall of the castle to the tower where my lady awaits.

Impatient now, I break into a run, ignoring the sleeping courtiers in my way, ducking through shadows, and sidestepping the sun's lethal rays.

As I approach the tower door, my path is blocked.

A woman dressed in white, her hair like driven snow, her skin creased and worn as parchment, bars the door. A sole moving soul in the sleeping castle.

"Witch..." I hiss. "Was it a long wait?"

"Demon." Her voice creaks with disuse. "I hoped you were gone for good. My vision predicted a prince."

"Will you settle for a prince of darkness?"

Blue fire crackles at her fingertips.

"Begone." Her voice rises in fury. "You will not have her."

"Why do you people keep saying that? Why don't we wake Rose together and ask her what she wants?"

"Never. Not if she must sleep for a thousand years." Her voice rattles the walls. *Very inconsiderate considering everyone is asleep.*

"Can you wait so long?" I ask, softly. "I can."

Her stance crumples, an infinitesimal dip. My enemy has a weakness. Doubt.

"You were wrong about me," I insist. "Like your misguided prophecy..."

"Was I, demon?" She raises a gnarled claw.

I'm wary of the blue fire, but I'm too close to my goal. I cannot fail now.

60

"Your prophecy was warped. 'On her sixteenth birthday, she will prick her finger on a needle and die'. How do you confuse a spinning wheel with the needle-sharp teeth of a vampire?"

The witch scowls. "The interpretation of prophecies is not an exact science. But she did die."

"Briefly. It didn't take. She died and rose again, more powerful and more beautiful than ever."

"You cannot have her."

"Ah, once again you are wrong."

I take a step forward, my teeth lengthening in anticipation. I don't have time for snacks, but I'll make time to take the life of the harpy who kept my beloved from me.

The witch approaches, her amber eyes never leaving my face. The blue magic crackles as she tosses it, hitting my chest. The charge sizzles, flaring against my bare skin, powerful enough to stop a human heart. A shiver runs through me. The smell of ozone is overpowering. My muscles twitch and spasm, bringing me to my knees.

The witch cackles in triumph, moving closer 'till she stands above me.

I lift my head to face my nemesis, yet as I face my doom, my eyes are drawn over her shoulder, past her maniacal grin.

Despite the disrepair of the castle, the tower door doesn't creak as it opens.

I still my un-beating heart at the vision of loveliness standing in the doorway. Her midnight eyes are tinged with red, yet she is as beautiful as the day we pledged our lives, and our deaths, to each other.

Her bare feet make no noise on the carpet. Her lips part, the sharp points of her elongated fangs just visible between her plump red lips. Silently, she slips behind the aged witch, her eyes finding mine as she clutches the witch's neck with superhuman strength.

The witch struggles in her grasp as Rose drains her of blood.

"Why?" The hag gasps, slipping to the ground. "I only wanted to protect you."

Rose stands over her, hands on her dainty hips, licking a drop of blood from her red lips. "The princess shall not die, but fall into a deep sleep for a hundred years." She taunts. "Do you know how thirsty I am after a century of sleep?"

The witch croaks, yet no words pass her wizened lips. Her body falls limp. Her eyes close for the last time.

Rose reaches out her hand to pull me to my feet.

"It's you." She flings herself into my arms and I crush her to my breast. If my cold dead heart could beat, it would be hammering out of my chest. "I promised I would wait forever," she murmurs against me, "but the witch prophesied a prince would save me. I thought I'd never see you again, but you came. My knight in tarnished armor..." she tips her chin up, gazing into my eyes as her fingertips run over my bare shoulders, sending delicious shivers up my spine. "Or even better. No armor at all."

I thread my fingers into her golden hair. "No witch, no forest of thorns, could keep me away from you, my love. I've waited for this moment for one hundred years."

She smiles, tilting her head to expose the smooth white skin of her neck.

"From this day on, nothing will part us again. I am forever yours."

As I kiss her lips, sound fades away. There is nothing but the rasp of her silk gown beneath my hands, the touch of her palm on my neck. Only when we break apart do I hear the sounds of waking courtiers, stirring around us. Dogs bark outside, servants cry out, and birds take to the air once more.

The spell is broken.

"Are you hungry, my dear?" I ask, taking her hand in mine.

The joyful cries of the court awakening soon turn to screams, music to my ears. Those who tried to keep us apart pay in flesh and blood, for one hundred years of longing, one hundred years alone. Now hand in hand, my Rose and I feast and celebrate our reunion.

And we will live happily ever after.

The End

Twice Shy of Truth, Once in Love

Also Known As

Rose's Thorn

Sarah Parker

"Such a beautiful creature," they cooed over me when I was a babe. Though they'd probably rather not come across adult me in the woods. Within the castle walls, I presented myself one way. With my true love, I presented another. He was shown no mercy for loving me, an act above his social station. So I'll show no mercy on those who called us damned, and I will put their fanciful ideas into proper place: reality bites.

I've been locked up here now for many a lonely night. You know, waiting for someone to release me from the highest tower, where I'm sheltered away from the dangers of the world as

I slumber "in peace". Restless, I sleep, though it's something my body no longer needs. I'm left alone with my thoughts. Ready to rewrite history, to speak of heresy.

On occasion, the witch who called herself my fairy godmother, aka Wanda of the Wonderful Vision, walks my room. She thinks she blessed me with some future opportunity. Believes she preserved me for my Prince Charming, but that's PC BS. I believe it's best to get to the point. Wanda wanted to find a way around that prophecy spoken over me. For decades, she's spent her mornings muttering words to keep me from waking, from walking the earth until a hundred years have passed.

"Sleep it off," had been her answer to everything when she was known as Nanny. Father often noted how much like his own nanny she was, but he didn't give that enough mind. He minded that witchy woman more than me. More than Mother. More than his own mother. They should all be dead and gone now. But she preserves them for what will come to pass.

"Sit a spell with me," Nanny Wanda goaded when I was still a gullible girl of fifteen, then spilled the secret of the prophetic words spoken over me. Words which wrought a future she couldn't wrap up nicely. She only wanted to protect and serve, she says now, as if she offers an apology. As if she didn't see the consequence of her actions. Her own rash response to words of another. Another fool who attempted to foretell my story, to write it for me. And the cycle continues. Another will bite the dust. The Ever-After Wheel continues to turn. Happily, I've plenty of time now, so I'm in no rush.

I dream of my response, my revenge, as I lay entombed here in my internment. I recall every detail that destined me here, awaiting the kiss of true love to awaken me. I seep myself in the words and actions that ferried me to this unfortunate turn of events.

"Now, now," Nanny Wanda consoled me after Glenora, the most glamorous of my ladies in waiting, teased me for being ignorant and innocent. In this conversation I first heeded spell-binding words.

"The ways of the world hold no weight on you, for you are the matter around which the masses merge. You are the one to inform and lead and set the standard. You do not need the world's education." Nurse-maid and nanny, perpetual nurturer, she suggested there was little for me to know outside my place within the castle walls. Little to lament missing out on. Still, I was a cagey child.

Wanda cautioned me, and might as well have been waving a magic wand. "Question the depth and multiple meanings of words. Spoken brazenly, rash utterances lead to ruin. One needs to be fully informed before they make a choice." She spoke in the voice she used when her words cast about in the future.

I understand the conveyed warning in retrospect. Possess now the knowledge she had. She was always after illumination. Ironic t'was a creature of the night who made the way for me and my true love. The lady among my maids who had the darkest heart served to secure my foretold future. They all knew of my reciprocated affections for the soldier boy. They were all bound to serve me to my heart's content. I saw how cruel they could be, but saw too how they conceded readily to the power of love everlasting; how they thirsted after life.

Mind you, I didn't quite grasp how literal that truth expressed their essence. I admired how they were tireless. When I spoke with fondness of that observation, Mother explained how these families who served us in-waiting were age-old within our midst, driven by duty. I didn't understand this was not a generational matter. But neither did Mother fully know of what she spoke; she silenced her own retrospection. She and Father, both blind to that in their midst.

"You spy on us," I accused Glenora. She broke through the glade after dusk to meet me beneath the tree where my love, Vincent, and I'd just spoken of our eternal and undying love and devotion to one another. The tree where he planned to return to me under cover of midnight, and we'd steal away together by the star's light. Rather romantic, all in all. I let a sigh slip.

She ignored my words, knowing that I knew it to be her job to keep an eye out for me.

"You want to be together forever?" Glenora's eyes glinted as she spoke. There was an edge to her inquiry. I considered how the words could be a double-edged sword.

She licked her lips. I would assume her nervous, but sensed it was another matter entirely.

"I can make that happen, you know." She offered, eager.

No, I don't know. The retort didn't leave my mind. Yet, I would take any help I could get. Any path that allowed Vincent and I to remain together. I knew him to be my once-in-a-lifetime love. I'm sure t'was a vacant expression she saw upon my face. My thoughts flowed after him, could not fathom her suggestion.

My other ladies joined us, forming a tight circle around me.

"Silly me," Glenora giggled. "Of course you don't garner my meaning. Let's go to the rose garden."

I agreed, but sent Leila to fetch Vincent back for me. I told her the post where he'd reported for duty. Glenora informed her all hush hush in whispers behind her hand where they could find us waiting. I side-eyed their off-sides conversation but remained willing to sidle up to any plan that could absolve any wrong-doing of my choices made so I could be with my love.

I wondered after pruning, but said nothing, and followed after her as obediently as she'd followed after me. As we entered the maze the rose garden had been shaped into, it seemed more and more like she was the one at home.

She confidently walked as if she knew this labyrinth better than those who'd walked it since their youth and still managed to get lost within its winding ways.

We emerged from the rose garden maze to enter the woods. We stopped at another tree.

My lady Glenora turned to me, silently appraising. Quick about the summons, moments later Vincent was at my side and she addressed us both. "Will you make a pact to spend the rest of your lives together? To reign here together, forever?"

Forever did not have finality in it as she spoke. The word lingered. I reflected briefly on the lot of rulers and gentry. How their lives were already bound to something for all their days.

Her tone harsh, she asked again. Prodding. "We don't have much time. Another draws near. Make your vow to do so before me now and I will turn your future into your hands."

That promise of holding my future in my own hands swayed me. I'd already exchanged words of this weight with Vincent. I could commit to forever.

I looked over to Vincent, who was already looking to me. "Forever?" I asked.

"Forever," he affirmed.

"A blood oath seals your union." Glenora began to explain. I'd turned to seal our vow with true love's kiss and assumed she'd turned to give us privacy. When I broke from his embrace, she handed me a goblet I figured to be celebratory wine. After I sipped from and dropped the vessel, about the same time she brought her lips to my neck and I looked down to see her slit wrist; only then, in that moment, did I comprehend how Vincent and I would be together forever.

But we didn't have forever in that moment. Her sharp hearing proved true as the King's guard crashed upon our ceremony.

I pressed my lips and teeth to Vincent's neck, hoping the blood I sipped transferred saving power into him as well. Seeing the blood upon Glenora, they assumed what transpired; an attack, they surmised. My lady-in-waiting swept me up as my legs gave way underneath me, portraying herself as my protector while hiding her healing wrist. My eyes closed as the men seized Vincent. "By the tree," I murmured.

When I awoke, raging, the news that my love had been sentenced to die did nothing to quell that rising within me. I could not see that proclamation as a concluding sentence. Glenora cloaked and cautioned me from being out of doors at that time. The sun would soon rise. I knew her words held multiple implications.

But I smelled his fear and heard the cries for justice. My love's first offense was letting me befall danger. The second, leading me into it by being out of doors after dark. Rumors already shrouded our land. The people within the walls feared that outside their understanding. Feared some evil creature who lived in the woods; one that craved blood. I had to be protected. My image and associations kept pure. For I was deemed the fairest of them all; a fine delicacy. But I'm strong now. I'm sure of my future now.

Hellbent on gnashing the rope they tied around his neck to bind him away from me, t'was a sore temptation to tear out their throats, but I kept thinking during that first rescue attempt of how I couldn't dare let them see my face. I don't know what I'd been trying to preserve, now that I think more on it. Before sunrise, I broke him free from the dungeons and brought him to a place where we could begin our new lives together.

I left him to hunt, for he claimed he must be the provider, and I knew that would give me enough time to properly tend to the guards who turned against him, all because his heart turned towards me. New to the demands of my new life, I found I did not have the energy to evoke my vengeance. I needed to feed before I could best men conditioned to preserve and protect.

When I awake I am alone, back at that first tree; that shaded place under which we first promised ourselves to each other. I walk just a bit further and find myself in front of the door that grants entry to our castle.

The sentries are sleeping. Never have they fallen so in their duty. Our guards have always proven honor-bound to our family. Reflecting on my own honor, I hurry to my chambers. Vincent was not by my side below the tree; he must wait for me sequestered in my room-- the one place inside the confines of the castle walls we'd been free to be together.

Nanny meets me at the threshold. I open my mouth. Can't close it fast enough as she blows dust at me. I'm coughing. But, if the tales I've heard of bloodletters are true, there should be no effect upon me.

My body stills, though my mind races, and my eyes remain open. I feel each tender touch as I'm changed into a midnight blue sleeping gown. I hear the murmurs as shouts while Nanny whisks away tears and spews damnations and repetitions of "always supposed to wait a generation," "wait a generation or significantly alter appearance."

She turns to chide Glenora, gliding in without a sound. It surprises me as I can hear the rustle of the rose bushes in the wind.

"I turned him loose in the woods," Glenora tells Nanny, who nods gravely. "He will become known as the forest creature they fear, if folklore serves us, as it so often does."

"Witch, we do not have an accord here. Only shared loyalty to our princess." Glenora's voice is cold.

Wanda seems to ignore their differences, choosing to focus on common purpose.

"Those limbs and roots will be twisted to prevent any entrance until it is time." The witch speaks words and bends elements to her enchantment.

I'm aware, but consciousness is not there, as my body is carried to the highest tower. All must be according to plan. Witch Wanda speaks of it to me as she settles me in for the next century. "Slumber will allow people to forget. Time to pass. We will be able to present a new tale in time. A fortified future. I promise."

Promise. That word lingers, and memory is pain. I think back on when I first spoke to a sentry of love. How I'd guarded my heart until it became his to hold. How we'd promised each other forever.

Our pact had an impact neither of us anticipated. We fulfilled a curse, aided by the turning conducted by my shrewd lady. That foretold looms now nonetheless. I now know myself to be cursed by this faerie godmother to gather dust and cobwebs as I await an awakening.

The silence that surrounds me is broken by footfalls. It's time; the anticipated prince has arrived. I wonder where he heralds from. If he's ready for me. I suppose if he suffices, I can turn him. If not, I'll have my first supper in a century.

I've wrapped my mind around the story spun about my condition. The witch has spoken no words over me today. Today I will rise. I will settle the score, though it will be four-score and four years since my sixteenth birthday bound me. Endings are beginnings, after all.

Ever after, ever here. Those who heard the tale will have passed it down to the next generation before passing into death. If we keep our shrouded forest, we'll have no need to leave our home. I can repurpose the past to preserve our future. But first, I must quench my thirst.

The ever-watchful witch doesn't see me coming for her. I'd say Vincent serves as a distraction, but that really only applies to me. I'm sore tempted to attack him, albeit in an entirely different manner. First things first; eliminate the barrier between us.

Glenora and her sisters gather as our counsel once Vincent and I are reunited. Stepping out of the shadows near the tower door, my chamber door, the grand hall door. They stayed as sentry, serving my family faithfully as we slumbered. Now we are an eternal family. Our future is nigh. We're fortunate to never know death and to always have love. We toast to our good health, laying to waste those who wished to refuse Vincent and I our love.

based on

Die goldene Gans

collected by

Jacob & Wilhelm Grimm

Goose Bastardly

Darius Bearguard & Mara Lynn Johnstone

Goose Bastardly
Darius Bearguard & Mara Lynn Johnstone

Wild Fortune

Darius Bearguard

"War is what happens when language fails"
— Margaret Atwood

Philip adjusts his pack as he walks through the woods to fetch firewood to sell. A lunch packed by his mother in his bag, and his father's axe resting on his shoulder, he walks with a beaming smile, and not a care in the world.

"Darn you!" someone shouts off in the distance.

Against his father's advice, he leaves the road and heads into the thick brush in search of the voice. After a few moments he is ready to give up, when from behind a fallen log peeks the head of a goose. But not any goose Philip has ever seen, for the goose's golden feathers shone brightly in the mid-morning light. The goose does not see Philip as he snatches the fowl up.

"Was it you shouting?" Philip asks with a chuckle. The goose honks and strains against Philip's grip, bringing a smile to the boy's face. "No, I suppose not."

"Oh! You found him!" a tiny man in grey clothes shouts excitedly, coming upon Philip.

"Is this your goose, sir?" Philip asks.

"...Yes," the man says meekly.

"I'm sorry, sir. I'm not trying to steal him. He's a magnificent creature! Would you be willing to trade?" Philip asks, imagining the praise his father will heap upon him.

"You want to trade for him?"

"I don't have much," Philip starts, but upon seeing how small and skinny the man is, he beams and holds out his lunch bag. "But I'll trade you my lunch if you—"

The small man, fast as can be, snatches the food and takes off. "A fine trade indeed!" he shouts over his shoulder as he bounds through the woods.

Philip holds up the goose. "Well, Mr. Beakers." His smile broadens at his cleverness, "wait until my family gets a look at—"

"Are you barking mad?" Brom asks.

"Hit your head in the woods then, eh?" Tom questions.

"Dad'll 'ave your head, he will," Dom chimes in.

Philip, dejected by his older brothers' comments, looks at his goose running around the kitchen, scared by their laughter. "He's a golden goose! He could be worth loads of—"

Just then Philip's mother opens the door and the goose takes off, with Philip not far behind.

The goose runs into the village, dashing down the streets, and narrowly avoiding Philip. The boy starts to fall behind, but just before the goose rounds the last bend, a man clad in black trips over the waterfowl and tumbles into the street, cracking his head on the cobblestone.

"Mr. Beakers!" Philip shouts, pulling the honking bird out from under the man in black.

The sheriff comes around the corner. "You, boy! Did you trip this man?"

"Y-yes, sir! Sorry, sir!" Philip says nervously, not wanting the goose to be hurt in recompense.

"Sorry? 'Sorry,' he says!" the sheriff shouts to his men, who all laugh as they pick up the man in black. "This fellow here has been robbing folks blind for a fortnight now! You stopped the most notorious thief this town has ever seen!" The sheriff looks him over and unstraps a sword from the criminal's belt. "Here, a reward for yah! Young man like you shouldn't be out without a weapon anyhow!"

Philip hands the sheriff the goose as he straps the sword around his waist. "Wow! I've always wanted a—"

The goose honks and flaps, startling the sheriff who drops him, leaving the bird free to run into the busy street. Philip sees the traffic but doesn't hesitate to go after the wayward fowl. He weaves in and out of carts and horses, chasing after the bird. As Philip is about to grab the goose, stunned still in the street, a horse-drawn carriage strikes his head, and the boy is knocked unconscious.

"Woah!" the driver shouts, bringing the carriage to a halt. Other drivers are prepared to raise a commotion, but they see the gilded seal of the mediciner on the carriage doors. The goose stands over the boy as if remorseful for his actions when he's snatched up by the driver, and a well-dressed mediciner steps out of the carriage. "Bloody boy come outta nowhere!" the driver says. "Chasin' this 'ere bird, I reckon!"

"Yes," the mediciner says, giving a brief glance at the bird still honking and hissing away, "I can imagine." He examines Philip and gives a smile to the driver. "Not to worry, Bartholemew, you've merely knocked his wits out. We'll prop him up against a store and—"

"Sir, I don't be thinking that's such a good idea." The driver nods to Philip's waist.

The mediciner sees the sword, and recognizes the wolf sigil on the scabbard. "What is a boy from house Verrater doing here? No matter, we should bring him into the city. No sense angering what's soon to be the most powerful noble family in the kingdom."

The driver puts the goose in the carriage and helps the mediciner lift Philip in before taking off for the city.

"I don't have a clue who this boy is."

"What do you mean?"

"I mean I've never seen this child a day in my life!."

"But he carries the Verrater sigil?"

"Where?"

"Unnngh." Philip groans, as he awakens on the examination table of the quaint mediciner's office. The two men turn their attention to him as he starts to get up.

"Take care now, young man," the mediciner says, reaching out to steady Philip as he rises. "That was quite the bump on your head."

"Am I— unngh!" He moans, his head giving a big throb. "Am I going to be— Mr. Beakers!" Philip proclaims, remembering his golden goose. "Is Mr. Beakers alright!?"

"Mr. *Beakers*? Oh! The goose!" The mediciner points to the other side of the table where the goose is preening himself. "Yes, quite alright. I had my driver bring him along."

"Excuse me," a well-dressed man interrupts, "but I would have a word Mr...?"

"Oh! Philip, sir, my name is Philip. I'm from—"

"Well Philip, the good mediciner here tells me that you said we know each other, but I've never so much as laid eyes on—"

"I never said he told me *anything!*" The mediciner says, growing irritable. "I said his sword bears the sigil of your house!"

"What are you talk—"

Suddenly the goose begins honking and flapping its wings, coming around the table and launching himself at the nobleman. With unusually quick reflexes, he grabs the bird mid-flight. As he goes to toss the bird aside he nearly falls over, still clinging tight. "What sort of nonsense is this?" He flails the bird around, eliciting a honk from the goose every time he does. "Did you put something on this foul creature, sir?"

"What?" The mediciner asks, then looks to Philip who shakes his head. "What do you mean, put something on it?"

"Him," Philip corrects.

"Whatever," the mediciner replies.

"It, he, *whatever*, is stuck to my hands!" the nobleman shouts as he again swings the bird around, trying to loosen it from his hands.

The mediciner rolls his eyes. "I've no time for this nonsense. I am behind on my duties as is."

"What do you mean you've no—"

"Sir Whendam, while I appreciate your plight, I am not a veterinarian, and even if I were one, clearly there are magical properties to contend with, what with the golden feathers and all. Go see Madam Portia."

"Who is Madam Portia?" Philip asks.

Within the hour, they arrive at the castle gates, Sir Whendam still trying to dislodge the goose from his grip, all while Philip looks with wonder at the castle before him. Philip had never so much as strayed from the village or the woods behind his home, let alone been to the city, nevermind the castle. And now he was about to have an audience with the high court wizard Madam Portia. The nobleman explained to Philip that she was a battle sorceress for years before being promoted to court wizard for her bravery and exceptional knowledge of spells.

Soon they climb the tower and enter Madam Portia's study. Various books and scrolls on magic are strewn throughout the room, along with vials and bottles of brightly colored potions on tables and the floor.

"Well, well, Sir Whendam, let me take a *gander* at the problem, hm?" she laughs, seeing the bird looking around frantically. "My my, such a beautiful specimen indeed. The bird is yours, I take it?" She asks Philip while examining the goose.

"Yes, Ma— Madam Portia," Philip studders. "Hi—his name is—"

Madam Portia smiles at the boy. "There's no need to be nervous, I don't bite. Usually," she adds with a wink. "Sadly young man, I will have no choice but to offer you compensation."

"Compensation?"

"For the bird."

"Mr. Beakers? Why?"

"... Is that really what you've named him?" Madam Portia asks incredulously.

"Yes?" Philip replies meekly.

"Well, I doubt he likes that very much. Irrelevant; a magical creature like this? No spell will unbind him. I'll need to destroy him."

"What!?" Philip shouts.

"What?!" Sir Whendam exclaims.

"I'm sorry gentlemen, but I don't have much in the way of options. I promise, young Philip, you will be rewarded handsomely. Now hold still, Sir Whendam!" She levitates her staff from across the room into her hand and takes a few steps back. "One... Two... Thr—"

Before she can finish, the goose falls from the hands of the nobleman and dashes for the door.

"Mr. Beakers!" Philip shouts, rushing after the goose, clumsily knocking over a potion as he passes. It spills on the nobleman.

"Philip! Look out!" the wizard screams. Philip turns back to see, standing awkwardly in the nobleman's clothes, a goblin. Before the goblin can finish thrashing free of the clothing and armor now far too large for his true form, reaching for a weapon, Philip draws his own sword. He thrusts it into the monster, killing him instantly.

"Philip!" Madam Portia says shrilly. "You've saved us all!"

"Saved us all, you say?" the king asks, seated upon his throne.

"Yes, your Majesty." Portia motions for Philip to rise from his knee, which he does while clutching his goose under his arm. "If he hadn't acted so quickly after the potion of revealing was spilled on the goblin assassin, who knows what havoc the creature could have wreaked. Not to mention…"

"Yes. My daughter." The king shudders. "I cannot bear to think what would have become of the realm if he had been allowed to marry the princess as planned." The king looks to Philip. "What is your name, my boy?"

"Philip, Your Highness."

"Majesty," Portia corrects.

"Whatever," Philip replies looking at his feet, prompting a smile from the king.

"Young Philip, you have saved the realm and all her people this day. I don't know if I could ever truly repay you, but I tell you this: pick something, anything. Whatever your hand touches next shall be yours for all eternity. So swears the crown."

"So swears the crown," the assembled nobles echo through the throne room.

Philip's mind is ablaze as he looks around at all of the priceless treasures in the throne room, prompting a knowing grin from the king. Just a ruby from one of the vases could change his life forever.

However, in his moment of stupor, his grip loosens from the goose and it takes off down a corridor at the back of the hall, with Philip not far behind. "Mr. Beakers! Come back!"

The king and the assembled court all laugh, watching the boy chase after his bird.

The goose quickly weaves down the hallway, dodging Philip as he dives for him. The bird is nearly to the window when he's suddenly scooped up by the princess leaving her bedchamber.

"Oh my, and who might this be?" she asks of the bird, who honks and flails.

"That's— He's mine, your High— Maj— uhhh." Philip fumbles his words, catching up to the two of them.

"Princess Liesa will do fine." She smiles at him, looking him over. Tattered clothes notwithstanding, she finds him quite handsome.

"Yes, Princess. Sorry."

She smiles, amused by his bashfulness. "And your name? Or shall I call you 'The Man who Owns the Goose'?"

"I'm Philip."

"Philip?" A flash of recognition comes over her. "The boy who killed the goblin assassin! You're the one who saved me!" She embraces him in a hug.

"The boy has chosen!" Madam Portia exclaims gleefully, her robes flowing behind her as she comes up the hall.

"This is preposterous!" the king shouts. "You cannot possibly expect—"

"Now, now, Your Majesty; the old magics of sacred bonds, especially the sacred bonds of kings, cannot be so easily trifled with," she says, menace in her voice. "Lest they invite dark omens, as they have done so often in the past."

"Please, Daddy," the princess says, instantly bringing calm to her father's red face. "Maybe it won't be so bad." She looks at Philip with a wink and a bite of her lip.

And so it was that Philip wed Princess Liesa, making him Prince of the realm, but not before Liesa had a magic leash made for Mr. Beakers so he couldn't run away anymore. And when Liesa's father passed, Philip was crowned King. He ruled justly over his kingdom with his best friend, Mr. Beakers, ever at his side.

Intrepid Hero

Mara Lynn Johnstone

It had started as a normal day for The Almighty Honk — Ruler of Sky and Surf, He Who Outwitted the Fairy Queen, Legendary Troublemaker, Cleverest of Birds, Slayer of the First Goblin King, As Golden as the Sun and Twice as Bright, First of His Name.

The current recipient of his attention was growing tiresome, as humans go, insisting that the Thief of Golden Magic behave like a common waterfowl, which simply wouldn't do. One would think the man ungrateful for such delights as goose poop, surprise peckings, and sudden hisses, not to mention the rampant rearrangement of his terrible interior decoration.

Goose Bastardly, Destroyer of Hordes, was taking a leisurely scuttle through the forest (giving his human some exercise), when he was unceremoniously scooped up by some young ragamuffin in torn clothes.

Flapping and swearing in the goose language did nothing to gain him freedom. If only he had his old battle magics handy! Then he'd show this brigand what for.

But here was his human. Perhaps the man could be useful.

The man *sold* him. Of all the insults! And for nothing more than a meal!

So be it. If this peasant's home was unsuited to be graced by He of the Tongue-Teeth that Strike Fear into Housepets, then he would be a free goose once more.

It was unsuited.

Three more loud humans crowded the room, and there was hardly anything edible or breakable about the place. The moment the door was opened, he darted outside and led the youth on a merry chase.

So merry! Many humans were startled by the sudden presence of The Intolerable Menace, and one even tripped over him, landing with a satisfying smack. He lingered to see whether he'd managed to knock a tooth out (human teeth were so comically smooth).

That was when the youth caught up to him, managing a capture while those unconscious legs were still hobbling the Golden Wings. Most undignified.

Oh, but this was interesting. Other humans had been chasing this one — and now they were thanking the boy for his capture, instead of the Conqueror of the Woodlands who was truly responsible. How dare!

Well, enough tarrying. He would wait for an ideal moment… and there it was, when the boy was given a trophy taken from the conquered villain. (Rude. A goose had nowhere to fit a sword belt, but it would have been nice if they had asked.) The boy went to accept the blade, handing off The Instigator of Havoc to another human.

A human who was unprepared! After a honk and flutter, the chase was on again. The youth who dared to claim The Water Viper's valor was quick, that was certain, but not bright. Despite chasing the Glorious Golden Feathers into traffic, the boy did not think to look around himself when his quarry stopped in the middle of the street.

The horse missed him. The carriage didn't.

With the boy sprawled unconscious and the carriage stopped, He of a Most Dickish Disposition honked in triumph and looked for teeth.

He really had to stop doing that. Someone caught him this time too.

The humans from the carriage dithered, arguing over whether to leave the boy to recover (yes, please) or to get involved (dagnabbit). Apparently, the sword was more valuable than it had appeared, which made the situation more infuriating when the busybodies loaded everyone back into the carriage.

Said busybodies were treated to a symphony of honks, hisses, and befouled seats on the ride. They deserved no less.

A look out the window, between bouts of havoc, showed increasing proximity to the capitol city. Hmm. The Master of the Long Game settled as the carriage came to a halt. This deserved observation. He would choose the most satisfying route to chaos from the many he would undoubtedly be presented with.

And so it was that The Gold that Will Kill You behaved with docility the human in the woods would have given much to see. He behaved while he was carried out of the carriage in the wake of the unconscious youth, and while the doctor did all manner of inspection to make sure the boy's head had not cracked permanently. He behaved while a nobleman was summoned who wore a symbol matching the one on the sword.

He caught a whiff of something he didn't like, but he behaved.

It was only after the boy had woken and talked with the nobleman that the Mighty Beakstrike recognized the scent of an old enemy.

Goblins. The nobleman smelled like goblins. And not the tame kind that ate mushrooms and bothered no one. This was a member of the raiding clan: thieves of magic much darker than his own, casters of illusions, and performers of deeds most foul.

The Vicious Wingbeat, Master Tactician sprang into action. He activated the magic that had served him well in the past, and flung himself at the false nobleman in a flurry of golden feathers and mighty honks. The man caught him, and his feathers stuck fast.

Good, thought The Most Courageous Waterfowl. *Now take me to your den.*

He did not. But the man did take him to the castle, which was almost as good. There was great potential for excitement there. He of No Bothers to Give kept his calm on the trip to see the highest-ranking human wizard in the land.

He wondered if she would recognize him. He'd distinguished himself in the goblin insurrection some years ago.

She did not recognize him. Nor did she detect the scent of malevolence clinging to the "nobleman" like a rancid perfume. Useless human magickers and their useless human noses.

If that wasn't enough, this wizard had the gall to go straight for a destruction spell, without trying a single unbinding first! *Useless* human magickers!

The Hiss that Shatters Stone deactivated his own magic and made for the door. Let them deal with the disguised invaders on their own.

But the youth lunged after him, nearly upending a table in his haste. The crash of glass was eclipsed by the shouts of the humans. That caught the attention of He Who has Befouled the Tallest Rock, who paused in the doorway. Goblin scent filled the air.

Well, look at that. They *did* deal with the invader. Who knew the kid could handle a sword that well?

Oh ho, and they were off to see the king. This sounded worth sticking around for.

It wasn't. They just talked. And not even about rooting out any other goblin sneaks, either. Useless humans. But this was the castle, full of potential for mischief. He Whose Courtesy You Do Not Deserve slipped free from the foolish youth and dashed away, webbed feet slapping the polished floor, eyes open for shenanigans.

Despite this, he was caught unaware by a fast-moving human in a poofy dress, who had no right being so talented at waterfowl capture. Great, the one human who wasn't useless, and she was eavesdropping on the conversation in the main room.

But wait. This new conversation had promise. The foolish youth would be marrying into royalty by the looks of it, which meant continued access to the seat of power in this kingdom. And the youth insisted on claiming the Feathers That Outshine The Sunset as his own.

Hmm. Playing along would mean that he, Blessed By No God But Himself, would also have access to castle intrigue. That was definitely worth sticking around for. What excitement would the future bring now?

A leash. The future brought a leash. A magical one, crafted specially for him, to keep him from inflicting his particular brand of pandemonium on the kingdom at large.

But that wouldn't last. He Who Is Surprisingly Stealthy for Someone So Brightly Colored would find his way to freedom soon enough, and much fun would be had.

He would cause a glorious mess, then sneak into the war effort and unleash feathery hell on the goblins. Everyone would see what it meant to get on the bad side of The Most Glorious of Geese.

based on

Troldens Datter

collected by

Svend Grundtvig

The Daughter's Toll

Imelda Taylor & Sarah Parker

The Daughter's Toll
Imelda Taylor & Sarah Parker

The Tale of the Troll's Heart

Imelda Taylor

This is a tale of a misunderstood father. How a creature so feared was capable of love so pure.

Once, in a land where kingdoms vied for power and riches, dwelt the most powerful troll. Unlike any other trolls, he possessed magic and wisdom. He could disguise himself as whomever he desired and turn others into whatever he whimmed. His powers were enough to conquer any land he wished and the kings of every kingdom knew of this. Their forefathers provided him with the riches he possessed. Now they ask for financial favours. Through the years of war, nothing was achieved. They all squandered their riches and made the troll the richest of them all.

A witch from a nearby land heard of this renowned power. She left the cave where she lived to marry the troll. Such a union was dangerous, for he was the most powerful and she the most wicked. The moment she laid eyes on him, she knew he was rare. For he had a heart that could love and a brain that could never be fooled.

Yet, this witch was able to make the troll fall in love with her.

Years passed. The troll and witch gave life to a girl. The troll adored her. The witch despised her. She had the beauty of the queen, and the wisdom of her father.

The time arrived when the daughter came of age. The witch knew she must consume her daughter's heart for her to keep her youth, for as soon as the daughter blossomed, the witch would perish.

On the night of the ritual, the witch was about to kill her daughter when the troll found out. He could never slay his wife as she was still his beloved. Instead, he cursed her to become a fish. She was set free to roam the waters, and with her, she took the troll's heart.

Time passed. The troll's daughter grew more and more desirable. Not only for her beauty, but also as an heir to the troll's treasures. Kings, Princes and Emperors pursued her hand in marriage. However, their intention wasn't to marry out of love.

"I'm no fool to your game," the troll announced to the suitors. Each of them reassured him that their intentions were pure, so the troll thought to put them to the test.

"The one who is worthy of my daughter's hand will be the master of the air, land, and seas," the troll said. Each suitor was turned into an animal void of human tools to see how they survived. One by one, the troll watched them fail and remain the animal they were turned into.

Then a ruthless king tried to take the daughter by force. The troll had to make the hard decision to hide his daughter at the bottom of the sea, the only place no suitor survived.

The troll watched his daughter from a distance. His heart broke every time he saw her sad. Deep inside he wished she could have a forever companion. However, he could never choose for his headstrong daughter.

One day, the troll remembered the godson he had. The boy must be nearly a man. The troll thought it was time to pay him a visit.

On his visit, he learned that the boy had left. With the help of his magic, the troll found the boy and offered him an occupation. After all, he would need ample riches if he was to join his daughter. However, he must prove himself worthy.

First, the test of obedience: to carry out his master's orders without objections, no matter how peculiar. His task was to feed the animals in the troll's barn, unaware they were once human. Second, the test of mastery of the land. The troll chose to turn him into a hare for a year to see if something so small could survey the land. Then the mastery of the air. The troll turned the lad into a raven. For a year he watched the boy as a raven conquer the wind and the sky. Each time, the boy was paid handsomely upon his return. And finally, the mastery of the waters. The troll chose a humble fish.

Many of the other suitors complained and wished they were turned into some other animal: "If I was a lion, I'd rule the land... If I was an eagle, I'd rule the sky... if I was a shark, I would rule the oceans..." Everyone who made it to the test of the ocean was unable to return. Either they were eaten by a bigger fish or lost in the depths of the sea.

The boy completed the tests and found the troll's daughter. *"If only I was in my human form,"* the boy thought. Suddenly, he was struck by an idea. "If I say the words the troll used to make me human, will I be able to change myself as well?"

It was fortunate the boy was blessed with a sharp memory. As he recited the spell, he was returned to his human form.

There he was, standing in front of the startled princess. It was love at first sight for him-- for her, he was the key to her freedom. She knew he would not have reached this far if he had not passed her father's standards. It was her turn to put him to the test.

He had proven his obedience, the mastery of the land, air and water. He proved to be clever, as he was able to remember the troll's spell.

She had to know he was free from greed, for greed would distract him. She asked him to find the king who was in debt to her father. The very king who had attempted to take her by force.

Then, the boy should lend the wages he earned from her father to the king so the king could pay his debt.

"Will he be able to pay me back?" asked the boy.

"No," replied the troll's daughter. She waited for his response, and wondered. *Will he agree to continue, knowing he might lose his money?*

"Alright. What else?" he said.

The girl's heart leapt, for this was something she did not expect. Next, she wanted to test his humility.

"Tell the king that you will only lend him the money if you accompany him as a fool." There was nothing less dignified than being a fool, yet the boy agreed.

"When you're in my father's house, do as fools do and break the windows as well as anything that has value." As the girl said this, the boy felt uneasy. He didn't want to betray the master he came to know and serve. Yet, he must earn the troll's daughter's heart.

"As the king's fool, my father will ask the king to pay for the damage or die. The king has nothing left in his possession to repay my father -- other than you. Offer yourself as payment. My father will ask what your worth is, then tell him you can answer any question. He will ask three questions to which you will answer," the girl instructed.

"What if I cannot answer his question?" asked the boy.

"I will reveal the answers to you."

The girl told the boy the questions and the answers he must give.

The day arrived when the plan had to be executed. The boy returned to his master to collect his wage. The troll, pleased with his services, offered him another year of service where he could double his wages, enough for him to become a master himself. However, no other treasure was worth more than his beloved's heart. He went on his way to fulfil the rest of the plan.

The troll asked the boy the first question, "Where is my daughter?"

"Under the sea," answered the boy.

"Will you recognise her?" The troll asked the second question.

"Yes," answered the boy.

Several women circled around him. Each one looked exactly the same as another. Finding his love was a feat. The troll's daughter reached out her hand, which he caught.

"Very well, where is my heart?" The troll asked the third question.

"It's in a fish," The boy responded, pleased that he was able to answer the third question. He was prepared to reveal himself and ask for the girl's hand in marriage.

Until the troll asked another question. "Will you recognise that fish?" asked the troll.

"Ah but, that is the fourth question," answered the boy, quick enough to see through the troll's deceit.

"You said you could answer any question. You are worthless to me if you cannot answer this question," argued the troll.

Both the girl and the boy were taken by surprise.

"Yes, of course," the boy bluffed.

The girl was speechless. She looked the boy in the eye, hoping he could read her thoughts.

"What is in it for me if I answered the question?" The boy asked courageously.

"Your life and my daughter's freedom-- free to choose the course of her remaining existence, including who to wed, or not to wed," answered the troll.

"I await your question," answered the boy.

To this the daughter interfered, "Father, no, please," she pleaded.

"This matter is between me and this lad. It does not concern you whatsoever!" The troll scolded.

"But it does father! He's doing this for me. Please father. He will not be able to answer this question. Please, father, spare him." The daughter repeated as tears fell from her face.

"And how do you know that the boy is unable to answer?" asked the troll.

"Because I gave him the answer to all the other questions. Forgive me father for I have deceived you," the daughter confessed.

"Did you put this boy under a spell?" interrogated the father.

"No, father," answered the daughter.

"And you shed tears in fear of losing his life?"

"Yes, father, yes," the girl said as she wept.

"My darling daughter, you have found your heart," said the troll to his daughter. The girl wiped her tears off and remained silent.

"However, the boy accepted the challenge and must fulfil it."

"Do not worry, my love," said the boy to the daughter, "I will set us all free." He then nodded at the troll.

Hundreds of fish circled around him, each one looking exactly the same as the other. The boy remembered the spell that the troll used to turn him back to human. When the boy spoke the spell, the fish turned back into a witch, the troll's beloved and mother to his daughter.

The troll was surprised to see her after all those years. The witch was now indebted to the boy, bound to a spell that held her powerless.

"Here is your heart," said the boy to the troll.

The troll, in tears, embraced his beloved. The boy asked for the daughter's hand in marriage. The troll gave his blessings. As the girl accepted his proposal with a kiss, the troll and the witch vanished.

A Wickedly Powerful Love

Sarah Parker

Sit still, boy. You were the one asking for the telling of tales. I believe you'd benefit from hearing one about settling down. Originally this story was about the father, see, but named after she it's really centered on. And it's high time someone focused on the choices of that poor boy who set his sights on the Troll's daughter.

The lad wasn't looking for a place, but to belong. Be long, and you shall know if a place suits you. So an adage about spending time together should go. But when one should go, or should stay, a crone never knows, nor a wizard. Neither are eyes blinded by love any wiser to intent and best interests. Many are too easily bewitched.

Our protag prince had not been raised on stranger danger, and the promise of perpetuating funds appealed-- good wages, twice the second year, and thrice the third year. Count him in. He

108

could love anyone a bushel and a peck for that!
He was willing enough to heed the man who
introduced himself as his good godfather. A lad
could always benefit from one of those, much
like a fairy godmother for a lassie.

The first warning sign; the troll required
obedience. This meant one must step to, step
carefully. But the boy was one to acquiesce and
ready for any adventurous path. He had no
problems with obedience and no fears. While
she'd been raised to fear the unknown and took
precautions. She, our femme fatale, was ready to
be out of fear's way. To seize hers and the day.
But he didn't yet know her role in the
arrangement of this meet cute. We so often get
ahead of ourselves when we consider the future
and promises.

The troll paid the tolls, and so he got to lay the
way. The troll assigned the lad his duties. Always
summoned to feed the wild animals on the first
day of the year. Then to become one. He
recounted the tale of how he spent his time for
her; at first the lad was a hare, he then became a
raven, and finally a fish, which was when and
how they crossed paths, for she lived under the
sea, a queen to be.

She caught him; enticed him. The land and
air offered little, so she of the sea lulled him in
the final year. By the by, the troll had promised
him play, and taking to flight had suggested

peace. She offered permanence. Marriage to her would mean pre-eminence.

She, daughter of the troll, was ready to overturn her father-- ready to toll a new time for them both. And so she helped the lad with the coming choices he'd have to make. Survival of the fittest, her father had touted of the tests he'd prepared. But she knew the lad toasted to her good health, and that red would flow freely for her.

She advised him he would be asked the following: First, where is my daughter? Second, can you recognize her? Third, where is my heart? The three questions illustrated how the heart of the old man already lay with the fabled treasure at the bottom of the sea.

She knew she held both hearts. She knew she could wield them both to flow along with her will. She knew the stays of power when one possessed a heart. How a heart could hold one prisoner. How one set free was bound by heart's allegiance. Many a heart had called out to her.

All unfolded as she'd foretold. At the sight of the glass castle, her man began to act a fool. He was quick to take a knife to the fish and that held within it. Timing was of the essence, she'd suggested to him.

As you've heard this tale told before, child, you know the old man's heart lay inside the fish. The lad hadn't seen how that fish had been the first to accompany his lady within the glass castle which lied deep. All eyes on her; the stories all shored up upon her beauty, a mer maid; a free-flowing dream, a weaver of words. Words of warning would have been apropos, I suppose, but everyone already knew of her father too.

When the terms and conditions were met, it was as if a table of contents splayed open. The animals were all released to roam as created. Humans were released from bondage. The kings bowed to the new power roaming the land. But this troll's ending was only the beginning.

The princess of power turned to the lad to explain, "There was no third question, for I'm done with the third degree. There are always two parts to any probing question. There were only two tests to pass. My father's weak heart and his deep concerns no longer imprison me."

He'd not exactly drawn and quartered her father, only his heart. But the boy had known how hearts entangle. She suggested a reasonable way to frame that before them once again. Bleeding hearts can't sustain strength for long. Another apt adage for the ages, mind you.

She reached for him. His arms too contained memory, and reached for her. The words the troll had told him once again faded into echoes.

The feelings ebbed, but the soul tie remained. She pushed; he pulled, and their relationship buoyed. He bobbed, always swept up in her current schemes. She'd sunk him long ago. He fell for the hook and lines. Her body and words continued to sway him.

He learned the ropes, the riggings, after they were married. Reckoned there was a reason she'd needed to be free of her father. Objected to any obvious aspersions cast on her character. Wondered why things had gone right enough by the plan, but rang a wrong tune. But he did not say a word. She'd taken his voice, offered him little real choice in any matter. All ways are the queen's ways, as many a husband knows.

He heard the call, the echo, as that which heralds from the conch shell. Reminiscent of the need to attune to the troll's words that transformed and transported him, brought him before and bore him away from her; his destiny. There was deceit and duplicity to her words, as there had been in his. He'd not actually learned their ways, but had assimilated them. That fordaining him had proven fortunate enough. But enough is never enough.

Off he goes one day, galivanting to present himself as knight before the other kings, as was the role cast for him by his beloved. As was expected, for the High King should lord over all, after all.

He'd been positioned to offer them words to win the troll's favor. Now they favored him with words which made wise doms of their own fool sons.

"The fool never holds the answer," advised the first king. "Had your name been Tom, you'd be cited a peeper. She knew you were watching her. Peter, and you'd have to eat it. You cannot beat her at her own game. She betook you and called you beloved. And so you belonged. Became bound to her." This king had learned much from the guppie which returned to him, his lost firstborn.

The second king assured him, "you passed the test when you saw her and no longer desired the wild and free life lived as a jackalope or creature of the air. See that she is always your greatest desire, and you will remain richly rewarded." His eldest had been a blowfish when borrowed body bore him about the sea.

The third king fought folly. "Quick rising, as both rabbit and bird you were like the leavened bread. You grew to have an inflated sense of self, despite lack of nourishment. Don't you see what she feeds you?" His aged son had been bound as angelfish.

I tell you now, my son, the lad and the troll were both indeed fools (one might say tools). They shared a heart; one full of love for the daughter. One that could fathom no evil. Speak no slander. See no damages. Hear not their lot. They refused the refuge. Ignored the flotsam. You know what they say about birds of a feather, about the curse of the rabbit's foot.

After searching lands and looking high, the fish saw what was below the surface. The fish knew her crafty ways, how she calculated the cost, and how she too chose him. Prices must always be paid for happiness. She'd spoken such resplendent words and readied him for a whole new world.

What's the moral of this story, son? Fate, foibles, folly; all forge a future, in accord with one's designs. Listen to your father, now. The troll was a father, and a wise one at that. He knew his daughter would distinguish tempting trickster from lovefool. He knew well the boy would heed heart, play a part. How within his role, the daughter would become. The troll was the keeper of the toll because he knew the truth; hearts are always tested, but words do not always hold true.

Now, I know you know there is another version of this story. One of those neat happy endings. But sit a spell with any couple together for more than a few years and you'll learn it's not all roses and sunshine. There's light and dark. Just be sure you see what's illuminated and where the heart lies before you act on feelings or the words of others. Had the lad done so, this story would read differently. That's the trick with fate; one's free will. Your choices craft the conclusion.

115

based on

Die Riesen und die Herden Junge

collected by

Dr. Heinrich von Wlislock

The Herdsman and the Herbalist

Dewi Hargreaves & Alex Woodroe

The Herdsman and the Herbalist

Dewi Hargreaves & Alex Woodroe

The Herdsman

Dewi Hargreaves

Somebody had seen a giant.

Giants were evil creatures, the village elders said. You never knew what they would do. Some could speak, others couldn't. Some would whisper kind words to you, only to follow you home and cast a curse on your unborn children. Some were not so devious—they would simply chase you and eat you whole or rip the flesh from your bones. With big legs, they were fast runners.

Dornei perched on a rock, placed his staff on the ground, and watched as his flock of czarnai scattered and munched on the bright heads of summer weeds, their short, armoured legs pounding the ground. He was already sweating. Up here on the hillside, there was no respite from the sun.

There were plenty of places to lose a czarna, though. Dips, valleys, and gorges broke up the terrain—perfect places for his herd to disappear. Or for ambushers to hide.

Such thoughts were usually far from his mind when he led his flock up the hill. But today was different.

Dornei shuddered. *Giants are just fairytales*, he thought.

He grinned when he saw the girl.

She made her way up the hill, bright golden hair reflecting the sun. Her blue dress was stained around the hem by mud and dew.

"I haven't seen you for days," he said.

"I know," she replied, her pale face turning away. "I'm sorry."

He frowned. "There's nothing to be sorry about. I'm happy you're here."

That made her smile. Her soft brown eyes rested on his, the kindest he'd seen.

They'd first met a few weeks ago. She had come to him with a bruised face, having slipped down one of the gorges. He'd tended to her wounds, and she'd curled up beside him like a stray cat. Though they rarely exchanged words, he felt strangely protective over her.

Perhaps it was his herdsguard nature.

"You look stressed," she said, catching him off guard.

He waved a hand as though it was nothing. "One of the village elders says he saw a giant. I don't believe him, but it's still a little scary."

He was afraid his words would spook her, but she wasn't fazed at all.

"Have you never seen a giant?" she said.

"No. Have you?"

She nodded. "We see them all the time in our valley."

He could hardly believe her. He scoffed. "No. You see giants?"

"Every week," she insisted. "They come to trade things."

"Where do you live?"

Those four words made her tense up. "It's far away."

"If you can walk it, I'm sure I can too."

She said nothing.

"Can I come with–"

"No," she said, with surprising force.

"Why not?"

"Your people aren't welcome in my village."

Warmth rushed to his cheeks. "My people?"

"Outlanders. Especially people like you."

"Our people are just fine," he said. "We've never hurt anyone. What's wrong with me?"

She looked away, and he realised his words had cut deeper than he expected. Her hands clenched. "It's—it's not that. Please, don't raise your voice," she said.

He swept to her side, putting a hand gently on her shoulder. "I'm sorry."

She sniffed, ignoring his hand. "You can't come to our village. You can't."

He nodded. "All right. If you say so."

Shortly after, she stood. He hoped to catch her eyes as she brushed herself off and walked back down the field, but she ignored him. He worried he'd upset her.

She turned around. "You'll be here again?"

He smiled. "I will."

She smiled back, and then she was gone.

###

He sat still as the sun drifted across the sky and the hours passed, and he wondered about the girl's village.

It must be a strange place, he told himself. But curiosity gnawed at his gut.

A voice carried on the wind.

"*Help*," it said.

Dornei was on his feet in a second, staff in his hands. Leaving the herd behind, he set off in the direction of the words.

As they grew louder, he was relieved it didn't sound like the girl's voice. It was far, far deeper.

"Help me, Dornei."

He stopped when it used his name.

How could it know him? It didn't sound like anyone he knew from the village.

The voice appeared to be coming from a steep, rocky gorge ahead. He knew a steady stream cut through the bottom of it. He used to play there when he was younger.

Peering over the edge, he saw something that made his breath catch in his throat.

Lying in the stream, the water trickling over his limbs, was a giant. He was twice the size of a man, with grey, stony skin and long hair down to his shoulders. The giant's heavy brow was furrowed in pain.

His leg was twisted at an alarming angle.

"Dornei," the giant said, his yellow eyes widening when he saw the boy.

Dornei stepped out of view, trying to stay calm.

"I know you're there, boy. I need you."

He looked away, steadying his breathing. *Don't speak to them*, they'd told him. *If you see a giant, no matter what you do, don't speak to them.*

"I can't move," the giant said, his voice sounding like an avalanche. "Rain is coming. If you don't help me, I'll drown."

Just go back, he told himself. *Back to the herd. Leave him.*

"That girl," the giant said.

He froze.

The giant laughed. "You like her. You want to go after her."

"I don't," he said.

"You do," the giant said. Dornei could hear the smile in his voice, even though he was out of sight. "You want to see her village."

"She told me not to. That's enough for me."

"You trust her words?"

"Why shouldn't I?"

"Things are not all they seem in that village."

There was an edge to the giant's voice that made the skin on his neck prickle. "What do you mean?"

"Why do you think the girl comes here, instead of staying home?"

It was a good question. No, he thought, shaking his head. Giants are tricky creatures. "Maybe she likes to walk."

The giant laughed. "The truth is there, but you refuse to see it. Perhaps you are too cowardly."

"Why not just tell me, then?"

"Come here. Help me, and I'll show you."

Giants are dangerous, a voice said. But it was too late.

If the girl was in danger, he'd help her.

Making his way down the slope, he followed an old path cut into the gorge, a path he'd followed many times as a youth. He paddled through the water.

The giant seemed even larger up close. There were deep patterns cut into his skin, shapes Dornei found unpleasant to look at. Wide ears stuck out of his hair.

His leg wasn't bleeding, but it was twisted. It looked broken.

"You know what to do," the giant said.

It was true. Long ago, one of his friends had fallen off the back of a czarna they were riding as part of a game. Dornei had watched how his father bound the girl's leg, scolding her for her stupidity.

He found two large branches, using them to fashion a crude splint.

The giant rolled onto his front, pushing himself up. "Help me, boy."

Dornei wriggled under the giant's arm, shoving with all his strength. The giant's folded skin smelled like the rancid czarna cheese at the back of his family's cellar.

Eventually, though, the giant was on his feet. He tenderly stepped on his leg, wincing.

"It will be some time before I can walk," the giant said, "but thank you."

He handed Dornei three gold coins the size of the boy's palm, then unclipped his belt and slung it over the boy's shoulder. It, too, stank – strongly enough to make Dornei's head spin.

"Tell me about the village."

The giant smiled. "I don't need to. That belt will take you there."

"How?"

The giant reached over, fastening the clip. As soon as it clicked into place, Dornei's body vanished.

"You can walk wherever you want when you wear that belt. No eyes will see you. Not even your own."

The next time the girl visited, he didn't mention the giant, the belt, or her village. They spoke a little about czarnai, and she asked about his father.

Hers was not like his, she told him.

As the day drifted towards evening, she stood, brushed herself off, and walked away.

"You'll be here again?" she asked.

"Of course," he said.

When she passed out of sight, he retrieved the belt from behind the rock, threw it over his shoulder like a sash and buckled the clip.

He disappeared.

With one last glance back at the herd, he followed the girl.

"Take care of yourselves," he muttered and offered a small prayer to the gods.

She walked for a long time, leading him through dark forests, open plains and rocky highlands. Two or three times he had to hold back as she waded across a stream, keeping quiet and staying low to the ground. Though he was invisible, he didn't want to take any chances.

The sun dropped behind the trees as he walked along the edge of a wide lake. He'd never seen such a large open body of water before. He watched the surface ripple for a moment, mesmerised. Around its edge grew plants he'd never seen in such unsuitable land before, and the fruits were bigger than usual, their flesh so ripe. When he looked back, the sky was black and the only sign of the girl was a small, flickering light – the glow of her lantern.

He followed it until he reached a village.

He couldn't make out much in the gloom, but more lights flickered behind her lantern. As he drew closer, he saw a dozen huts, their windows glowing, clustered around a large unlit pyre. The square was deserted, but the pyre was tall and ready to be lit. It would have taken days to gather that much wood.

On a hill overlooking the huts sat a compact stone castle. The girl approached the door, knocked, and was allowed in.

He slipped through the door behind her, holding his breath. His heart pounded.

He crouched in a corner, surveying the main hall. A long table stood in the centre, purple cloth lain over it. Cutlery and plates for two diners lay ready on the mats.

The air tasted bad, wrong. As though evil had been done there.

The hairs of his arms prickled and stood as though there were a cold wind. His head spun.

No wonder she hated it here.

A door crashed deeper within the castle. The girl flinched, dousing her lantern. She darted down a corridor, flitting away like a mouse. Footsteps approached the hall. From one of the corridors, a long, thin shadow stretched towards the fire.

Dornei hurried after the girl, stopping at the door. Within he heard soft sobs. "Please, please, please."

Unsure of what else he could do, he drew the giant's coins from his pocket and slid them under the door.

He fled the castle, and traced his steps home.

Whatever the elders said, the giant's words seemed true: there was something strange happening in that village.

When he next met the girl, she told him about the coins. She hugged her chest and spoke of fairies and good fortune and how she never thought she was worthy. A part of him regretted giving the gold away – but it was worth it. Because he didn't need to understand everything to know that he had to help her escape that place.

He was sitting on his rock, watching the czarnai, when the girl came to him again. Her face was bruised, and tears glistened on her cheeks.

"Did you fall in the gorge again?" Dornei asked, jumping to his feet.

She shook her head slowly, and more tears fell. "Father found the coins. He took them."

The rage that filled Dornei led him to one conclusion.

He would break her out of the castle that night.

The village was alive.

The pyre was burning when he arrived, lighting up the woods surrounding the secluded village. The flames licked high into the sky, gulping the night air. People danced around the base, wearing tattered shawls and long hair and beards. They leapt back and forth, balancing on their heels, their hands waving in the air in fits of madness, grins carved onto their faces. Occasionally they let out wild yelps, which, together, created a savage song.

The giant's voice echoed in his mind. *Things are not all they seem in that village.*

He wondered if the giants were responsible.

The castle glowed orange in the light of the fire. He crept slowly up the hill towards the heavy doors.

Their chanting grew louder.

Foreboding gripped his chest. He didn't like any of this.

His hand wavered on the door. The voice in the back of his head screamed.

Go home.

He shoved the door open.

Cold hands gripped his arms. Something swept him off his feet. A hoarse scream slipped from his lips as a soldier carried him like a baby, marching through the hall.

A pair of dark, predator eyes locked on him and grinned.

"Our little gold fairy."

He thrashed and punched, but it was no use. His captor was built of muscle, his head heavy and bald and lacking a neck, and he seemed not to feel it.

He carried Dornei deep into the earth, down endless flights of stairs.

In his head, the giant laughed.

The Herbalist

Alex Woodroe

A cheerful spring day drifted towards a solemn evening, and a nagging itch of fear rose in Malina's chest. It was time to get home; before anyone noticed how long she'd been gone or questioned why.

She rose from her stump by a plum copse and dusted herself off. "You'll be here again?"

"Of course." The herdsman, Dornei, stood as well, looking almost surprised.

There was a hint of something in his eyes that worried her. There had been for weeks. The desire to ask more questions; to follow her home, perhaps. So many lads had tried that she knew the look. Without giving him any more time to come up with something they'd both regret, Malina scurried through a thicket of young hazel trees towards her village. Home, as some would call it.

The woods were cool and inviting as she rushed down her well-worn deer trail, stooping here and there to pluck fragrant mint, tansy, and pennyroyal from the undergrowth. Often, she yanked out fistfuls of plants that had no use at all, but would quickly fill her basket. They'd scold her for being slow and clumsy, she'd apologise, and nobody would be any wiser about her weekly trips.

A sudden crackle like that of a snapping branch drew her gaze away from a patch of nasturtiums. She stood still, holding her breath, the succulent nasturtium leaves crushed in her fist. A heartbeat, then two, then five. Nothing further stirred; even the distant baying of czarnai was muffled. She rose, breaking into a run, dodging and weaving through the trees. Meeting Dornei at all was such a risk. The last time a stranger wandered close to the village because of her, she had to scrape him from between the floorboards. She was the one picking teeth out of her hair all night. Never again.

Familiar as the soles of her own feet, the forest rolled past her in her rush. Plain birch and simple aspen gave way to lush fruit-filled elder and mulberry as she neared the lake. A rich forest of out-of-season fruit was one of the many blessings her village boasted from their trade with the Giants. Rainbow-scaled fish leaped from the water, crab apples hung heavy in the orchard, wheat plumper than plums swayed in the breeze. There was so little that couldn't be done with enough blood, sweat, and tears, and her community knew well enough how to harvest those.

Between the squat houses, up the little hill, and to the fort doors she ran, thinking all the while how nice it might be if someday, it'd be the last time she walked that path.

"Who goes there?" A ragged voice boomed from beyond the massive wooden door.

Knowing the right answer was no answer at all, she raised her fist instead. Two knocks, pause. Two knocks, pause. One last look down the hill to make sure the coast was clear as the door swung open. Then, as she stepped forward into the dark, rough hands grabbed her shoulders and yanked her brutally forward.

"There ye are. Well, lassie. You've sure done it now."

The chair they'd tied her to was uncomfortable for the first five minutes, and excruciating for every minute after that. A circle of village elders stood around her, eyes hard and mistrusting. The herbs from her satchel lay spilled across the floor before her. Griselda, the healer, rifled through them.

Cross-armed, her father lorded over their work. "You must think we're really stupid."

It didn't seem like Tanase wanted an answer, and it was a good thing, too. He wouldn't have liked it.

132

"Griselda kept telling me about what a slow lamb you are. On and on she went. Takes her five times as long to gather herbs. Always brings the wrong ones. Eventually, she got me thinking."

What a terrible time for him to start a new habit. Malina should have been long gone; she should have run away when they were still lax and trusting. She'd been a coward, and now it would be too late.

"See, my daughter's not that dumb, I thought. No. Every time she opens her mouth, she's twice as clever as she's any right to be. Especially when she mouths off at me. Slow? Malina? No."

His eyes shone with a feral fire she'd rarely seen before. The seriousness of the situation hit her. They wouldn't do anything to her. Would they? She was precious to them. It was her job to lure in the menfolk they'd sacrifice to the Giants. Hers, still, for a long time, before she was old enough to retire into a different job.

Griselda stood, a wicked smile on her lips, and lifted a sprig of something ending with a round white flower. "Calmille. See?" She held the flower up to Tanase. "I told you."

Malina finally worked some spit down her dry throat. "It's only a herb, like all the others."

"Ha!" The crone cawed, visibly excited. "Calmille doesn't grow here, you dolt. You'd know if your head wasn't always elsewhere. We don't allow white flowers. To get this you'd have had to be picking far beyond our woods." She turned to Tanase again, straightening, weaselling. "Maybe as far as the fields. Maybe further."

The implication hung over the gathered crowd like a rank mist. As far as the fields, maybe further, where other people were. Where one could talk to other people. Whispers rose, then mutters, then howls.

Malina's legs shook so hard her knees ached. "Please." She couldn't tell if anyone heard her. "Please, please." She didn't know what she was pleading for. "Please."

Her father picked the flower out of Griselda's fingers, raising his other hand to silence the crowd. "You know what?" He smiled. "It's fine."

She almost sighed in relief.

He crushed the petals and let them fall, wilted and bruised, to the floor. "I've been looking for an excuse."

Before she could reply, her father jerked his head to the door and raised his hand for silence. The crowd fell still in an instant, and in the space left over by their cruel suggestions, hurried footsteps thudded from beyond the front door, getting dimmer and dimmer. Tanase yanked it open and glared into the hall; at what, Malina couldn't see. Would that be enough for him to forget about her? Or, at least, postpone her punishment for the next day?

Still silently, he bent to pick something up off the floor and turned on her again, every bit as fierce as before. In his raised hand, three gold coins sparkled with firelight. Three gold coins that hadn't been there before; proof that she'd been followed. She could easily guess by whom.

"You gave me an excuse, and now you've given me a plan. What a fruitful night this turned out to be."

Under guard, like some sort of herd animal.

They'd couched it under new rules and kind words, talking about how she was free to roam the fortress as she pleased, but would be chaperoned outside of town. After all the frustration and isolation made bearable only by occasional visits to the outside world, their solution was to keep her even more deeply locked away.

No longer.

She grumbled and huffed, her fingers carefully rolling underthings into as tightly-wound packages as possible and stuffing them into a little satchel. As soon as there was a right time, she'd bolt. No more being locked away for her own good. No more rules. Dying of hunger in a ditch somewhere was better than what they had in store for her.

They'd have to let her out, eventually. She was certain. Tanase had a plan; to lure the generous herdsman back to the village and sacrifice him at the new moon, as they had countless others. Everyone the giants marked with their coins ended as delicately butchered flesh, the one task giant hands weren't suited for.

The village traded bodies and suffering for wealth and plenty; and her father was convinced that was what everyone did.

Malina didn't want to doom him, but saving more than just herself would be hard. And why should she?

She shook her head and blew her candle out. Now was not the time for sentiment.

A week passed, and it was time.

Griselda has watched her every move every day; and she was watching now, hidden in a hazel thicket, as Malina met with Dornei one final time.

When she approached him, his soft eyes made her heart melt.

"He took all of it." Her voice was cold and empty, tears already cried every day that week, thinking about what she'd have to do to him. "All the gold you left. He's never going to let me go, and I'm sure he has some terrible plan for me."

It was the most she'd ever told him about the way her family treated her, and it was such a shame to have to do it for a horrible cause.

As she'd hoped, he reached out to her, filled with caring and desire to protect her. She pulled away, distraught, and ran into the woods. This time, she made sure to do so slowly, stumbling around apparently due to the tears in her eyes, fumbling and making as much noise as she could. Making herself easy to follow. Making sure Dornei did, as Griselda surely was.

Every step was agony. The nearer she drew to the village, the more she saw signs of their grisly trade. Charms in the trees marked their borders, so the Giants would know where to spread their blessings. The pyres by the village were lit, so the Giants would know there was a new sacrifice in store. And behind her, following closely, was the gift for the Giants.

Stifling any further thoughts, she sprinted the last hundred paces to the gate, hoping maybe he'd change his mind and turn around. Once inside, she huddled in a dusty corner, whispering to herself.

"Please let him change his mind. Please let him change his mind." But then, she'd still be trapped.

It was hopeless, anyway. The next time the door opened, one of the soldiers walked in, carrying a struggling, kicking, yowling Dornei. The look in his eyes when he saw her crouched in her corner of shame was like an ice bath.

Griselda walked in after them. "Good lass. You know the drill. Don't be late after dawn for the clean-up. Then we can talk about setting you free."

The slick smile on her teacher's face made her doubt any such thing would be talked about at all.

The moment the old woman had her back turned, Malina dashed to her room and grabbed her perfectly packed satchel, already buzzing with excitement. Nobody would guard her, nobody would be looking.

"Except you'll be looking, Mal," she muttered to herself. "And you'll judge yourself faulty."

Why was Dornei different from all the others? She dismissed any notions of love with a shake of her head. He was different because he'd been her choice. So far, she'd only been the bait, drawing strangers to the village with her beauty and promises of marriage. This time, she was the fisher, and it made her feel guilty enough for all the other times.

Resigned to herself, Malina took her first step outside her father's hall as a free woman, and rather than continue in that vein by walking into the sunset, chose to circle the outer wall in search for the dungeon window. There was no stone she wasn't familiar with, no crack in the wall and no ivy shoot she hadn't run her fingers over. There were only six windows where he could be, and she whistled into each of them in turn.

On the third, someone whistled back.

"Don't move!" She whispered, and heard back only grumbled complaints.

The window was small; probably too small for most of the villagers. But she was young and little, kept lythe to better impress and lure travellers. Hopefully, he'd fit too, on the way out.

She found him chained to the wall, filthy and glaring at her like he wanted to eat the nose off her face. She gestured for silence, the voices outside the wooden door making her shiver.

There were at least four—maybe six? And they'd only be waiting for midnight. Not a lot of time.

Malina crouched next to him, digging through her satchel. He only breathed warm air on her, smelling like hay and fear.

"I'm gonna get you out of here."

"I knew you weren't—"

"Shh."

Finally finding the plant she'd been looking for, she threw it in her mouth and chewed at it with a vengeance. They may have all thought she was feeble in the head; a terrible lazy herbalist with no use and no training. But in truth, she'd learned to do as much in an hour as took others a whole day. She'd learned to make powders to give her more energy and oils to clean her after a day with Dornei and the flock. And she'd learned which plants make good grease.

She spat the now-gelatinous wad of Spokeflower petals onto his wrists, causing him to recoil.

"Be still."

It was no time to be coy. Outside the door was murder, and it was coming. She grabbed another mouthful of petals, all the while working the oil she'd already made into his skin and under his shackles. It wouldn't be easy, and he'd hate her for it, but she could get him free.

Once both his wrists were thoroughly greased, she handed him the strap of her satchel. "Bite down on this."

Even as he said "Why?" She pushed it into his mouth.

"Because it's going to hurt. And you have to be very, very quiet."

His eyes went wide, but a shuffle outside the door made her heart race. Were they fumbling at the lock? There was no time.

Bracing with her feet against the wall, she yanked at his elbows as hard as she could. A muffled "mmf" escaped him, and she paused for a moment to listen for more sounds at the door. His heavy, rapid, breaths were all she could hear. Pulling again, she released one of his arms, bloodied and torn, from the shackles. Still chewing on her satchel strap, he helped her pull on the second, grunting hard as a strip of flesh pulled off the side of his palm.

"Did you hear—"

Voices rose outside, and the lock rattled. Malina flung herself at the window, abandoning her satchel where it lay. As soon as her hands were on the edge, she felt her feet lifted and pushed. She slipped out effortlessly, and turned to find Dornei already making his way through, arms outstretched.

"Don't you dare leave me here!"

She had no intention to. Broader of shoulder than she was, it was harder for him, but with a final brace and pull, she yanked him out into the dark. He'd be battered and bruised and torn, but alive. And maybe the same could be said for her.

The cell door poured armoured guards into the room behind them, but they were far too hefty to make it out the window.

Curses chased Malina and Dornei as they vanished into the night.

based on

Den Lille Havfrue

collected by

H.C. Andersen

The Giant Battle of the Little Mermaid

Perseus Greenman & Nikki Mitchell

The Giant Battle of the Little Mermaid

Perseus Greenman & Nikki Mitchell

Prince Alik's perspective by Nikki Mitchell

Crescentia's Perspective by Perseus Greenman

Thump. Crescentia is fretting over Prince Alik and ignores the first sound, but another comes soon after. *Thump*. Crescentia looks over the port gunwale. A pod of dolphins swims at the ship. *Thump. Thump*. Several now swim away in a wide circle that will likely bring them back for another run--

A spray of white erupts from the starboard side, heralding a black tentacle which reaches straight toward the clouds above. Crescentia looks to the pilot who is already spinning the wheel away from the monstrous thing.

Her hands blur across her drum as she bangs out a command. Harpoons! Take aim at the dolphins. They are the greater threat, she knows.

She points to the port drummer and gestures for him not to mimic her, then makes eye contact with the starboard drummer and drums to bring forth the Trident Cannon.

The Sea Witch appears above the waves, giant and ever-changing. Tentacles become giant arms or legs which turn to fins. Her face is that of an eel one moment, a dolphin the next.

"Queen Sea," the first mate reports. Crescentia quietly likes her nickname. "The large tentacles have only delivered glancing blows, but the damage to the hull has been substantial. Also, the bilge is overflowing due to cracks in the boards. We believe that sharks have been hitting us below the waves where we cannot see them."

She silently curses the loss of her voice, and its ability to command the creatures of the sea. The best she can do right now is command the humans with her drum to keep them moving in the right direction.

She will hold this ship together as long as she can; she hopes Alik will return in time.

Almost three years earlier, Prince Alik strode across the deck of his ship, his waist stripped bare and his arms overflowing with coiled rope.

"To stations!" he yelled, throwing the excess lines where each belonged. A gentle rocking—his stance easily and immediately adjusting—told him that his weapon was finally aboard.

The young prince had spent his last four years creating the very sight that now graced his dark eyes. A monstrous thing, the Trident Cannon was chest-height and stretched further than he was tall. He had taken the schematics for a regular canon and adapted it specifically for his purposes. Instead of a ball, a trident slid into the mouth of the great cast-iron tube and fired with a much greater speed and precision.

With a thrill of anticipation curling in his belly, Alik yelled to his men, "Hoist anchor and set sail!" His rich baritone, afire with his emotions, immediately set his men to action, and the ship began slowly moving out to sea.

It was time to prove to his people that he was no longer just a boy; that he would faithfully rule his country when it came time to take his father's place on the throne.

Finally, his Siren Hunt could begin.

Dodging the anchor, Crescentia swam eagerly alongside the chain toward the sunlight, hoping to get her first sight of a man. Her sister said that she was too young to go above the waves, but she would only take a peek.

The boat was so much bigger than her sister had described it, descending deeper into the water than the length of a dolphin. She broke the surface, brushing her emerald tresses from her eyes. Well above her, men laughed and talked, illuminated by the last rays of the sun.

It was time to sing.

Crescentia pulled herself up onto a large rock. She could see the wooden carving of a mermaid on the prow. It actually looked a little like her sister, Ada. She was sad that she was about to break that beautiful wooden mermaid.

She opened her mouth and the music was barely audible at first. The waves have a way of dulling sounds, and the young mermaid was still unsure of herself. But with each note, her confidence grew and her singing crescendoed. Notes echoed from the cliffs behind her and she harmonized with her own voice.

As if pulled by an invisible cord, the boat turned slightly toward her. It was a small change, slight enough that those on board probably didn't notice, but it would be enough. The boat would crash and the fishermen inside it would stop hunting her friends.

Shouting erupted from a part of the boat she could not see. Perhaps they had noticed that they were sailing into the rocks? She sang louder, hoping to draw in the one who was shouting. He had a lovely baritone voice.

As the wooden mermaid approached, almost close enough to touch, a man's face appeared above the deck. His sandy hair contrasted with his dark brown eyes in an intriguing way. Crescentia felt something begin to flutter inside her. He was beautiful!

"There she is!" he shouted. "Fire the cannon!"

Crescentia didn't know what "fire" or "cannon" meant, but the anger in his voice told her to flee. She rolled off the rock into the sea just in time to hear a *clank* behind her. Looking back, she saw a trident stuck into the rock where she had just been.

The boat turned just in time to avoid the rocks. Crescentia descended into the darkness of the ocean depths, her heart leaping. She knew that she should be afraid, but she was filled with a strange joy at the beautiful face she had seen.

Alik hauled his trident back onto his ship as his men manoeuvred away from the rocks, staring at the place where he'd glimpsed the siren. He had heard stories aplenty, mostly from his father congratulating the young men on their ascent into manhood, but none had mentioned how stunningly *beautiful* the sirens were. Of course, the men spoke of the lilt of their voices, lulling the uncareful into the rocks... but nothing about their physical beauty. In fact, all of the renderings of the sirens were plain, like the carving on his own ship. It was a beautiful piece of woodwork, but the siren itself was rather average.

He shook his head as he reloaded his canon, readying himself for another shot. The beauty of the monster was irrelevant. They preyed on humans, so it was his duty to protect his people by hunting the foul creatures.

A fortnight passed and only twice more was a siren spotted. Alik failed both times, the empty clang of trident hitting rock mocking him. In each case, it seemed to be the same siren from that first day. It hadn't even tried to redirect the ship, simply taunting his inability to so much as graze its magnificent body. It was infuriating.

He needed a new plan.

He remembered a legend woven into a tapestry in the back rooms of the palace library. As a boy, he had hidden there from his lessons and stared at the wall hangings for hours. Most of them depicted glowing warriors fighting grisly battles against the sirens on the backs of ruined ships as the fiends had encroached upon the humans' territory ages ago. But one, unlike the rest, showed a vision underneath the water, in a cave not far from the palace.

Within that cave, the tapestry showed a sandy-haired human kneeling with bowed head and arms upraised before a giantess with tentacles for limbs. Her face bore kindness, and she placed a brilliant object in the man's risen hands.

In the panel beneath, the man was shown to swim unhindered toward the ocean's depths.

The rest of the tapestry ended in singed tatters; fire had consumed the lower sections in an accident that predated Alik's birth by many years. But the message was clear. If he could find the giantess, he could procure the means to take the battle to the sirens' homeland.

Crescentia knew what she needed to do. When she had complained to her older sister, Ada had told her to stay away from the big ships… but *he* was on a big ship. Wrecking small fishing boats protected the fish of the sea, but didn't bring her any closer to that beautiful face. Unfortunately, this "cannon" shooting at her didn't bring her any closer either.

She would swim to the cave of The Sea Witch. She needed the help of magic to solve this problem. Maybe The Witch could let her swim through the air, or give her scales all over her body to protect her. Then she could stay in the world above the waves with him.

As she swam out of the civilized portion of the sea, the view below her changed. There were no more palaces, no more roads, no more people or homes or statues. Just the open ocean.

She swam up, following the coldest currents she could find. She had heard that The Sea Witch's cave was deep in the heart of an iceberg which thrust far into the sky. By the time that mountain of ice appeared before her, she was trembling with the cold. It was only the cold.

She had expected a dark cave, but was instead greeted by a pale blue light emerging from the entrance to an inviting home. Carpets taken from some palace above formed a path on the floor at the entrance. As she swam in, she saw round glass bottles providing the light that had guided her here. Its refraction through the ice gave it the cool blue color that she had seen from outside, but it was yellow and warm inside.

"Can I help you, dearie?"

Crescentia spun, startled at the voice. She had been so caught up admiring the furnishings that she had not noticed The Sea Witch swim in. She had thought she'd seen a bright green eel swimming into the room, but when she looked directly at The Witch, she saw a mermaid like herself, perhaps a bit younger. The Sea Witch's bright red hair contrasted with Crescentia's dark green.

"The Eastern Tide tells me that you have been swimming too close to humans, and one of them has managed to catch you, though not with a net." The Sea Witch admired herself in a floor-length silver mirror.

"No, I--"

"I have what you need," The Sea Witch cut her off. "I have the magic to give you legs and allow you to walk among the humans. But I warn you: you will never see your family again. They live beneath the waves, and you will be trapped in the realm of birds and boats. Will you be able to live with that?"

The little mermaid nodded solemnly. Her voice came out barely above a whisper.

"I love him."

Alik stood in the cave, his head lowered and shoulders hunched to account for the low ceiling. His sandy hair brushed the rock, sending little showers of debris upon his shoulders. He'd been surprised to find the giantess' home fully furnished and burning with a warmth that leaked out of small glass bottles in the rock and into the night.

His crew had sailed for two days and two nights to reach this isolated mountain-cave. His ship was safely anchored a few miles off-coast-- he'd had to make the final leg of the journey on his own. Swimming through the ocean waters had been crisp, but the air was so warm inside that the freezing droplets on his skin instantly evaporated.

Finding the cave had been easy--he'd recognized it from the tapestry almost immediately. Even so, relief had flooded him as he'd broken the surface of the water and saw that the cave truly did exist--meaning the tapestry must have also told the truth about the magic.

"Hello?" he called into the empty cave. His voice reverberated back a hundredfold.

Almost immediately, a dark shape appeared under the water, and he stepped back from its edge, pressing his back against the cave's wall. His eyes were wide, but they grew even wider as the shape broke from the water.

A fire-haired siren arose from the water, but immediately transformed into a dark being with eleven ink-black tentacles that curled incessantly. She greeted him with a smile that bared sharpened teeth. She was even larger in life than the tapestry had depicted, and Alik immediately went to his knees, bowing in supplication.

"What do you seek, dearie?" The giantess' voice boomed around the cave, sounding like the rush of water along time-smoothened rocks.

"Great giantess, I have come for a way to capture a siren and make her mine." It would no longer be able to pop up next to his ship and then turn tail and escape under the waters, taunting him. Once he killed the emerald-haired siren that haunted his dreams and ship, he would take its body to his father as proof of his manhood. He planned, even, to have its likeness painted and hung next to the singed tapestry in the dusty corner of the library, a token of appreciation for the hint of help.

"You have asked, and so shall it be," the giantess intoned. "Raise your arms to receive your gift, as all I ask in return is this: the first daughter you bear."

Alik winced, but he would have given anything for this chance at the siren. And there was no guarantee he'd ever even have a daughter. He nodded and raised his arms. The giantess placed a brilliant object in his hands. A small vial of golden liquid.

He took the large boning knife strapped to his hip and broke the vial's seal. Throwing his head back, he downed its contents.

"Do not drink it here," The Sea Witch had told Crescentia. "Wait until you are near the surface. Once you drink it, you will no longer be able to breathe under the sea."

Now, Crescentia sat on a rock above the surface and watched the sunset. The cold hardness pressed against her tail's scales as she contemplated the vial in her delicate fingers. The Sea Witch had given her warning after warning about the power of this potion, all the changes she would undergo, but that wasn't what she was thinking about. She was thinking about the price the witch had asked: her voice. She would no longer be able to protect her friends by singing fishing boats into the rocks.

Crescentia watched a school of tuna swim past her. They couldn't see her up on the rock, she knew. They didn't know what she was contemplating. All they knew was that they were safe, protected by her family. And they would still be protected, she realized. She wasn't the only one protecting them. She wasn't even supposed to be swimming so close to the surface yet. She was too young! Her sister would carry on without her. She was in love, and she would do what she needed to do.

She idly looked to the west, toward the distant spire above The Sea Witch's cave. It rose above the horizon, a dark dagger in the dwindling daylight. That darkness sent a shiver down her spine, and she unconsciously tried to sing. No words came out. The Sea Witch had her voice now. There was no turning back. She brushed her emerald hair out of her face as she raised the potion to her ruby lips.

The potion slopped unevenly out of the bottle, impurities scraping against her tongue like sand. It tasted like the water near a shark attack, all iron and rotten flesh. And then it was gone. All that remained was the sour aftertaste.

She wondered if it had worked. Then her body informed her that it had. The pain started in the pit of her stomach and radiated outward. She felt like she was being cut open. Her lungs began to burn. She tried to scream, but the air passed through her throat without a sound. She could feel every bone in her tail breaking all at once. Her scales fell from her one by one, raining on the stone as twilight fell upon the sea.

And then it was done. A pair of pink legs revealed themselves where her tail had been. The hair that framed her vision had lost most of its color, now a dark brown. The wind suddenly seemed colder to her.

To the west, in front of the dark spire of The Sea Witch's cave, a ship came into view. She implicitly knew that she would see a wooden mermaid on the front which looked like Ada.

Crescentia attempted to leap into the sea, but her new legs didn't move right. She flopped off the rock, falling into the ocean. She tried to swim, but could barely support herself in the water. She knew that humans could swim; she had seen them do it. How did they keep themselves above water with these pathetic legs? Her head dipped below the waves and the sea water felt alien in her mouth. She splashed above the surface, frantically trying to get air into her lungs.

"Man overboard!" she heard. Something splashed into the water beside her. She grabbed onto it desperately, a large ring which floated on the surface. She heard two more loud splashes, and men appeared on either side of her. They tied a rope around her waist and she felt herself lifted up onto the ship.

Alik had been ready to try out his new ability to breathe underwater, but his sense of responsibility had taken him up to his ship and crew, first. The giantess beamed down at him as he left the cave, and his neck prickled as if she were hiding something. But if this helped him get close enough to the siren to catch it with his weapon, the bargain was well worth it.

He'd just been informing his men of his success and his plan to bring the attack to the sirens' own turf--figuratively speaking, of course--when one of his lookouts gave the shout for a man overboard. Immediately, he sprung into action; spotting the man in the sea, Alik tossed him a life preserver and then leaped over the railing. He and his first mate helped the man grab hold and hoisted him up onto the deck.

But as they flopped the man over to check his breathing, Alik's eyes widened. That was no man--it was a *woman*. And one of the most beautiful women he'd ever seen. Alik stared down at the sopping wet, *naked*, woman on his deck as a vague familiarity tugged at the corners of his memory.

She smiled up at him and moved her mouth as if she were trying to say something. Likely, the dunk in the sea had coarsened her throat, and a tea would help set her right. But before that... he shrugged out of his own coat and gently wrapped it around the woman. Only noticing that it was sopping wet from his own dunk in the sea when he saw her shivering.

"Here, come with me to the cabin, and I'll find you some drier clothes."

She allowed herself to be led. She was pretty sure she had heard the word "cabin" before. A cabin was the leader of the ship. She didn't know why he would have drier clothes, but she was disappointed that the beautiful man holding her was bringing her to someone else.

She stumbled as her sandy-haired support stopped suddenly and she fell against him. With a slight cry of surprise, he put his arms around her and held her. Wordlessly, she looked up at him through her newly darkened locks. She felt a warmth flush through her whole body, despite the chill.

Her gaze, with those big, glistening and confused eyes but with a swirl of pure *her* shining through, hit him like a cannonball to the gut. He held her tightly against him, unable to let go. This woman, whoever she was, had come to him for a reason; he could feel it in his bones. He had been destined to find her on this gods-forsaken hunt for the insidious emerald-haired siren.

With a roguish grin for the woman nestled against his chest, he yelled to his men over his shoulder, "Hoist anchor and set sail!"

"Where? Did you find the siren?"

"For home!" he bellowed back, grinning at the momentary astonished silence of his men before the regular sounds of a readying ship drifted to his ears. He wrapped his arms tighter around the still-shivering woman and gently pulled her into his cabin.

When they awoke, the palace was in sight. Crescentia had seen the castle before, but had never gotten this close: the bay was clogged with wooden ships. She could only imagine nets running from pier to pier.

Alik led her gently by the hand into the palace, and then he was gone and she was surrounded by babbling women who wrapped her in cloth and attacked her hair with a spiked club they called a brush. Women were like men without beards whose muscles were hidden under floofy fabric.

When they finally led her to the stone dining room, talking ceased and mouths gaped. Her blue-green dress fit her perfectly, and her fountain of black curls framed her pale face, reddened with makeup.

Acclimated to the dry and tasteless rations on the ship, Alik marveled at the opulent feast his father hosted for his benefit. Even though he had not taken a siren, he'd found something better: his to-be betrothed. Once they were married and the bloodline successfully continued, he would go back out to the seas to hunt that emerald-haired beauty. Strange, the thought of it no longer quickened his heart as it had back on the ship.

A hush fell upon the dining room and Alik looked up from the plates of meat pies, rolls, and decadent fish in all categories of sauce. His eyes met the woman that now walked his dreams and stole the breath from his lungs.

Far from the bedraggled and shivering woman he'd hoisted onto his ship so many days ago, Sea--when he'd asked her name, she'd made a "C" symbol with her hand. He'd found it appropriate that he would call her Sea, for it was the sea that had brought her to him. Eventually, he would find her true name--was a shimmering Goddess, clothed in a floor-length dress that accentuated every perfection of her body.

Crescentia staggered into the room on the stilts which the women called "shoes." The smell of the place was overwhelming: she was not used to any smell except the ocean. This room was filled with scents which made her realize that she hadn't eaten since before visiting The Sea Witch.

The sandy-haired beauty who had inspired her transformation, Alik, came to greet her. He stood taller on land than he had on the ship, and his feet moved differently. He extended his elbow toward her.

Crescentia looked at Alik's elbow, confused. After a moment, he placed her hand on his bicep, making her flush, and led her to the seat next to him. She looked at all of the brightly colored bowls and cups and trays of food, trying to decide what to eat first.

Then she lost her appetite. On a plate directly in front of her was a tuna fish. She was pretty sure it was one of the tuna who had swum past her last night before she took the potion.

She knocked her chair back as she stood up, horrified. She had known that humans ate fish, like sharks, but to see it up close... To be fed a fish for her dinner…

"What's wrong?" Alik asked. Crescentia blinked and looked at him. She pointed at her plate. "You don't like fish? Oh!" He clapped his hands. "She is a vegetarian. Please, provide her with a different entree."

In a flurry of activity, her plate and several others were removed from the table in front of her. Alik helped her back into her chair and pushed it in, just as a fresh plate of steaming vegetables was placed in front of her. While she ate, Alik kept touching her arm in a way that felt protective and safe. She soon forgot the tuna as she filled her empty stomach.

After they had eaten, the band began to play. Alik took her hand.

Stumbling as though he had fins for legs, he guided her to the dance floor as his heart hammered in his chest. He knew this woman was his *one*, even with her refusal to speak, and it terrified him. He needed no words from her lips; her smile was enough.

They danced the night away, his father watching the beginnings of their union with heavy eyes. And all were swayed by her grace and radiance. She would make an excellent wife, and a grand Queen.

Crescentia anxiously rode in the open carriage away from the sea. She had never been so far from the ocean before, but Alik was holding her. That would be enough. He held the reins with a sure hand, keeping the horses at a steady pace. He had told Crescentia where they were going, but it was not a name she recognized and she had already forgotten it. She snuggled in against him, and he wrapped his muscular right arm around her.

They sailed in this strange land-ship over roads and through fields. They passed trees with pink blossoms and fields with ragged green stalks sticking straight up out of the ground. She was delighted as a kaleidoscope of butterflies flew over the carriage from one flower garden to another.

Alongside the carriage, two guards rode on horseback. Their blue and green uniforms with the shiny buttons made them look like the sparkling waves, and the white plumes on their helmets looked like whales spouting. Having them there was like bringing a piece of the sea with her.

She drummed her hands on the edge of the carriage, and the guards responded by trotting their horses in a tight circle. They appeared to be quite fond of her, and had apparently decided that, since she could not speak, they would respond to her drumming hands as if they were military commands.

Crescentia looked up as the carriage came to a stop.

Alik smiled down at his new wife as she peered up at the surrounding mountains. As a boy, he had loved riding among the forever snow-flaked trees and sliding on the ice-encrusted lake. He'd never been bothered by the cold; not when there was a roaring fire ready for him to strip off his sodden clothes and snuggle up next to in his family's cozy cabin.

She was beautiful, his darling Sea. Of course, he now knew her true name, Crescentia, but the endearment he'd called her for the first few months of their courtship still held a firm grip on his heart--and seemed even more apt after she'd told him of her past. In fact, it had been one of his own men who had told him her name, after she'd tapped it out on a table.

It had seemed that she'd told a soldier before her husband, even if the man had been the first to realize her finger-drumming was a method of communication. And not only that, but he'd noticed his men becoming much too… familiar with his wife. They waited on her beck and call, ready to die for her with a single tap.

It should fill him with joy that she'd won their hearts so easily. Instead, he felt a prick of jealousy; it'd taken him years and several provings of his worth for them to take him half as seriously.

But as Sea--Crescentia--smiled up at him, those intrusive thoughts melted away as quickly as did the flecks of snow sprinkling her dark hair. They had the mountains and the cabin to themselves for an entire week, and he meant to make the most of it. So far, his lovely wife had had to deal with the intricacies of court life with little time to enjoy the world around them.

Now, he wanted to show her *everything*.

The Sea Witch? He had promised her firstborn to *The Sea Witch*? Crescentia went numb at the news. She looked down at her belly, not yet showing. When she looked back up at Alik, a sense of determination shone through her eyes.

Without taking her eyes off her prince, she drummed on the door to their rooms and a guard came in.

"Yes, milady?"

She drummed the command, "Ready the ship."

A fight that devoured the sum of all their other fights over their last two years of marriage--that's what Alik was faced with as he watched his men ready his ship. And Crescentia, his land-locked siren, stood on that rocking piece of wood, her feet spread apart as though she'd been born to pilot a ship.

"It's what brought me to you!" He'd tried to reason with her, but she would have none of it. Her mothering instincts were already prominent. She would do anything to protect their child.

And as he stood there, he realized that he would, too. There must be some way to protect this child of land and sea. They would keep her safe. Whatever the cost.

--

"Queen Sea, look!" She shakes her reminiscences away. A pod of orcas comes straight for them. Even having survived the current threats, that many whales directed by The Witch can easily crush their ship to splinters.

Crescentia drums, "Turn about," but she has no illusions that they can get away in time. They will be sent to the bottom of the sea.

But then she hears it. Singing. It almost sounds like her own voice... but no, it's her sisters. Over a dozen of them. They sing the Orcas toward her!

She grins.

Alik hangs onto a whale's fin as it drags him to the surface. The sirens flow behind him with Orcas and the other animals of the sea uncorrupted by the giantess weaving between them.

His heart bursts with pride and amazement as they speed toward his boat and wife. He sees her on the deck, drum in hand, as beautiful as the day he first laid eyes on her.

But then he spots the giantess.

As the monster with ever-changing form leads her forces in the middle of the ocean between Alik and Crescentia, darkened dolphins and scarred sharks fight against Alik's ship, attacking his men and destroying the only thing between the men and the deadly sea.

Alik waves his arm over his head, signaling to Ada to take the sirens toward the giantess, while the creatures of the sea face their own kind in the battle-water. The water froths with blood and flesh as the sirens' creatures dominate their unthinking brethren.

The giantess sees them coming and begins slicing her way through the water, heading directly for the ship.

Alik screams, but he is too far away for his darling Sea to hear. With acid in his core, he watches as the giantess descends upon the ship and slings herself directly onto the deck, mere paces from his wife and unborn daughter. Desire gleams in the giantess' dark eyes.

"You are mine now, Crescentia!"

A chill runs down Crescentia's spine at the sound of her name from that booming voice. She freezes, caught in The Sea Witch's spell. Her limbs won't move. She screams in her mind, but her body can't form the sound even if it would respond to her.

Instead, she finds herself walking toward the prow. Her legs move woodenly, like one of those puppets on strings that she'd seen in the mountain village. The sailors rush around, each knowing his duty by the drumbeats, even if their queen no longer drums. She walks through the chaos toward the naked form of The Sea Witch.

But behind The Witch, she sees a glint of golden hair. A whale drags Alik toward her. In front of the whale, Ada leaps from the water and sings for a golden moment before descending beneath the waves.

But that single moment was enough. Crescentia feels control return to her. She looks around wildly and sees the Trident Cannon beside her. The sailor who had manned it, gone. Crescentia lunges and points it at The Sea Witch. She lights the fuse.

"My name is Sea!"

With a boom, the trident erupts from the cannon. It hangs in the air for a moment, then pierces The Sea Witch through the chest. She looks down at herself and emits a horrifying howl. A rainbow of color swirls from her at the site of the wound, washing over Crescentia and the ship.

The Witch's skin loses its pink sheen, turning a scaly green. As she falls into the sea, she shrinks into a green eel. She floats on the surface with the three prongs of a trident pointed to the sky.

Their daughter now safe, Alik and Crescentia thank their land and sea compatriots, who return to their respective homes. Alik and Crescentia, king and queen of the land, set sail for home. And as they embrace one another on the ship's tattered remains, they begin to dream of a beautiful, powerful child, master of both land and water.

based on

La Chasse-Galerie

Honoré Beaugrand

&

Wilde Jagd

collected by

Jacob Grimm

The Wild Hunt

Reneé Gendron & David Simon

The Wild Hunt

Renée Gendron & David Simon

A New Start

Renée Gendron

Arthur Osborne pressed flat in the brush alongside the road, his fingers curled around the stock of his Brown Bess. One squeeze, and he'd drop the enemy soldier in his sights.

Henry lay to Arthur's right, face darkened with soot, blending into the shadows of the forest. Manon Fortin lay to Arthur's left, a dagger in her hand, a blue handkerchief holding back her mane of brown curls.

The American flag snapped in the wind, the drummers played a quick march, but the platoon shuffled along the winding road towards the fort.

Enemy.

An attacker with supplies.

Henry made to stand.

Arthur scowled at Henry. Three against a platoon were never good odds.

Henry shrugged the indifferent one-shouldered shrug of all younger brothers when caught stealing a cookie from the jar.

The footfalls of the American platoon disappeared over the hill.

Manon rose and shook the dirt off her skirts. "Think the woman at the tavern was right?"

The crown of her head came to Arthur's shoulder. What she lacked in size, she made up with boldness. Much to his mind's contention but to his heart's desire.

"You can't be serious," Arthur said. "We're here to steal horses."

"Manon's right," Henry said. "We need to steal their supplies."

Younger brothers were never of much help.

"We steal their cannons and munitions and use them against the *Amércains.*" Manon strode into the forest, paralleling the road.

"From inside the fort?" Arthur grabbed his musket and fell in beside her. "The munitions are *in* the fort. The *heavily guarded* fort. The place where over one thousand soldiers are massed, *that* fort."

"You saw how those troops marched," she said. "They're exhausted and not expecting a fight. By sundown, they'll all be asleep. Besides, we can take the canoe home."

"The story your grandmother keeps saying?" Arthur asked.

"*Grandmaman* saw it with her own eyes." Her accent thickened, the way it did when she was excited or angry.

"Make a deal with the Devil to fly away in a canoe?"

"We can make a pact," she said. "Get the gunpowder and fly away before they stop us."

"It'll be like the time we got the tea." Henry jogged alongside Arthur. Thicker in the shoulder than Arthur, Henry was also thicker in the head.

"Then there were four armed guards protecting the warehouse." Arthur extended his hand to help Manon over a fallen tree. "This fort's defended by an entire regiment."

They stopped one hundred feet from the end of the treeline. Shadows elongated in the forest as the sun disappeared behind pines and cedars.

Beyond, a swath of land had been cleared of trees, but stumps protruded from the ground—wooden pocks jutting out of ankle-high grass. The wind carried disgruntled male voices from the direction of the fort. Melancholic notes from a fiddle filled the evening air.

Shaped like a jagged square, a pine stockade walled Fort Detroit stood at the edge of town. The city stood between the Detroit River and the fort. Less than two miles and they'd be in Upper Canada. Home.

"See that roof in the northeast corner?" Manon asked. "That's where they keep their gunpowder. The powder's worth a lot." Her eyes were dark honey, proud and determined. Eyes that never accepted no. Even from Arthur. Even in the face of overwhelming odds. "Two powder kegs, and we can make it. *We* can make it."

Make a new life—one free from the shackles of farming and brigandry and the threat of chains around his wrists and ankles.

Lit torches hung along the fort's sides. Cannons sat silent. Soldiers patrolled the walls, casting bored glances towards the forest. A wooden gate barred the entrance. Twice the height of a man, the fort's walls were scalable with a boost.

The Fort. Gunpowder. Risk, but freedom.

The forest. Homesteads with bony-hipped horses. Easy, but empty cupboards after one week.

A spark filled Manon's eyes, fanning the flames of deep emotion reserved for him. He never wanted to see that fire dwindle.

Risk it was.

"It's a new moon tonight. We wait until after midnight." Arthur stepped out from behind a pine. "Manon will secure a wagon, and Henry and I will go after the gunpowder."

Manon kissed the spot under his Adam's apple but before his collarbone. The spot that turned his bones to mashed potatoes.

When was the last time they had eaten?

His hand looped around her waist and drew her closer. Soon they'd spend every night in each other's embrace.

Beaming, Manon handed him a piece of jerky. "You've got the look of a starving man."

For her. He could never get enough of her.

Hours passed with them lying in the shadows of trees. Activity at the fort slowed.

A low rumble emerged from the darkness of the forest.

"What's that?" Henry raised his musket.

"Thunder." Arthur ignored the hairs raising on his forearms.

"It's not humid enough for thunder." Manon lifted her chin, but the defiance didn't reach her eyes.

The ground heaved and buckled. Pinecones dropped from the trees.

Arthur's muscles jerked, urging him to run.

"Cavalry?" Henry asked.

"I don't know, but we're not finding out." Arthur pulled Manon to his side.

The air shifted. Gone was the tang of fresh pine and dirt, in its place an overpowering stench of wet dog. The air thickened with iron and copper, coating his tongue with a metallic aftertaste.

A flash of fangs and something lunged at Arthur, sending him crashing to the ground. One hundred pounds of muscle and claws smothered him.

Arthur's head banged against the ground. Ribs cracked, and his organs rattled. Stunned, he punched at the beast, burying his knuckles in thick fur.

Manon shouted, and a shot went off, then a second shot.

The beast roared, its howl tearing the fabric of the night. It stumbled backwards, jaws snapping, eyes wild, hind leg limp.

"Get up," Henry yelled, but the clatter of snarls and hooves overwhelmed his voice.

Something wicked growled from their right and a fierce snarl came from the left. A rumble of ancient oceans rolled from behind them carrying with it the blow of a horn. Summoned, thunder and lightning clashed in the night. A second horn blew, drawing curtains of grey clouds across the sky, turning it into a swirling abyss. Riders with horned helmets and wolf-fur capes on powerful steeds charged from the darkness with a pack of wolves beside them.

Arthur scrambled to his feet, stumbling towards Manon.

Manon reloaded her musket and aimed. Her shot landed between the eyes of the wolf with a puff of smoke.

No. Not a wolf. Three times the size, with fur darker than tar, a muzzle twice as long, fangs the length of Arthur's hand, and claws the size of his foot. A primal predator summoned from hell.

A bugle sounded inside Fort Detroit.

"Run." Arthur collected his musket, grabbed Manon's hand, and ran past the pain that rocked his body.

They ran through the clearing between the forest and the fort.

Twenty-pound cannon balls rained down. Every boom from cannon fire was answered with howls. The air thickened with gunpowder, scratching the back of Arthur's throat. The pack spread through the forest, turning into a furious flurry of fangs and claws.

Manon ran towards the back of the fort. They raced over tree stumps and rounded the eastern wall, stopping at the far corner under the guard tower.

Gasping for breath, she motioned for a boost. "I'll get the barrels."

"We need to cross the river." Sharp pain stabbed his chest. A broken rib, likely two. "*Now.*"

"They're distracted. We can get the powder." Manon's handkerchief hung by her neck and a mess of Medusa curls sprang from her head. "Us. We do this for us."

"Those beasts aren't natural," Arthur said. "We have to put distance between them."

"The Devil's out to help us," Manon said. "We need the powder."

Henry boosted her over the palisade. Henry Osborne. Thicker than a plank of wood. Faster than a deer. Traitor to blood.

Arthur cursed.

"Save your sour face." Henry cupped his hands for Arthur to use as a step. "You'll thank me when you've married and settled far from here."

Who thanks someone for getting them killed?

He gave Henry his musket. "Get a wagon." Arthur scrambled up the wall and dropped over its side.

The stench of fear mingled with wool uniforms drenched in sweat. The American artillery sliced through the night. A high-pitched feral yelp rose above the fighting. Staggering into the clearing, a hellhound collapsed to its side with a gaping hole in its chest.

A rider with flowing hair blew a horn, low and long. It's terrifying sound was enough to frighten the dead back to their graves.

Four-tusked boars stampeded forward, lowering their heads against the fort's battlements. Thick logs splintered under the assault.

The medieval armour of the riders reflected the orange glow of torches of the fort. Blue flames licked the edges of the attacker's swords.

A squad of soldiers ran from the rear fortifications to the front battlements. Panicked shouts called for more fire and all artillery to be moved forward.

Manon flattened against the wall of the gunpowder room. "A barrel each."

"No. Keep watch." Arthur slipped around her into the room. Five barrels lined each wall and more barrels in the back. He grabbed the first and rolled it forward.

A shadow blocked the exit.

His heart thundered against his sternum, and he straightened, ready to drive his fists into whatever nightmare stood before him.

Manon crouched by the barrel and rolled it forward.

"Don't do that," he said.

"Help?" Her lips twitched in a half-smile. "Scare what life I have left out of me."

Compared to the scene before Arthur, chaos was a neatly stacked pile of folded napkins. The yells, the troops running from position to position along the palisade, the stomach-churning stench, the metallic air that thickened tongues, amplified the mayhem.

They rolled the barrel to the gate where Henry waited. Henry lifted the barrel to the cart.

Manon was half-way back to the gunpowder room when Arthur caught up. They rolled a second barrel to the cart, with Henry taking a third. Arthur tossed his brother a curious look.

"Two for you, one for me," Henry said. "You're not the only ones that have to start fresh."

"We still have to make it out alive." Arthur held Manon's hand. "There's no time for a fourth."

Arthur strode to the front of the cart and picked up the shaft. Manon fell in behind, and Henry behind Manon. They pulled the cart towards the river, towards safety, away from the horror behind.

Every window in the town was dark. A few frightened faces stared out at the fort, bibles clutched to their chests.

"There's a boat," Manon said.

They eased down the embankment and loaded the gunpowder onto the boat. The small craft bobbed and rocked under the weight.

"We leave a barrel behind." Arthur helped Manon into the boat.

"No," Henry said. "It's less than a third of a mile across the river. We can row faster than this thing sinks."

On a good night's sleep, with full bellies and muscles that didn't ache.

"Take all barrels." Manon settled in the middle bench.

Arthur sat and took an oar. Henry pushed the boat into the water and hopped aboard. The hull sunk nearly to the oarlocks.

The current increased, pushing the boat away from the Canadian shore further down the river—still more distance between them and Detroit.

"We'll land in Sandwich," Manon said.

One hundred feet from shore. Fifty feet. So close.

Arthur bullied his shoulders into rowing faster, promising his body ale and a soft bed, if they would row on.

Manon bucketed water with cupped hands. "We're almost there. Keep rowing."

Water seeped into Arthur's boots. Keep rowing, indeed.

A black shape, large and fast, swooped from the sky. Lightning crackled, reflecting against its onyx talons. Dark and graceful, a powerful form dove from the hellish sky towards the boat. An enormous bird of prey clutched Manon by the shoulders and lifted her from the boat.

Fighting and kicking the eagle, a pained cry erupted from her mouth.

In two powerful flaps, the eagle took flight.

"Manon." Arthur lunged for her, reaching for her ankles, but they slipped through his hands.

Arthur fell back onto the rowboat, helpless and terrified. He reached for his musket and fired two shots, the small rounds insignificant against the bird's armour.

"How do we get her back?" The words sandpaper on Arthur's tongue.

"What was that story she told us about?"

"What?"

Manon was carried higher and higher into the night, disappearing towards thick clouds. The higher she was, the deeper his heart sank.

"The canoe," Henry said. "The story about the canoe."

"The one about the pact with the devil?" Arthur asked.

"Aye, that one."

"The devil doesn't exist."

Henry jerked his thumb back towards Fort Detroit, the bone rattling shrieks of death carrying over the river, the flashes of hell lighting the darkness. "That says otherwise."

Cold settled in Arthur's bones, one that infused ache and longing and torment into his soul.

"Devil." Arthur screamed. "Bring Manon and us back safely to Sandwich." His words echoed off the water.

"Your hands mustn't touch a rooftop when you fly over the village," a voice whispered in his ear, low and dark. "Or all of your souls will be mine."

A chill cloaked him, robbing his hands and feet of heat. "We understand. No touching of rooftops." Arthur slid his gaze to Henry.

Paler than a full moon, Henry nodded.

With a groan, the boat lifted from the water and flew towards Manon. Refusing to peer over the edges, Arthur's heart seized.

Arthur lifted the oar in her direction, and the boat caught up to the eagle. They whacked the predator's talons with their oars, but the eagle shook them off. Undeterred, Arthur yanked the bird's tail feathers, pulling out three. Henry yanked four wing feathers.

The eagle veered off course, flapping its wings but unable to gain its former steadiness. Confused, it dropped Manon into the canoe and spiralled towards the river.

"Are you hurt?" Arthur clutched her.

"*Non*." She trembled against him. "Don't let me go."

He couldn't if he wanted to; his soul needed hers.

The boat descended over the darkened houses and cold chimneys of Sandwich. Churches rang their bells, calling parishioners to pray.

The boat flew to a pasture, coming to an effortless stop. They sat in the boat on the ground, exhausted, dragging in long breaths.

The murky confusion cleared from Arthur's thoughts. They were safe with enough gunpowder to buy anything they wanted.

Manon slid to his lap and wrapped her arms around him. "A new start."

The Wild Hunt

David Simon

Tattered clouds swept across the face of the full moon like wolves stalking prey.

Karl Ottweiler and his son Michael, sprawled in a hollow between two massive fallen oak trees, were muddy, exhausted, and wearing mismatched, castoff uniforms of the 4th U.S. Infantry Division. They were lost somewhere in the primordial forest along the United States/Canada border, surrounded by towering birch and aspen, walnut and cedar, pine and maple. Swarms of black flies and mosquitoes were thick in the humid air. The oppressive August heat was a physical thing, draping them like a wet wool blanket. They had stumbled through the dark between tree trunks and dead falls, ankle-deep in mud from torrential rains, and had become separated from the other members of their company.

Somewhere behind them, lost in the gloom, were the hopefully impregnable walls of Fort Detroit, constructed of earthen embankments and thick log walls, topped with sharpened stakes. Somewhere in front of them, a regiment of British soldiers, aided by warriors under Shawnee leader Tecumseh's command, had massed for battle.

Michael leaned his musket with fixed bayonet against the tree trunk, peered into the dark, and fell back with a sigh. "Papa," he said. "I know we're surrounded by two armies, but I have never felt so alone."

"Ja," Karl answered. "This place is like the Black Forest when I was a boy." He opened his rucksack and rummaged inside, pulling out a greasy roll of paper wrapped in twine. "Come, let's eat something. We'll need our strength for the long night ahead." Karl handed Michael a hunk of salt pork and a crust of hard black bread. "Eat up. That's the last of it for now." The entire contingent of American troops had been on half rations for the past few weeks.

Michael smiled, but there was little humor in it. "Mmm, salt horse." He tore off a bite and worked it with his teeth until it was soft enough to swallow. He shook his canteen and, realizing it was nearly empty, raised it to his father. "Ein prosit."

"Ein prosit." Karl lifted his own canteen.

"When do you think they'll attack?" Michael asked. "It's not that I'm afraid to fight. These are hard men on our side. I've gotten to know them, and they're the equal of any army, even Tecumseh's. It's this damn waiting."

"Patience, boy. The battle will be here soon enough. Before daylight probably, tomorrow at the latest."

"You're right, Papa, but patience is hard. I guess none of this is what I expected when we left home." Michael drained the last of his water. "Do you think the farm is safe?"

"Ja," Karl said. "Don't worry. Your mama and brothers will take good care of things." He chuckled. "Your mama is harder than these men here."

Michael surprised himself by laughing at that. "True, true." He watched worriedly as his father stretched his left leg out, wincing in pain. "Papa, how's the ankle?"

Karl had stepped into a hidden badger hole and turned his ankle on the journey north, and the pain still lingered.

"I fight for my adopted country," he said. "My ankle is a small thing."

They had left their farm outside Dayton, Ohio, months ago, joining a regiment under Brigadier General Hull's command. Draft horses carried their equipment and supplies, and the men marched, using roads at first. They may not have been professional soldiers, but they were all farm boys, strong as the oxen that pulled their plows, and they made good time on the level terrain.

All that changed when General Hull decided to forge a new route to Detroit, directly through the Great Black Swamp in northwest

Ohio. Sycamore and cottonwood trees grew shoulder to shoulder, the trunks mired in a thick black mud that made every step agony. Wagon wheels foundered, and draft horses sank to their hocks in the muck. Mosquitoes tormented man and horse alike. By the time the troops reached the Maumee River, they were exhausted and half starved. General Hull was forced to load the horses, heavy equipment, and the sickest of the men onto ships. The soldiers that finally staggered into Fort Detroit, Karl and Michael included, were broken. Hollowed out.

Now they found themselves alone in the dark, on the brink of battle.

Michael startled awake. At some point, he had slipped into an uneasy sleep, his dreams filled with thousands of clutching, skeletal hands reaching up from the mud, blindly grasping. He expected to see his father still asleep, but Karl was standing, musket in hand. Michael scrambled to his feet. "What is it?" he asked. "Have the British attacked?"

"No," Karl answered. "I don't think so. I've heard no musket fire, no artillery. But there's something wrong. The temperature is dropping."

Michael realized his father was right—he was no longer sweating. He tugged his uniform jacket tighter around his body. Then he noticed something else. The hairs stood up on the back of his neck. His breath fogged in the sudden cold. "Papa, look at the moon. It's moving." The full moon was juddering violently, the light pulsing from bright to dim.

"Gott im Himmel," Karl said, his voice shaking. "I saw this once before, back in Germany. We have to move. Now. Back to the Fort if we can."

"But the British—"

"Forget the British. A much older evil is on the way." The two of them shouldered their rucksacks and clambered over the downed oak behind them. Karl took a step and staggered. Gritting his teeth he pushed on in the direction of the fort. They had gone mere yards when a vicious wind emerged from the west, swirling through the forest, tearing off branches and uprooting bushes. A howling came with the wind, a shredding cacophony that doubled and tripled in volume as the trees around them shook. The moon vibrated in the sky, its afterimage burning against the stars.

A shorn-off tree limb whistled through the air, smashing Karl in the shoulder. He stumbled and fell to his knees. "It's too late!" Karl screamed to Michael above the din. "They're here!"

Michael put his arms around his father, tried to shield him from more flying debris. "Who, Papa? Who is here?"

"The wilde jagd!"

Michael shook his head, not sure he had heard right. "The wild hunt? But those are just stories you tell to scare the kinder. They're not real!"

Karl took his son by the shoulders, pulled Michael to him until they were face to face. He still had to scream. "Michael, listen to me. The wild hunt is real. They are here to foretell the coming battle. You must run. Now!"

"Not without you, Papa!"

"Go, boy!"

The wind died as swiftly as it had risen, the forest suddenly silent, not a whisper in the icy, still air. The moon pulsed brightly one last time, then dimmed to almost nothing.

An unnatural, sickly glow lit the forest to the west. A low, guttural growling, and a crashing came through the underbrush. Michael pulled his father to his feet. Moving like drunks, Michael half-dragged his father away from the murky lights, into the shadows. The growls, mixed with piercing barks, grew louder, the light brighter, and they tried to hurry. Karl's breath came in ragged gasps. He tripped. A wave of twisting fire roared up his leg. Karl screamed in pain, nearly passing out. He clutched Michael's arm and kept moving.

Michael realized his father had nearly reached his limit, and searched for shelter. They stumbled into a large clearing, the ground—a remnant of the last glacial age—too rocky for anything but underbrush to grow. "There, Papa!" he shouted.

On the far side of the clearing, the devil wind had torn a mammoth walnut tree from the earth, roots and all, leaving behind a deep pit. The two staggered across the last few yards, and half-slid, half-fell into the wet black hole. The tree's roots arched over them like the open maw of some ancient beast as they waited, silently, muskets at the ready.

Revenant dogs came first. Dozens of them prowled into the clearing, shaggy heads swinging from side to side. The size of dire wolves, they slunk low to the ground, their heads wreathed in the steam blowing from their nostrils. Their lips curled back from wicked teeth, and their high-pitched barks chilled Michael to the marrow. The dogs were translucent—Michael could see the outlines of the trees behind them. Still, they were solid enough. Their paws snapped branches and scattered clods of dirt. Where their slavering jaws dripped saliva, the ground sizzled. The dogs glowed the putrescent color of curdled milk.

Karl touched Michael on the shoulder, held one finger to his lips. Michael nodded grimly, gripping his musket until his knuckles were white as bone. Despite the cold, both men found themselves sweating.

The dogs fanned out across the clearing in formation. They pawed at the ground, restless, and began to howl as one. The trees shook, limbs raining down. The ground trembled beneath his feet.

"Möge Gott uns beistehen," Karl whispered.

An armored hunter astride a warhorse burst into the clearing, surrounded by an army of spectral warriors. Glowing like the dogs, light radiated from their bodies like cold flame from a tallow candle.

The hunter was clad in heavy, battle-scarred armor of leather and mail. He wore a horned helmet, long hair streaming from beneath. In his left hand, he gripped a round wooden shield trimmed in iron, three interlocking triangles painted in the center. In his right hand, a massive two-sided battle axe. His horse, black as pitch, heavily muscled, and lathered with sweat, wore crude leather barding to protect its head and body. The hunter raised his axe and screamed, the sound echoing across the clearing. His horse reared, slicing the air with frenzied hooves.

The warriors raised their weapons—spears, swords, and axes—and screamed with him, as the dogs joined in. They were lean men, some in leather and mail and some bare-chested, some with helmets, long hair and beards braided. They moved among the dogs, ruffling fur.

The hunter shouted, "I kveld jakter vi og kaller frem kampen!" in a voice like icebergs calving into the ocean, and the wild hunt surged forward.

Karl pulled his son to him, hugged him tightly and whispered in his ear, "Take care of your mama." He pushed the boy down into the furrow. While Michael struggled to stand, Karl climbed from the hole, dragging his musket behind him. Ignoring his pain, he charged away from the pit, bellowing, "This way, bastarde!" The wild hunt rushed him, the dogs barking, the men whooping excitedly.

Michael screamed, "Papa, no!" but it was lost in the pandemonium. He scrambled up, intent on saving his father. He ran directly at the hunt, staying low, with no real plan except to attack.

While the rest of them circled Karl, one ghost dog saw Michael and peeled off from the pack. It bounded toward him, paws churning up dirt, mouth open in a snarl. Michael braced himself, bayonet forward. The dog leaped. The last thing Michael saw before impact was a mouth full of jagged teeth opened impossibly wide. Then boy and beast were locked together, tumbling. Michael's only thought was to hang on to the musket at all costs. He rolled to a stop with the full weight of the beast on top of him, open jaws inches from his face, and Michael waited for death.

Instead, the dog's head lolled to one side, the infernal light in its eyes extinguished. Michael pushed the dog off him and got shakily to his feet. His bayonet had found its mark, piercing the animal in the throat. As Michael watched in horror, the dog dissolved into dust around his bayonet and swirled away on the wind. The glow dimmed, and was soon gone like the dust.

Michael spun around at the sound of laughter. He fell to his knees.

The warriors had cornered Karl, surrounding him. They crowded in closer, shaking their weapons and laughing, the circle shrinking. Karl crouched, watching them warily, bayonet ready. The hunter dismounted. He strode through the men and dogs, as they parted for him. When he reached the inner circle opposite Karl, the hunter stopped, one hand holding fast to a dog's scruff. The dog whined, straining, as if ready to attack.

Karl faced the hunter. He stood up, ramrod straight, and threw his musket to the ground. In a strong, clear voice that rang through the clearing, he said, "Go back to hell, all of you, where you belong." He raised his voice, chanced a glance at Michael, and said, "Auf wiedersehen mein sohn."

The hunter said, "Velkommen til jakten," and released the dog. It snarled and leaped—and its body passed straight through Michael's father. Karl's body jerked. It crumpled to the ground. In his place stood a spectral warrior, sword in hand instead of a musket. He had Karl's face. Younger, stronger, but it was his face. He glowed with a fierce brightness, like he was on fire. He clasped arms with the hunter, and the entire wild hunt erupted, the men howling to the moon along with the dogs. The hunter remounted, and they moved off through the trees, back to the hunt. The spectral warrior who had been Karl never looked back.

Michael watched them leave, head hung low, racked with sobs. When he could no longer hear the hunt, or see their pale light, he dried his eyes and went to his father's body. He dragged it to the pit where they had hidden and dropped him in. Without a shovel, it was the best he could do. He said a prayer, then staked his father's musket there as a grave marker. Michael buried his sorrow deep inside—when this was all over he would grieve.

The sky above him lit up with artillery fire arcing toward Fort Detroit. The battle had begun, as the wild hunt had foretold. Michael had been a farmer before taking up arms, and hopefully would one day be again. But for now, he was a soldier. He would fight for his country, and now for his father. Michael headed off at a brisk trot in the direction of the British forces.

based on

Das Bürle

collected by

Jacob & Wilhelm Grimm

The Little Peasant of Cransley Manor Boys School

Sean Southerland-Kirby
&
Mickey Hadick

The Little Peasant of Cransley Manor Boys School

Sean Southerland-Kirby & Mickey Hadick

Archie's Story

Sean Southerland-Kirby

When Archie and his mum first walked up the long drive to Cransley Manor Boys School, she had assured him he would fit in just fine despite his late start. Being mid-November, the rest of the pupils had already been there for two months. However, due to an admin error with his scholarship papers, his admittance had been delayed.

She stopped on the path before reaching the main lawn. Archie stopped too.

"This is a big day, Archie. Remember what your dad always says. Grab every opportunity by the scruff and hold on for dear life." She loosened the clenched fist she had been holding in front of her and smoothed Archie's lapel and tie.

"Don't worry Mum. I'm looking forward to it. I'm going to make the best friends and learn everything the teachers can teach me." He beamed an infectious smile that his mum mirrored. Setting off once more, they rounded a corner. The surrounding trees fell away, replaced by a sprawling, manicured lawn and perfectly trimmed topiary. The hulking edifice of Cransley Manor dominated the view. Its red brick walls and sandstone columns seemed to erupt from the very earth it stood on. A monolith, hidden by trees, in the middle of leafy Hampshire.

Archie thought about that now as he sat on his bunk in the dormitory. He had been so enamoured by the sheer enormity of the building, he had been in a daze the first time he met Mister Rutherford, the headmaster. The slender grey-haired man who had greeted them at the door that first day insisted on being their guide and telling them all of the history of the four-hundred-year-old manor as they went. The stories of priest holes, hidden passages and magic wells had long entertained the boys of the school, though nothing more than an elaborate cupboard was ever found by pupils and the well was strictly off limits.

Archie smiled at the other boys as they walked around the building and everyone seemed especially polite and smiled back. It wasn't until someone overheard the word scholarship that whispers spread like a virus among the students at Cransley. By the time the tour was over, everyone knew.

Archie discovered a well-established hierarchy among the student populous. At the very top was Digby Lennox, the youngest prefect Cransley ever had. A fact that, if someone didn't know, then one of his cronies would inform you of. Chief among these was Nathan Snell, a boy who looked like he was raised on growth hormones and children's television. He had cornered Archie in the first week. Surrounded by several more of Digby's deadbeats, he spelled out exactly how things worked at Cransley. It had been a shower of spittle, swearing and grunts as Nathan pinned Archie to a wall single handedly and stared at him with his little piggy eyes. From what Archie had pieced together, the top dog was Digby, followed by Nathan, Birley, Lucas, Toby and Dune.

Being from the wealthiest families, they had private rooms away from the rest of the boys. Of course, officially the rooms had been awarded to the boys on merit, but everyone knew it was money. Below them, the rest of the pupils. The rest except for the fat, spotty, effeminate and of course the poor, a collection of around a dozen pupils. A dozen including Archie. They were considered fair game by all for bullying and simply referred to as *the inferiors*. Archie had been dubbed 'Little Peasant' by Digby Lennox.

Since coming here, he had been pushed over, spat on, tripped up, and had graffiti written about him in the toilets. What the others hadn't considered was why Archie had obtained a scholarship to begin with. He was brilliant, scoring off the charts in standard IQ tests. He had an amazing memory and he spent his free time playing strategy games, which he almost always won.

Today though, deflated, he lay back on his bed, looked up at the slats on the underside of the bed above, and sighed.

"What's wrong?" came a voice from above, followed by a blonde mop of hair and small face.

"Nothing Zachary," Archie said with another deep sigh. "I just can't think in here. It's too loud." When Archie first saw the dormitory with its high beamed ceiling and neat rows of bunk beds, he thought it an orderly and pleasant place to sleep. In reality, it was little more than a warehouse of bottom burps, belches and body odour. There was no peace, but a constant low murmuring, punctuated at intervals with whoops, hollers and occasional fights.

Zachary, a fellow member of the inferiors due to being gay, tutted and flicked his hair back, carrying on the motion to flop back on his own bed in a dramatic fashion. "The only

203

way you'll get peace in here is to have your own room," he said with a sigh of his own. "And that's never going to happen."

The words lodged in Archie's brain. It was like a pebble rattling around in there. 'Your own room, your own room...' For days it rolled around. It gathered other thoughts and small ideas.

In a week, Archie had formed a plan and today presented the perfect opportunity to put it into action. In art class, the boys had all been given homework to depict a cow as realistically as possible. So when everyone was leaving, Archie approached the teacher. "Excuse me sir. Could I have some clay for my cow?"

"Well of course, um..." the teacher flicked through the class register quickly- "um, Archie, yes, Archie. It's always nice to see pupils push themselves and try something different. Clay is over there." He pointed a boney finger to a large bin in the corner. Archie took a plastic bag and filled it with as much clay as he thought he needed. Returning to the dormitory before his next class, he stashed it under his bed.

Finally, the school day was finished and he set about putting his plan into action.

First things first, the cow. Archie was no master sculptor. He didn't need to be. He found a quiet corner and spent some time making the best-looking cow he could. Sure, the legs were wonkey and it was cross eyed, but it was undeniably a cow. With a little luck, everything else should fall into place.

He strolled down to the corridor where the teachers' living rooms were and weighed up his options. Mr. Brown was too deaf. Mr. Williams too mean. Mr. McLachlan would be perfect. He knocked on the science teacher's door.

"Hello?" came a voice before the door opened. Mr. McLachlan stood in the doorways wearing a smoking jacket with half-moon glasses resting on the tip of his nose. "Ah, Archie. To what do I owe this unexpected pleasure?"

"Well, Sir, I was hoping you might give me permission to dry this over the radiator there." Archie was pointing to the large bar radiator under a window. "The one in the dorm is covered in towels and I'd like to have this dry by the morning for art class. It's a cow, see?" Archie held the cow up for Mr McLachlan to inspect.

"So it is," he said with a smile. "I'll tell you what. Why don't you get it where you want it and I'll make sure it stays safe till the morning."

"Thank you, sir."

"You're welcome." Mr. McLachlan closed the door and Archie positioned the cow on the windowsill over the radiator. Time for the next part of the plan. The teachers' corridor was adjacent to the pupils' private rooms. Archie didn't have to wait long for none other than Nathan Snell to walk around the corner. Archie pressed back into the corridor and whistled to himself whilst adjusting his cows position. The whistle yielded its desired effect. Moments later, Archie felt the steely grip of Nathan's chubby fingers grasping his shoulder.

"What have you got here then little peasant?" he snorted.

"It's nothing. Leave it alone," Archie protested and tried to shrug off Nathan's hand. Nathan laughed and with little effort pushed Archie away and to the floor. He picked up the cow.

"Aaawww it's a little moo-cow. Getting in practice for living on a poor farm." Nathan laughed as he held the cow over Archie.

"Give it back!" Archie shouted as loud as he could into the corridor.

"No chance. They say pigs don't fly. I wonder if cows can." Nathan opened the window, took a step back, hooked his arm and *whoosh*. The cow flew out the window and onto the flagstone two floors down. It landed with a wet thud. Nathan crossed his arms over his chest and laughed. That is until a larger hand than his own gripped his shoulder. The colour drained from his face as he turned to Mr. McLachlan who had stepped out to see what the fuss was in time to see everything.

"I think we need a chat, Master Snell. Don't you? You too, Archie." He beckoned for Archie to follow as they all marched to the Headmaster's office.

Archie's plan had been a success. Since there was no debate that Mr. McLachlan witnessed the flying cow, Nathan was to be punished for his bullying. His first punishment was one month of labour, after school, with the caretaker. Second, and worst of all for Nathan, his private room had been taken from him. As recompense for Nathan's action, his room now belonged to Archie.

He had done it. He had successfully carried out his plan and now had his own room.

Archie sat on his bed, getting together his things, ready to move into his new room. They had been given two days to make the switch, and Archie couldn't wait.

The familiar mop of Zachary's hair, followed by his face, peered over from the bunk above. "Miracles really do happen."

"Hi Zach. Can you keep a secret?" Archie asked. He barely finished the word 'secret' before Zachary launched himself over the edge of his bunk and landed with arms in the air as if finishing a gymnastic display.

"Secret is my middle name. Well, not really, but I'll never tell what it really is," He slumped down on Archie's bed and sprawled out next to him, kicking his legs behind him with his chin in his hands. "Spill the tea."

So, Archie did.

A small Welsh accented voice piped up. "No wonder Digby is out to get you."

Archie and Zachary noticed Hew Hughs, a small, pale lad whom Digby had dubbed Ghost Boy. Another member of the inferiors.

"What do you mean?" asked Archie. Hew had an unnerving ability to appear unexpectedly and quietly, which meant he knew more than he should. That and his monotone speech were more than enough reason for his nickname.

"Word is, Digby is planning to have you kicked out of school. He's going to steal some exam papers and plant them in your new room."

"When?" asked Archie in a panic.

"I think they're doing it tonight. Or so I hear. Taking maths papers from Mr. Woodcock's class." Hew wiped his nose on his sleeve, turned, and silently walked away.

"What are you going to do?" Zachary flapped.

Archie, stunned for a moment, smiled. "I think I have a plan. Come with me."

Archie and Zachary waited in the corridor opposite Mr. Woodcock's class, out of sight under the stairs with a box of Archie's belongings. They didn't have to wait long. All alone, here was Digby, picking the lock to the classroom and letting himself in. As soon as he was in, the trap was sprung. Zachary rushed off and Archie peered inside the classroom to keep an eye on Digby. He was still rooting through papers when Mr. Woodcock appeared with Zachary.

"I hear you wanted to speak to me, young man." Mr. Woodcock had a kind face and smiled as he walked towards Archie. Digby, hearing the teacher's voice, jumped into a cupboard.

"That's right, Sir. I know it's late but I just wanted to ask about fractions and decimals," said Archie. He winked at Zachary who left them to it.

"Well, then you had better come in."

They spent a few minutes talking and Archie took a magic 8-ball from his box and started to roll it between his hands.

"Is that a magic 8-ball?" asked Mr Woodcock.

"Oh, this?" Archie held it up. "My dad gave me this. Sometimes I just like to hold it and think of him."

"Remarkable things. An icosahedron suspended in blue liquid inside a sphere. Just a fun toy," said Mr Woodcock.

"This one is not just a toy," said Archie. "My dad told me it was special. You could ask it two questions a day and it would absolutely tell the truth. On the third shake it will reveal a secret. Want to test it out?" Archie asked.

"Alright," said Mr. Woodcock, amused. "What do I have in my top drawer?"

Archie shook the ball and peered inside. "Jelly babies," he answered, a piece of information Hew had told him.

"How did you know that?" Mr. Woodcock scratched his head. "Ok. What is my birthday?"

Archie shook the toy again and peered. "July 24th." *Thank you Zachary and your need to send all teachers birthday cards.*

"Astonishing." Mr. Woodcock sat down. "And the secret?" Archie shook a final time and peered into the round window of the ball.

"There's someone hiding in your cupboard." Before they could both turn to look, the cupboard door burst open and out popped Digby with an arm full of papers running as fast as he could out of the room. Mr. Woodcock ran after him shouting, leaving a satisfied Archie to collect his things and leave.

The next two days saw Digby have his prefecture taken away and be put on lunch duty in the cafeteria. He kept his room, not that Archie minded too much. He could lock his new door and shut out the world. It was, however, very clear Digby wanted revenge.

As Archie walked to the bathroom, Digby struck. Birley, Lucas, Toby and Dune jumped out from the shadows. Grabbing Archie, they pinned his arms to his side, clamped a hand over his mouth, and marched him outside. They trudged along the slick, muddy path until there, at the well, stood Digby with a large barrel. Without a word, he lifted the top and the four other boys threw Archie in and secured the lid with a couple of nails. The barrel was full of holes. At one appeared Digby's eye.

"You little rat faced peasant. Do you know what we're going to do? We're going to throw this barrel into the well, you included. Who's going to care if a peasant like you drowns. Accidents happen all the time. But before that, we're going to let you sweat a bit. Come on boys!" With that they trudged up the mud towards the house.

Archie started to panic. What would he do? He didn't have time to think of a plan.

"Need a hand?" a dreary voice came from beside the barrel.

"Hew? Hew, is that you? Please help me out of here!" Archie pleaded. A few moments later Hew had pulled the securing nails and popped the lid. Archie gulped a huge breath of fresh air.

"What were you doing in there then?" asked Hew.

"They were going to drown me." Archie's voice shook.

"Those horrible bullies. I wish someone would just get rid of them." Hew said, slinking away into the darkness.

Get rid of them? Get rid of them. An idea solidified in Archie's mind. He only needed to wait a little longer in the barrel.

No more than ten minutes had passed when his quarry was in sight.

"I don't want to do it! Please don't make me! Choose someone else! Let me out!" yelled Archie loud enough for Nathan Snell to hear on his way back to the house from garden duty. It worked. Nathan made a b-line for the barrel.

"Well well well. What do we have here then? A little peasant all locked up in a barrel." He laughed.

"Nathan. They want to make me Prefect. The teachers said this is how they decide. If I can stay in this barrel until they come back, they'll make me Prefect," Archie called from inside the barrel. The lid was snatched back and Archie stared up at Nathan's lumpy pig face.

"I want to be Prefect. You don't deserve it." He grabbed Archie by the lapels and lifted him out with one hand, then stuffed his bulk into the barrel himself. "Put the lid on or else. I'm going to get it, not you."

"Yes, you are." Archie said to himself as he secured the lid and tacked it in place with a couple of nails. He hid out of sight until the boys came back, expecting them to open the barrel and let out "Archie" and end their joke. But no, they each took hold of the barrel and unceremoniously dumped it and Nathan into the well. Brushing their hands together in satisfaction and laughing.

"Let's go get cleaned up," Digby said as they all went to the showers. Archie darted off to his room and prepared to finish the job. He grabbed several old exam papers, placed a chair outside his room, and sat in the corridor reading them. Soon enough, the now clean bullies came up the corridor and were stunned to find their victim reading papers, unharmed.

"Oh hi, guys," waved Archie, noticing them, and turned back to his book.

"What the.. How did you... but we drowned you!" stammered Digby.

"The well you mean? No, there's no water in the well. It's a big room where the teachers keep confiscated items and the new exam papers." He held up the paper for emphasis, making sure to keep the date hidden.

A fever hit the bullies. They murmured to themselves, growing excited. Then, before they could talk about it, one of them ran for the well, followed by another and then all of them were hot-footing it to the well to check it out. Looking out of the window, Archie witnessed Dune make it there first and peer inside, followed by Lucas who could barely stop before looking over the edge into the darkness. Bringing up the rear, the other 3 boys hit the mud simultaneously and lost their footing. The flailing arms and legs hit Dune and Lucas as they turned to see what had happened. The collision was solid and final. All five boys tipped over the edge and into the well.

The next day, in assembly, the headmaster looked grave as he announced the passing of six pupils in a tragic accident by the well. The well, which would be locked up, was now off limits to all pupils of the school. For his actions and informing teachers of the tragic accident -even if it was two hours later- Archie Hawkins was to be the new Prefect at Cransley. Archie, in his role as Prefect, designated the private rooms to deserving pupils, Zachary and Hew included. Cransley was now a bully-free school.

The Prefect's Story

Mickey Hadick

Digby Lennox rose from his desk when Rutherford, the headmaster, entered his dorm room. Digby hid his annoyance at the intrusion and clasped his hands behind his back, raised his eyebrows to show attention, and arranged the slightest of smiles to top it all off.

"I was wondering," Rutherford said, "if you might have a moment to assist me. We have a new student arriving—"

"Really, sir?" Digby asked. "This late in the semester?"

"Yes, well, they had some difficulties, but it's all sorted out. He's quite impressive, I think you'll agree. Smart as a whip. Reminds me a bit of you at that age. I thought it'd be nice for you to help me welcome him, tour the grounds. Perhaps you could help get him settled."

"I'd love to, sir, but I've got an exam soon and a paper due, not to mention my chemistry labs, and, you see, I'm just writing a letter to my mother who's not feeling well. Along with my other duties, I'm afraid I would be distracted."

"Of course," Rutherford said. "I just thought—"

"I'll see to it he's welcomed at dinner," Digby said.

"What should we do to him?" Snell asked. They were at the table positioned far from the faculty's table across the dining hall. Between Digby's table and the faculty's sat the other students. At the opposing corner, at a table by himself, the new student ate haltingly, his head down, but scanning the hall, watching the other students.

"What should we do with whom?" Digby asked.

"Archie," Snell said. "The little runt."

Archie was smart to avoid the boys. Smallest of his class, dressed in a tattered uniform, they had dealt him a poor hand. He didn't seem a runt though. He wasn't puny and frightened. A fox avoided a wolf, but it was quite cunning on its own.

"The little peasant?" Digby asked. "Do what you like. See if he learns his place."

What Snell lacked in imagination, he compensated with bodily girth. Straight off, Snell carried his dirty dishes to the kitchen, going the long way around, and bumped into Archie, knocking him off his chair to the floor.

"Clumsy idiot," Snell said. "You could have tripped me."

"Sorry," Archie said, picking himself up.

Rutherford rose from his place to observe the proceedings. Luckily for Snell, Dune and Birley had followed like jackals looking for scraps. Dune made a great show of helping Archie off the floor. Birley, giggling, provided cover as Snell grabbed at Archie's underpants and gave him a wedgie.

Archie yelped and laughter erupted from the nearby tables. That brought Woodcock, the maths teacher, to his feet and on his way. Digby timed his approach to arrive with Woodcock at the scene.

"What's all this?" Digby asked. Snell took a step back, and Digby moved between Archie and Mr. Woodcock.

"He pushed me," Archie said, his eyes downcast. "It's not my fault."

Digby turned to Mr. Woodcock. "Shall I have Snell get the mop?"

"Yes," Woodcock said. "That's a good start."

Digby cast a glance at Snell and sent him off.

"You boys should help Archie adjust," Woodcock said. "We all need help, don't we?"

"Of course, sir," Digby said.

Digby offered Archie his hand. "I'm the prefect. Digby Lennox, third year. Get yourself cleaned up and then come see me. Alright?"

"That's the spirit, lads," Woodcock said.

Digby, at the age of five, saw a trained bear perform at the circus. The bear towered over its handler, a slightly built man of dark complexion and mysterious background. Not once did the bear threaten or even complain about their relationship, despite the whip used to direct the bear to balance on a ball, ride a tricycle on a tightrope and play dead. Why hadn't the bear destroyed this annoying little man, forcing it to do things against its nature?

Digby pondered how this was so for many years, and it was never far from his mind as he learned how the world worked. Topics such as love, loyalty, and family jumbled up with the circus, the bear and its trainer.

Digby was the third male heir of a British man of some means; however, he'd been born of the man's second wife. One incident stood out from when he was to begin school. "Third time's a charm, right?" Digby's mother offered her husband, the elder Lennox. Digby's father, in response, said, "If he's no smarter than the first two, I dare say I'm better off drowning the lot of them."

The much-older half-brothers did not get along with their father, a man who raised his voice at the first provocation. They held a grudge over the treatment of their mother, who was from a "good" family and had not put up with Lennox's improprieties.

Unfortunately for the first Mrs. Lennox, being from a "good" family did not secure her financial life after divorce.

Digby's father made it clear that those boys — now young men — were fast approaching a line they oughtn't to cross. They could only get so far in this world with the Lennox name. They would also need something of the Lennox fortune. Digby overheard his father's ultimatum to them: "Mention your mother to me once more, and I'll never speak with any of you again. Especially regarding matters of money."

Meanwhile, Digby's mother did all she could to please her husband. It seemed she pulled something off to become the new Mrs. Lennox. At some point, during one of his tirades, she realized: if her husband had divorced one wife, he might well divorce a second.

Digby learned to agree with his father, and to do as he was asked in order to curry favor. It was at Cransley he learned smaller kids agree just as quickly.

When Snell returned with the broom and mop, Digby cast a glance at two of the younger boys, Hew and Felix. Without a word, they rose from their seats and took charge of the broom and mop, cleaning the mess while Snell looked on.

Along the prefect's hall, the rooms near the dormitory were shit, but Digby's, three doors down, was spacious and well-appointed. Opposite the room was a sitting space with windows, a sofa and two chairs. No one dared sit there unless invited by Digby.

When Digby heard the creak of the sofa's leather, he rolled off his bed and looked out. "You," he said. "Who said you could sit there?"

"No one," the little peasant said. He appeared even smaller on the edge of the center of the sofa.

"That's mine," Digby said. "It's all mine, you understand?"

"You said I should come see you."

"Did I?" Digby remembered, of course. He was gauging the little peasant's reaction. "Come in then."

He noticed how the little peasant paused in the doorway to admire the room. His eyes moved from the desk and shelves in the corner to the chest of drawers and wardrobe beside the bed, settling on the window overlooking the pitch.

"Listen, Alfie—"

"It's Archie."

Digby stared until the little peasant swallowed. "Archie, then. Listen Archie, you're new, so I'll cut you a bit of slack today. But you'll have to catch on soon. That thing you pulled with Snell—"

"He shoved me," Archie said. "It wasn't my fault."

"Snell's been loyal to me," Digby said. "He's helped me out quite a few times. You might think about doing the same, and I might help you someday."

"Help me do what?"

Digby counted to five before responding. "Things happen in the dormitory at night. People get hurt. You'd best watch yourself while you're sleeping."

Archie nodded. "Shall I go now?"

"Yes."

Digby was the youngest prefect ever selected at Cransley and with good reason. He had been precocious. What made him different, he concluded, was that he realized his precociousness. It wasn't fancy words and complex sentences, putting subordinate clauses in their place while never letting the listener forget the larger meaning at hand.

No, Digby knew others would be jealous of him. What is cute in a small child becomes threatening in a young adult. This happened to both of his half-brothers, smarter than their father, yet neither understood why the over-matched old man provoked and tormented them.

Digby understood.

The clever must be watched carefully, never trusted. The dull must be kept in the dark and in check, lest their ignorance turn to belligerence. Sort them properly and you can beat the clever and the dull with equal ease.

That self-awareness was Digby's gift. *Know how you stand in comparison to others. Don't think you are the smartest, even if you are. Control the situation.*

Never be the trained bear in the circus. Neither should you be the bear trainer. They are both in a cage, performing for pennies and scraps of food.

Be the circus owner, earning money from those in the cage.

Digby was summoned to Rutherford's office where McLachlan sat in the leather chair against the wall and Snell, a grim and angry snarl on his lips, stood before the desk beside the little peasant.

"Ah, Lennox." Rutherford poured tea for McLachlan. "There's a good lad." The old man motioned with his hand and Digby understood. He handed the tea cup to McLachlan and took a position before the desk.

"May I inquire what this is about?" Digby asked.

Rutherford slurped his tea. "Snell, here, tossed Archie's work of art out the window—"

"It was a stupid fat cow," Snell said. "I put it out of its misery."

"You're no expert in art," McLachlan said. "I saw you throw it out the window."

"There's no place for such behavior in Cransley," Rutherford said. "Would you agree, Lennox?"

Digby cast a glance at Snell. There was no use if the faculty caught the stupid sod in the act. "I agree, sir."

Digby sat on the sofa outside his room longing for a smoke. Down the corridor, Snell packed his meager belongings, forced to vacate so the little peasant, as recompense for Snell's bullying, would be given the room.

Dune and Birley stood outside the door, taking turns carrying each box or satchel to the cart. Dune brought a garbage bag out and tried to place it on the cart, but it brought half the cart's contents to the floor where they spilled open.

"You stupid idgits," Snell growled. "Pick it up."

"It's not my fault," Dune snapped back. "You pack like you live, slob."

"Piss off."

While Snell gathered his things, cursing under his breath, Dune and Birley approached Digby.

"Isn't there something we can do?" Dune asked. "This little peasant is going to be a problem."

"Yah," Birley said. "He's a problem."

"There is a thing," Digby said.

"Should I get Snell?" Dune asked.

Digby shook his head. "He's too angry. Besides, I can't get him out of his punishment."

"I'd sure hate pulling weeds," Birley said. "That's like actual work."

"But we can get Archie out of here," Digby said.

Birley nudged Dune. "That sounds good, eh?"

Digby stared at Birley until he had the idgit's attention. "If you'll shut your mouth a second, I'll explain what we need to do."

Digby would employ his first and most successful trick, which he'd only used once so as not to arouse suspicion. But this was an emergency.

The first step was to pick the lock to Woodcock's office, a skill Digby learned from the Prefect in charge of the boys when Digby first arrived at Cransley. That Prefect—was his name Smyth?—took a liking to Digby, how he seemed a natural at getting what he wanted. Smyth taught Digby to pick locks to send him round to various offices to steal exams, cigarettes, and the occasional flask of whiskey.

Of course, it took Smyth unawares when he was caught with copies of the final exams. He

225

blamed Digby for the transgression but, by that time, the faculty were all enamored with Digby.

Once Smyth and his crew—all caught with exam papers—were expelled, Digby was the natural choice to take his place as prefect.

Now he'd do the same to the little peasant and be rid of the problem.

Digby found the exams in the same place he'd found them four years prior, and looked around a bit, overcome for the moment by nostalgia. He'd always enjoyed these excursions and felt like a celebratory smoke and sip of whisky was in order.

For this, however, Woodcock had changed things around, and he checked all the drawers, the credenza and the file cabinet before finding the contraband in the cupboard.

His pockets full and the exams in hand, Digby headed for the office door.

He stopped cold when he heard Woodcock's voice. "I hear you wanted to speak to me, young man?" he said.

Digby didn't wait for the answer. He climbed in the cupboard—the only thing large enough—and settled himself.

A moment later, the office door opened, and he heard Woodcock and that little shit peasant Archie chatting about things. Digby calmed himself as best he could, focusing on staying quiet so that he could soon straighten his legs and get on with the plan.

"Is that a Magic 8-Ball?" Woodcock asked.

"Oh this?" Archie said.

Digby peeked out the cupboard door and Archie was, indeed, showing off a Magic 8-Ball.

"An icosahedron suspended in blue liquid," Woodcock said. "Just a fun toy."

"This one is not just a toy," said Archie. "My dad told me that it was special. You ask it two questions a day and it reveals the truth. Give it a third shake and it reveals a secret.

Rubbish, Digby thought.

"What do I have in my top drawer?" Woodcock asked.

Archie shook the ball.

"Jelly babies."

"How did you know that?" Woodcock said, laughing.

Yes, Digby thought. How did that little peasant know—

"What's my birthday?" Woodcock asked.

"July 24th."

"Astonishing." Woodcock said. "And the secret?"

Archie glanced at the cupboard as he shook the 8-Ball, and Digby's throat tightened. That little shit wouldn't—

"There's someone hiding in your cupboard."

Digby kicked open the cupboard and ran from the room, his only hope that Woodcock would somehow not see his face.

But as Digby ran down the hall, he heard Woodcock's voice calling, "Master Lennox! Master Lennox, return this second!"

Digby sat on his bed, considering his options. He hadn't been caught, but Woodcock was unimpressed with the explanation that it must have been someone else who looked like him crawling out of the cupboard and running from the office.

Called before Rutherford that same night, Digby presented himself with nothing about his person out of place, the papers, smokes and flask were safely hidden.

"I don't understand," Digby said. He repeated what he told Woodcock during the walk to the office: "It just couldn't have been me."

Archie arrived and confirmed Woodcock's version without a moment of hesitation.

That was enough for Rutherford to strip Digby of his Prefecture until they held a formal hearing.

"You may stay in your room for now," Rutherford said. "Your father pays for it, but I know he'll agree with whatever decision I make once the evidence is presented."

Things would not go well with his father if he was expelled. Even the loss of the Prefecture might doom him.

The smokes and whisky were forbidden even among the teachers. He could use that to work out a deal with Woodcock.

If this little peasant insisted on playing out his hand, he left Digby no choice.

Digby visited the old cooperage to get what he needed for this next, and final, move.

He found a barrel of the right size, drilled several holes around it, and rolled it to the old well. As he waited for Archie to arrive, he hammered the pry bar to loosen the rings.

Digby considered it a good sign that a moment after the barrel was ready, Dune, Birley, Lucas and Toby trudged up the path with the little peasant, his mouth gagged and stuffed with a sock.

"Well, well, well," he said. "Look who's going to fall into the well."

Archie squirmed and shook, but they lifted him up and dropped him in the barrel head first.

"Oh that must have hurt," Digby said as he nailed the lid shut.

By then, Archie had righted himself in the barrel and removed the sock. "Let me out," he said. "I promise I won't say anything."

"Say what you want," Digby said. "No one can hear you."

"We dropping him in the well now?" Lucas asked.

"Later," Digby said. "Not us, either. Snell would enjoy this, don't you think?""

229

"Won't it float?" Birley asked. "It's made of wood."

"There're holes in it," Dune said. "It'll sink enough to drown him."

"He'll have time to think about what he did," Digby said. "And wonder what he should have done instead."

"I've learned my lesson," Archie said, his voice shaking.

"Cry all you want," Digby said. "We're going to supper."

Digby moved his food around the plate, too nervous to eat. Snell should have finished the job by now. Why wasn't the stupid fat cow back yet?

At the inferior's table sat two empty seats. Archie's, of course, but one other. Digby racked his brain. Zachary was there, but who else sat with Archie?

Hew. The littlest of them all. That little creep was like a hungry mouse, showing up in every nook and cranny, his spectacles slipping down his nose. It's not like he'd be welcome at any other table.

"I don't like this," Digby said.

"What?" Birley asked. "The kidney pie?"

"No, you damn fool. Snell's not back. Hew is missing. Something's not right."

Birley waved his fork to get Digby's attention. "Are you going to eat your kidney pie or not?"

Birley's stupidity helped Digby understand the mistake. He shouldn't have relied on Snell, the dumbest of them all. Having made that mistake, he couldn't let it get out of hand.

"You told Snell to toss the barrel in the well?" Digby asked.

Birley shook his head, then nodded.

Digby took a breath. "What did you say to Snell?"

"I told him to go by the well."

Birley shrugged.

Digby closed his eyes. Snell had probably stolen some chocolate from the commissary and was shame eating in the basement. "Let's go lads."

"Where to?" Birley asked.

"To dump a barrel down a well."

Digby thought he'd feel triumphant with the little peasant drowned, but he only felt tired. As they returned to their quarters, they came upon Archie seated on the sofa outside Digby's room, quite content, flipping through a stack of papers.

"What the...How did you...but we drowned you!" Digby said.

"The well you mean? No, there's no water in the well. It's a big room where the

231

teachers keep confiscated items and the new exam papers." He held up the paper for emphasis.

Birley snatched at the papers but Archie was too quick. "Are those really exam papers?"

"Go get your own," Archie said. "There's plenty more down the well. Go ask Nathan Snell."

Digby chuckled. "Don't be a sap—"

But they didn't hear him. The four boys took off, running full speed out the door.

Digby, his arms shaking with fury, stood before Archie. "You talked Snell into taking your place?"

Archie nodded.

"How'd you find the exams?"

Archie shrugged. "I have friends here too. They're small, so you don't notice them watching."

As Digby ran up to them, the idiots leaned over the edge, arguing about who should go first.

"Stop it," Digby said. "He's fooling you."

He pulled at their trousers but he couldn't get a foothold in the soft ground. Instead, he was pulled toward the well. He let go, but one of them reached out to Digby and pulled him into the darkness.

It was chaos in the water. Birley screamed for his mother. The boys fought to find perch on the submerged barrel, but only pushed each other down into the water.

As his last breath ran out, Digby consoled himself that at least he wouldn't have to face his father again.

based on

The Most Dangerous Game

Richard Connell

Footprints

Rudy Alleyne & Pan D. MacCauley

Footprints
Rudy Alleyne & Pan D. MacCauley

Turnabout

Rudy Alleyne

The humans were out in mass today as I watched them scurry about like little rabbits around my domain. They amused me in their clumsy efforts of a hunt. Small, slow, and nearly powerless; their source of strength mostly in the sticks they carried around with them, which roared and expelled death at whatever prey was unfortunate enough to find its way in its path. A few of them laid traps all around the place – laughable in their assurance of its efficacy while I studied the circle of teeth protruding from the layer of dirt over some of them. *Pathetic*, I thought, when I would intentionally set them off to draw their attention, leading to a few of the human hunters astray, only to fall into the bone pit I had dug so long ago. It got to a point I did not even need to hide my trap with branches and leaves any longer. A couple of rocks thrown in their direction, a broken branch or two, and they would go running without looking where they were going. The sweet scent of terror and death filled the air throughout the day, when some of them would tumble into my trap: the sound of their flesh being pierced by the sharpened extremities of their own kind. One even pleaded for what they called "mercy," a gesture seemingly common to them, whenever they found no means of escape. It was something they cared not to offer for the various creatures they hunted but expected to be granted upon them when all was lost. So why should I grant them something they continuously deny from many of the creatures within my realm?

Normally they would be here to hunt the other animals foraging about the woods, but today was different, most of the hunters seemed determined on finding something bigger. Me, I assumed, when I checked the little light filled box one of the hunters had with him while he slept beneath a tree. It was filled with images of what looked like me, or at least what I would see looking back at me every time I drank water from the stream flowing in the middle of the forest. I studied the human for a bit as he laid propped up against the tree trunk, fast asleep. Many men have trespassed within my woods and most of them looked the same to me: puny and weak. This one, however, looked familiar. Was this the one who stumbled upon me when I was scrounging for food that one night? Yes, it was! Before him, the woods were calm and quiet; now it was filled with bloodthirsty humans disturbing my peace. I glared at him, thinking about how easy his neck would fit in my enormous hands, if I were to clasp them around it and gave it a good squeeze or a quick twist. But a better idea came to mind and I returned his picture box on the ground next to him. Unknown to him I had been stalking his movements as he laid his set of traps about the forest, now it was my turn to lay some out, specially made for him. The bone pit was already set but I decided that may not be enough, so I spent a few moments in the sunlit hours under the light rain preparing a few more ruses, as the human slept and the last of the foul hunters fell into my spiked colliery. When darkness fell, I was ready, and set my plan into motion.

I triggered one of his alert traps which filled the night air with the sound of chimes, signaling the hunter awake. It did not take him long before he came running to the spot. He looked confused as he searched the ground with that little box of his and I watched from the heavy thicket of brush that surrounded him: a light shone from it while he pointed what he called a "phone" around him. The hunter kept searching until he came across the tracks I had left on the ground, seemingly pleased with himself, even though I had intentionally left them there for him to find. I allowed him to follow the trail for a moment before I silently made my way ahead of him. I began to wail into the still night air and threw a hand into the toothy maw of the vice trap he had shrouded beneath a heap of decaying vegetation. It clamped violently around the limb I had chewed

238

away from one of the many hunters that fell prey to my pit earlier; a foul-tasting mound of flesh but it made for good bait, though. I could smell the fear emanating from the pores of my quarry as the hunter jumped and fell to the ground - shocked to find the dismembered appendage of his kind lying in wait for him. He jumped once more, when I let loose another blood curdling howl into the darkness and while the light disappeared from his phone-thing, visibly shaken by the experience. I had to give the human some respect, though, after he took a moment to gather his nerves and held the other box he had strapped around his next out in his hand, producing more light from it as he forged his way forward, right into the trap line I had waiting on the ground along his path.

He leaped out of the way moments before the sharpened log could separate his head from his body - *light on our feet are we now? Lucky little smallfoot!* I thought to myself with a growl. But that was alright, however, I had planned for this outcome. As weak as they may be some of them were agile enough to avoid something as easy as a log swing, and this one grew a little smarter, as he carefully avoided a few more of the trip wires I had set on the trail of my prints to follow. I knew what would get him, though, and I quickly climbed a tree and raced through the dense canopy above him to the spot where I had moved one of his signal traps. I triggered it and he came running like a madman towards the jangling sound of bells, and straight into my trophy pit. Covered with thickets of brush and branches this time around: a proud beast as I was not about to let a human get the best of me! He fell inside, or so I thought. Because just as I was sure he had been impaled on one of the many sharpened bones at the bottom, the hunter began to scramble his way out after being able to catch hold of the earth as he fell. *Oh, for fu-* I swore a bit; something of a habit I picked up from these humans, after years on the hunt. I could feel the rage build inside of me as I watched him survey the inside of the pit with the light box. *Why? Why won't you just die already?*

The anger bubbled within me until I could stand it no longer and I stepped from behind my hiding place. The hunter refused to turn around to see me coming after him, but simply took off running as fast as his puny little legs could carry him. But be it by my stride, or the snag he was about to run into ahead of him, he was not going to be fast enough to escape! It was the razor wire that won out in the end, as it wrapped itself around the hunter's ankle and sent him flying to the ground. Like a trembling bunny caught in one of the many traps I have seen his kind set up in my domain, I watched him try and free himself, frantically scratching at the wire around his leg. I approached, slowly, relishing the fear emanating my way from this arrogant human who dared to trespass into my world without the respect it deserved. The terror in his eyes felt satisfying as his light box flashed in my face; my teeth being the last thing he saw, before I sunk them deep into his clammy, warm flesh.

The Photo

Pan D. MacCauley

It wasn't that long ago that I saw him. Was the middle of the night and I got up to take a leak. Sure, it was dark, but who coulda mistaken that figure? I went home and started doin' research. Most of the sightin's seemed to be by crackheads and stupid kids playin' around, but then I found that website and I knew. I knew I really saw it. And if I done saw it once, I was gonna see it again. So, I grabbed my camera and loaded up my truck with my best huntin' stuff. If I may be so bold, I've taken to thinkin' of myself as somethin' of a trappin' expert. So, here I am again. I got my camera. I got my gun. My traps are set. Now it's just a waitin' thing. Folks pay big money for proof of the poor S.O.B., but too many pictures are way too fuzzy and easy to dismiss as a hoax, so I'm gonna make sure I don' make that mistake.

I've been waitin' most of the day. I hope the gunshots of the other hunters didn't scare him away. It's dark now and pretty quiet. Maybe he's... oh what's that word? Nocturnal or somethin' like that? Maybe he only comes out at night is what I'm tryin' say. Now, I'll admit, I did fall asleep, but then my bells started ringin' and woke me up. Grabbed my gun. Grabbed my camera. Found my trap.

Forgot my flashlight. That's alright. Got my phone. I pull my phone out, and turn on the little flashlight, and start lookin' 'round. It was kinda drizzly that day. Not a full on rain but just light enough that the ground was soft, but not so soft it swallows your boots. Forecast said it was s'posed to rain and I needed it to. Wet ground gives good tracks and I knew what I was lookin' for. Wasn't long 'fore I found it. The footprint. Now, my mama always said I had big feet, but my boots looked like kids' shoes next to this footprint. It was him. I was sure of it. Big dumb beast fell right into my trap! So, I start followin' the footprints.

I got my gun. I got my camera. I got my phone.

Another alarm goes off. Poor dumb thing set off another of my traps. This was goin' be like shooting fish in a barrel. I sprint off in the direction of that trap and as I get closer I can hear some sorta hollerin'. Sounds kinda like a bear. Better be careful, then. Bigfoot tends to be more gentle accordin' to the stories, but a bear'll take your ears off. I put my phone in my pocket. I grab my gun. I'm not lettin' no bear get between me and the prize of the century. Shoot. If I can capture Bigfoot, I'd be the hero of the century. If that Cash Me Outside little lady can get rich for bein' on a talk show, just imagine what I'd get for capturing THE Bigfoot.

As I walk up near the trap, there's nothin' there. Again. Just like the last one. I pull my phone back out. Look for tracks. Was it a bear or was it Bigfoot? SNAP! My bones near jump outta my body. One of my bear traps went off not that far from here! I hurry to the scene. Somethin's caught in its teeth. My phone's battery is startin' to get low. That's what I get for playin' on it earlier. I get closer to the trap. What is that? It's fleshy and looks chewed up, and there's something shin—

I jolt back and fall on my behind. It's a hand! A human hand wearin' a weddin' ring! Somethin' rustles nearby and I grab my phone. I grab my gun. I wanna puke but pukin'll do no good right now. I need to be alert. It's prolly just some wild animal dropped scraps off the… human… they were just eatin'.

I get up. Brush the leaves and the mud off my pants. I grab my gun. I look for my phone. There it is.

A bellow nearby. I jump again! Why are my nerves so bad? Get it together, John. You're a hunter and a trappin' expert. I take a deep breath. My phone dies. Damn that app. I put my phone away and pull out my camera. Won't need a picture if I just kill it and take the whole thing, right? I turn the light on on the camera.

244

Leaves and twigs are crunchin' as I make my way towards the creature. I got my gun ready, usin' the light to guide me through these here woods. I trip over somethin' and as I look down, there's some sorta string. Strange. I didn't set up any traps over here.

Somethin's clickin' away as I get up an— WHOA! I leap back as a log comes flyin' at my head! What in Sweet Jesus's name was that?!

I check around. There's gotta be some other hunter out here messin' with me or tryin' to capture my target. I shake myself off. Well he's gonna hafta do better than that. I'll have to be more careful from now on. The log settles down. I look closer. The end has been carefully carved. Someone took the time to whittle this thing down to multiple spikes. They were playin' to kill. I look up at the night sky and thank my lucky stars 'n' stripes that I managed to dodge in time. John, be happy God's on your side tonight.

Now where's them tracks? There they are. I carefully begin followin' the tracks again, this time keepin' my eyes locked on the ground. I don' need to be settin' off no more of them trip wires. That other fella thinks he's some kinda expert too? Hah! Trip wires is so amateur! When you have experience, like me, you learn what's effective and what is only used in kids' tales. Trip wires. Man's a hoot! He'll sure be jealous when he sees me on the cover of some paper with the body of Bigfoot.

Bells again! My own trap! I rush to where the sound is coming from and something gives out under me. My camera and my gun go flyin' as my hands barely manage to grab hold of the ground. I look down into the pitch blackness and scramble to pull myself outta this hole. What in the world? Some sorta pit? I follow the light and find my camera, goin' back to look at what fresh hell I just crawled outta. It was clearly a man-dug pit and the ground was lined with rows of... sharpened bones juttin' out of bodies in various stages of decomposition. It was a body pit. There was no denyin' it this time. I hurled into the pit, havin' to cover my eyes so that image doesn't get seared in. What in fresh blazes have I stumbled into?

A twig snaps nearby. Without thinkin', I just start runnin'. I don't have my gun. I don't have my phone. It's just me and my camera now. Twigs crunchin' under my feet and I swear it sounds like the trees are chasin' after me. Something slices through my ankle. I fall again. When I look back, a razor wire is halfway through my leg. I cry out and try to get free. I need to get back to my truck! I need to get outta here! Screw catchin' Bigfoot! It isn't worth gettin' killed by some rando serial killer!

Twigs crunchin'. I bite my hand to keep quiet. Crunch. Crunch. Crunch. And then a sinister laugh. I pant and reach for my camera. I turn it in the direction of the laugh. There he is. Standin' nine feet tall. He clasps his hands in front of him and if I didn't know better, I'd swear he was smarter than any man I'd ever seen. There's a hunger and a malice in his eyes and it was then I realize: these are his traps. He chuckles again and as he draws closer, the last thing I hear is the shutter on my camera.

At least I got my picture after all. Too bad no one'll ever see it.

based on

Hänsel und Grethel

collected by

Jacob & Wilhelm Grimm

Hansel & Gretel

C. Rathbone & A.R.K. Horton

Hansel & Gretel
C. Rathbone & A.R.K. Horton

The Kids

C. Rathbone

The forest was deep, dark, damp, and entirely uninviting.

Gretel shivered, looking over to her brother, Hans, who glanced back, his eyes filled with fear. It had often been remarked by the people at the home how alike the two looked. Then again, they were twins. Skinny, unlovable twins.

But this woman, Raven Baudelaire, had actually taken them away from the safety, the familiarity, of the home.

And now, here they were, making their way up the winding path from the little parking spot where she had left the car to find their new home. Raven, a few steps ahead of her reluctant charges, turned to face them. "You'll love it, children. It really is a lovely home. Some would say it's as *sweet as candy*!" she chirped, positively vibrating on the spot with excitement.

Gretel and Hans exchanged a look, barely noticeable by anyone else, rife with suspicion and fear. *Who was this Ms. Baudelaire? What did she want with them?*

She certainly hadn't been lying about her home. In a large clearing, at the center of the forest, was a sprawling house, built entirely from confectionery! Gretel and Hans stood in disbelief; they had never seen such a thing. The walls looked to be made from gingerbread, the roof resembled icing, window frames seemed to be moulded from candy cane, and the door handle... was that a cupcake!?

Ms. Baudelaire stood on the doorstep, arms outstretched dramatically. "Well, what do you think? Isn't it delightful? My family has lived here for generations. It's out of the way, peaceful, and lets me focus on my work without all of the interruptions of the outside world," she paused momentarily, brushing windswept hair from her face, "but do be careful! I admit to not being the most handy. Some parts of the house are a bit dangerous. Luckily, your bedrooms are in the safer part of the house, so you won't need to go wandering too far!"

The twins heard her all too clearly: *go poking around and you'll suffer.* Gretel shuddered just thinking of what that could mean.

Hallways of gingerbread and icing greeted them. Pictures of darkly dressed women posing with books, candles, and skulls adorned every room, as did fanciful ornaments, lamps and stacks of yellowing tomes. Ms. Baudelaire showed them to their rooms, small and spartan,

251

containing a single cot bed and nightstand in each. The woman allowed them to check these cells out before ushering them back to the main hall.

"Feel free to explore your new home, my dears. But don't stray into the woods. It's very easy to get lost out there, and there are all kinds of dangers after dark. I'll get some food cooked up for you. You look like you're half-starved!" their new captor smiled, before disappearing into a corridor and out of sight. They exchanged a look once again, they rarely spoke to each other, the staff at the home had always marveled, calling it a *telepathic connection*.

The haunted, skinny children set to work, pacing up and down the candy house's sprawling rooms and halls. What sinister things they found too! Bookshelves brimming with leatherbound volumes, pentagrams and other dark-looking symbology, skulls of various creatures. It all pointed to some very odd activity within the equally odd walls.

Then there was the cat. The little beast, black as the void and with twinkling, yellow eyes, followed them everywhere. It seemed to be keeping tabs on them, making sure they didn't pocket any trinkets perhaps, or try to escape. They were trying to coax the cat toward them, to get a closer look, when their strange benefactor reappeared, an eager smile on her otherwise unreadable face.

"Ah, there you are! I see you found my housemate. Don't worry, he's very friendly, maybe just a little shy. We don't often have other people in the house," she explained, crouching down and holding out a hand. The cat slinked over for a friendly nuzzle, casting a smug glance back at them as it went. "Well, dinner is ready at last. Shall we?"

The kitchen was large, stuffed with counters and shelving set up in a haphazard way. The shelves bowed with jars of herbs, strange ornaments and yet more old books. A huge cast iron range covered pretty much all of one wall. Pots and pans hung across the wall around it. The three human inhabitants sat around an old dinner table, the kind that had that experienced many life stories, in the middle of the room. The cat joined them, on an old cushion on the remaining chair, its pointy ears just visible above the lip of the table.

Despite their fear, Gretel and Hans were famished and powered through their meal of soup and rye bread like they hadn't eaten in months. They had no idea what was *in* the soup, but it tasted good enough that they just didn't care; it certainly beat the thin gruel from the home if nothing else.

Presently, it dawned on them that Ms. Baudelaire was watching them hawkishly, clearly satisfied. When they slowly looked up, she fixed them with a sinister smile. "I bet you have a few questions about my home, don't you? No doubt you've seen all of the... *interesting* gewgaws around the place?" she asked eagerly. Feeling that some response was needed, two heads nodded. A few seconds passed awkwardly, the woman's smile never leaving her face despite the silence of the children. Eventually, she pushed her chair back and stood, wandering over to the counter.

"Well, I shall tell you all about it, just as soon as you've taken your medication. Whilst I don't usually *believe* in that kind of thing, the administrator at the home was very forceful on the issue. Besides, I wouldn't like you two mites getting overly stressed on your first day, would I?"

Needless to say, the twins were very grateful for their medication. The grey, nondescript pills had been a mainstay in their lives at the home for a long time. How long, they couldn't remember; anything beyond a few weeks ago tended to be a haze to them. If the medication was missed then things became… *hazy*. As such, Gretel and Hans eagerly swallowed them down.

The strange candy house came back into sharp focus as Ms. Baudelaire led them away from the kitchen and into another room, asking them to sit down as she poured out some chamomile tea at a nearby cabinet. They had never experienced tea before. It tasted nice, in a subtle kind of way. As they sipped, Ms Baudelaire sat opposite them in an old armchair.

"I know that my home can seem rather unusual to newcomers," Raven explained. "Like I said before, I'm an author. I write about my journey as a witch," she said after a short silence, fixing them with a grin.

The writing had been on the candy wall the moment the twins had met her: Ms. Baudelaire was a witch. But to hear her actually say it so *openly* and as if it were no more unusual than playing golf, seemed to bring the whole thing into perfect clarity. The sense of dread made Gretel drop her cup, breaking it on the toffee-tiled floor.

They had been warned about witches many years ago by their old grandmother. Witches lured children into their homes with treats and promises, fattened them up, and, when they got hungry enough, threw them into the oven, cooking them for a special, sordid meal! Gretel caught Hans' eye, he was thinking the same thing as his sister. He always did.

Panicked by this horrible realisation, and knowing if they showed their fear, the witch might attack, Gretel hurriedly reached for the broken teacup, hoping to get it scooped up and thus not engage the evil witch's ire. Ms Baudelaire was faster though, already moving to cover the broken crockery herself, forcing both twins to shy back from her terrible aura.

"Please, let me clean it up," the witch said. "You've had an exhausting day and I don't want you to cut yourself."

Probably doesn't want us to lose a drop of tasty blood before she roasts us, they thought to themselves, exchanging a knowing look as she placed the broken cup upon a battered coffee table.

"I am what they call a kitchen witch," she explained, placing the broken china on her coffee table. "I grow herbs. I make healing recipes. I use my skills to help others. Witches aren't like what you see in movies. Not all of us."

But Hans and Gretel knew better. They knew this was *exactly* what a witch would say to her captors before throwing them into that big, blackened oven.

They spent the night locked away in their rooms. Great stout doors of dense shortbread barred their access to the rest of the world. The witch had said something about it being "for their own good", but they knew the truth. Separated every night since as far back as they could remember, they lay awake for most of the night, listening to wolves howl in the forest, unable to feel each others' presence.

When the witch Baudelaire released them from captivity the next day, she did so with a twinkle in her eye. "Rise and shine, wee ones!" she said in a strange voice, "Breakfast waits for you in the dining room. Try to eat as much as you can. You really need to fatten up."

And so it begins, Gretel thought. The fattening up. The beginning of the end.

Thankfully, the food intended to make the twins more appetising to the witch was really nice, and plentiful. It certainly beat the grey gruel the home served. Should this be the end, they may as well appease the woman and enjoy their food. They soon filled up on pancakes, bacon and eggs, but the witch lurked nearby, watching them. Despite their fullness, they felt they had to keep going, unless punishment fell upon them in the form of an evil curse, looking up constantly to see the dark figure standing over them.

When the amount of food had become too much, and they could hide their discomfort no more, Ms. Baudelaire relented.

"You can stop," she said. "You don't need to keep going just for me. I—I just didn't want you to be hungry."

Her eyes looked sad, something the twins weren't used to seeing from adults. *But they knew the truth, they knew why this woman was feeding them so much. They had to play along for now, as best they could; wait for their moment to escape from Baudelaire's clutches.* As Hans and Gretel shared this thought with nothing more than a glance, the witch's face split into a menacingly cheerful grin.

"You didn't see it because it's on the back patio outside, but I have a hot tub!" she cackled, clapping her hands together in excitement, "I even bought you bathing suits when I got your sizes from the orphanage. Go slip those on and I'll show you to the tub."

The patio was sprawling, but the hot tub dominated it, great gouts of steam belching from its innards. The witch swept past the children, showing them the steps that led up to the water. Hans hung back, too afraid, whilst Gretel took the reins, dipping a foot into what looked like, and probably was, a giant saucepan.

In her shock at just how hot the water was, Gretel broke her silence at last, her voice sounding frail and scratchy, "it's too hot, Ms. Baudelaire". The sound of her own voice surprised her, for each time the home tried to make them live with a new family, they stopped talking. It had resulted in them returning to the Home's safety more than once.

"Don't be silly," snapped the witch, clearly impatient to get them cooking. "You'll get used to it. I sit in this water all the time. I've not boiled away yet."

With no other choice, the twins lowered themselves into the water, convinced their skin was searing from their bones. Barely able to breathe, they sat and stared at Ms. Baudelaire, knowing the end was imminent. Finally, unable to take any more, Gretel leaned over the side of the tub, losing her breakfast all over the weed-strewn patio.

Hans watched in horror. His sister mumbled something before almost passing out and falling further into the water. The woman, plucking Gretel out of the tub with astonishing strength, no doubt afforded to her by her evil magics, quickly moved back toward the house.

Suspecting Gretel was about to be thrown into the oven, Hans hurried to follow, barely able to breath, such was his terror. His sister had always been the braver sibling.

Ms. Baudelaire took Gretel to her room, laying her out on a towel. "I don't want to eat your candy house, I promise I'll be good. Clean your house. Don't cook me for dinner." Gretel muttered as she came back around.

Hans was still panicking, thinking they were about to be killed. "We'll do anything you want," he squeaked. "Your cat will tell you we didn't touch any of your candy walls."

Ms. Baudelaire gave him a strange, unreadable expression. "I think the last two days may have been too much for you. Have a lie down. You don't need to clean my house. You can touch whatever you want. Just, please, be careful. You're awful weak."

Gretel, feeling better by the morning, regained her position as leader as they both walked into the kitchen, noting the witch pushing a tome away from view. *Probably a spellbook*, they thought, exchanging a knowing glance.

"I'm so sorry about the deck, Ms. Baudelaire, I'll clean it up," said Gretel, hoping to appease their captor.

Ms. Baudelaire gave a sinister smile. "No need, I'm just glad to see you both looking better. Would you like to go on a walk or read some books or—" she paused, eyeing them up hungrily. "Actually, you do whatever you want to. You don't need to run anything past me. Just let me know if you need my help."

The twins knew what was happening here. There were more pots of herbs next to the oven, and that spellbook was bound to be related to the fact they would be eaten soon. They could *feel* the end approaching.

"I think we would just like to spend some time alone," Gretel said. "Hansel and I together. If that's alright with you." She was hoping to buy them some time, hoping to nail down some kind of plan, to be free from this evil woman.

Ms. Baudelaire had some "writing" to do, and was happy to let them roam free. To keep the crone off their scent, they even engaged her in conversation from time to time, using their vocal cords for the first time in a long time. Despite their caution, they got quite into it: Gretel revealing a lifelong love of growing plants. Even Hans opened up about his joy of reading. Though Gretel suspected he may have overshared in telling the witch about the time he had blacked out and, in his fugue state, hit an adult who was looking after them. Neither twin remembered this, though the medicine could help them forget scary things that happened.

That night, when she ushered them to their rooms, the witch made a critical error: she forgot to lock the doors. Sensing their chance, the twins quickly dressed and crept out onto the landing. Using the moonlight as a guide, they made their way downstairs, where they saw a terrifying sight.

The oven door hung open. The spellbook was on the table, along with all manner of herbs and spices. Bending over the huge oven was the witch. The time was upon them. They were about to be cooked!

Wasting no time, Gretel dived forward, and, with all her might, shoved Ms. Baudelaire into the oven, trying to push her all the way inside in order to lock the door. But the witch, her strength superhuman, managed to regain her balance, and pinned Gretel to the kitchen floor. Hans moved to help, but was frozen in place by their enemy, with a cry of "don't you dare!" as she closed a cold claw around his wrist.

"You can't eat us!" cried Gretel hysterically.

"Why would I want to eat you?" the witch replied, her voice confused, "you're my children. You're all I ever wanted. I just want a family." The witch lied, her diatribe interrupted by the tinny ringing of her phone. Turning her back on the twins, she answered it.

This was it. Their chance to escape lay before them. The crone would be undone by her own lies and hubris. They would finally be free.

Gretel flashed Hans a meaningful expression. She moved to the counter. Picking up the meanest knife she could find, she hesitated. Only a second, overcoming her fear, she closed the gap and sank the blade into the witch.

Gretel struggled, pulling the weapon free. Baudelaire gasped. The waif plunged the sharp edge into the witch's ribs for the killing blow. Gretel yanked free the blade. The witch collapsed Blood pooled around her.

It wasn't enough. Hans scurried to deliver the ultimate coup de gras, stuffing the huge oven with oily rags from the storage cupboard, trembling with desperation and adrenaline. With a nod from his sister, he threw in a lit match. W*hoosh*. The kitchen burst into flames. Unable to contain their joy that the demon woman's days of cooking children were over, Hans and Gretel cavorted before the flames, before sweetly sharing a kiss.

"Free at last!" grinned Hans.

"At last," Gretel agreed, took her brother's hand, and lead him into the fresh air of the forest, toward their new lives, free from controlling adults and terrifying witches.

From the undergrowth, the black cat watched them walk away.

The Witch

A.R.K. Horton

Raven tried not to look at the social worker's embarrassing comb-over as he explained that her biggest dream was about to come true. She was going to be a mother. Sure, these were teenagers and they had a rocky past, but a single woman in her fifties wasn't exactly a prime candidate as an adoptive parent.

"Ms. Baudelaire, make sure they take this every night," the social worker said, placing a bottle of unlabeled pills into her hands. "They have rage issues. It's imperative they don't fall behind on their doses. If they do, they come back here. Got it?"

Raven nodded. Rage issues? That was scary. She would make sure they took the medicine and she'd keep everything really chipper, even if that wasn't her nature. Raven was a mother now— a mom—she needed to be whatever they needed.

On the drive back to her home, they stayed so quiet. It seemed as if they spoke to each other with only their eyes. They were thin, sallow, obviously malnourished. She would fix that. She would make them healthy. Obviously, life had been unkind to them. Even their names sounded like punishment. Twins named Hansel and Gretel. Was that supposed to be a joke?

Time in her family home in the mountain forest would be just what the doctor ordered. Their skinny legs shook walking up the path from the driveway to the house. Raven feared her old, creaky house might be dangerous. Based on their wide eyes and open mouths, she realized they must not have ever seen such a large, ornate residence. The Scandinavian branch of her family made sure to carve beautiful patterns into the rich wood of the house, which looked even more dramatic now with the dusting of snow glistening like sugar on every line.

"Well, what do you think? Ain't it delightful? My family has lived here for generations. It's out of the way, peaceful, and lets me focus on my work without all of the... interruptions of the outside world," Raven rambled. She caught how Hansel's twig frame trembled a bit and Gretel leaned into her brother for mutual support. "But do be careful. I admit to not being the most handy, some parts of the house are a bit dangerous. Luckily, your bedrooms are in the safer part of the house, so you won't need to go wandering too far!"

Raven turned to unlock the door and took a deep breath. Had she said too much and scared them? Was she going to screw this all up? *Not a motherly bone in your body.* That's what her husband said before he left with that blonde all those years ago. Just because she wanted to write her books on witchcraft. She always thought there would be time for children after she achieved her ambitions. Maybe he had been right. Maybe it was her.

She ushered them inside, watching them press into each other and gawk at her home's interior. She guided them down the hallway to their rooms, pointing out the photos of her fans posing with her books. Maybe they would feel proud to be adopted by such a famous author. She hated that their rooms were so stark compared to the rest of her home, but the social worker had been plain on the phone. They must be locked alone in their own rooms with no way to hurt themselves or others. Maybe, over time, that could change.

She let Hansel and Gretel know they could explore for a while. Then, she set about cooking a healthy dinner for them. She decided on making soup, with plenty of protein and nutrient-rich vegetables. Then, she sliced up the rye bread she had baked fresh that morning. She needed to put meat on those bones so they could spend some time outside and get some Vitamin D. She may not have the warmest personality, but she could at least make sure they spent the next few years healing from a life spent at an orphanage.

It took a moment to find the children—her children. This didn't surprise her. Raven knew her home was a labyrinth of books, witchcraft, herbs, and family history. When she did find the children, she saw Marlow watching them and her heart swelled. Marlow was a rescue, injured by a child with a pellet gun who had been scared of a black cat crossing his path. Since then, Marlow hid from everyone except Raven. He must be welcoming Hansel and Gretel to the family.

They all sat to dinner, Marlow included, and hope rose in Raven's chest. Hansel and Gretel tore through her bread and guzzled down her soup. Maybe she would be all right at this parenting thing. She couldn't help the wide smile stretching her cheeks to the limit.

"I bet you have a few questions about my home, don't you? No doubt you've seen all of the... *interesting* gewgaws around the place?" Raven said when they slowed down and finally looked up at their new mother with tired eyes. "Well, I shall tell you all about it, just as soon as you've taken your medication. Whilst I don't usually *believe* in that kind of thing, the man in charge was very forceful on the issue. Besides, I wouldn't like you two mites getting overly stressed on your first day, would I?"

Each took their pill with dinner, as they had done every night before. Raven supposed they had. It was familiar to them. They moved to the parlor and Raven poured them all some chamomile tea. She watched their bony wrists tremble as they lifted china cups to their lips.

"I know that my home can seem rather unusual to newcomers," Raven explained. "Like

267

I said before, I'm an author. I write about my journey as a witch."

Gretel's cup fell to the floor and splintered apart in shards. Raven sank to her knees before her new daughter could reach down.

"Please, let me clean it up," Raven said. "You've had an exhausting day and I don't want you to cut yourself."

In her mind, she swore at herself for not easing into that news. Most people thought witches worshipped Satan. She knew that better than anyone else.

"I am what they call a kitchen witch," Raven explained, placing the broken china on her coffee table. "I grow herbs. I make healing recipes. I use my skills to help others. Witches aren't like what you see in movies. Not all of us."

Raven sighed when she saw their frightened expressions. She could tell them she was harmless, but it would take a while before they believed it. It would take months of proving it over and over.

When they finished their tea, Raven ushered them back to their rooms and locked them in. This was another condition of adoption. She hated doing it, though, and spent the night dreaming of the children running away.

By the time morning came, Raven, brimming with determination, decided to make it a better day. She busied herself in the kitchen, creating a giant spread of food for the children to gorge on, and then unlocked their doors.

"Rise and shine, wee ones!" Raven exclaimed with her best interpretation of Mary

Poppins. "Breakfast waits for you in the dining room. Try to eat as much as you can. You really need to fatten up."

It became clear how seriously the twins took her instructions when they sat down at the table. They shoveled the food into their mouths like machines. At first, Raven assumed they were famished, but then she saw their wary glances in her direction and realized they continued to eat to please her.

"You can stop," she said. "You don't need to keep going just for me. I—I just didn't want you to be hungry."

Hansel and Gretel kept their cautious eyes on her and set their forks down on their plates. Raven could have cried right then. Did no one ever simply give these two anything just to be nice? They needed to relax, decompress, let off some of the stress bundling inside them from this transition. When the idea hit Raven, she couldn't believe she had forgotten to show them her big surprise.

"You didn't see it because it's on the back patio outside, but I have a hot tub!" Raven said and clapped her hands together to punctuate the end of her statement. "I even bought you bathing suits when I got your sizes from the orphanage. Go slip those on and I'll show you to the tub."

When the children came down from their rooms, Raven noticed the way the spandex of their swim clothes drooped instead of hugging their angular frames. Their malnourishment was worse than she thought. Bones shouldn't be this pronounced. She kept her chipper smile plastered to her face, hoping they couldn't see the worry in her eyes.

The water was bubbling and hot already, when she showed them how to get in. She couldn't wait to see how much they enjoyed it. Gretel poked her tiny toes in and winced. "It's too hot, Ms. Baudelaire."

"Don't be silly," Raven replied. "You'll get used to it. I sit in this water all the time. I've not boiled away yet."

The children kept their wide eyes and scrunched brows on her while they lowered into the water. Raven got the impression they felt like she had a shotgun drawn on them. Had she pushed too hard? She wondered if she should have let them choose their own activities in the house for the morning. Raven's wondering ended when Gretel leaned out of the hot tub and heaved her breakfast onto the patio.

"Ms. Baudelaire," Gretel croaked out. "I can't breathe…"

Raven rushed over and swooped the young girl out of the hot tub. Even though she was a teenager, she felt as light as a toddler. Raven had no difficulty carrying her inside to her room. Hansel trailed behind her, hyperventilating the whole way.

"I don't want to eat your candy house," Gretel muttered while Raven laid her onto a towel on her bed. "I promise I'll be good. Clean your house. Don't cook me for dinner."

"What is she talking about?" Raven asked Hansel.

"We'll do anything you want," Hansel said. "Your cat will tell you we didn't touch any of your candy walls."

Candy house; candy walls. Were these kids high? Raven thought of their nightly pill to keep their rage at bay. What exactly were they taking?

"I think the last two days may have been too much for you," Raven said. "Have a lie down. You don't need to clean my house. You can touch whatever you want. Just, please, be careful. You're awful weak."

Once Raven was sure the twins were resting and breathing normally, she headed downstairs and called her personal assistant. She asked that the prescription in her office from the orphanage be looked at by her personal doctor and pharmacist. Maybe there was a side effect causing this odd behavior. Raven mopped up the vomit on the patio. Then, she sat down to write, distracted by her feelings of inadequacy as a new mother.

A few hours later, Gretel came downstairs with Hansel trailing after her. Raven pushed away the little bit of writing she had managed to get done.

"I'm so sorry about the deck, Ms. Baudelaire," Gretel said. "I'll clean it up."

"No need," Raven said with a smile. "I'm just glad to see you both looking better. Would you like to go on a walk or read some books or—" Raven stopped. She was pushing too hard again. "Actually, you do whatever you want to. You don't need to run anything past me. Just let me know if you need my help."

"I think we would just like to spend some time alone," Gretel said. "Hansel and I together. If that's all right with you."

"Of course it is," Raven replied, sitting back down to write. "You two enjoy yourselves. I have writing to catch up on."

The rest of the day passed with such peace. At dinner, the twins even joined her in conversation. Hansel loved books and Gretel loved plants. She had even grown some from paper cups in her room before they were confiscated by the orphanage. Hansel could only read while visiting the library. They'd spent their nights locked alone in their rooms because of an incident where Hansel hit a foster parent years before. Something felt wrong about that story, though. Neither of them came out and said it, but Raven could see the signs of abuse there. Had Hansel simply defended himself?

The twins took their medicine and Raven ushered them to their rooms. Then, she stood in the hallway staring at their doors. She was supposed to lock them, but she couldn't make herself. These weren't prisoners; they were children. Why did the orphanage insist on treating them this way?

"No one needs to know," Raven whispered to herself.

She smiled and turned away from the unlocked doors. Tomorrow, for breakfast, there would be a feast of cookies. These children could use a little whimsy. She thought of all the books she would buy Hansel and how she could teach Gretel all about growing herbs, while she mixed the batter and spooned it onto the trays for baking. They had a rough start, but there was enough in common for them to become a family.

Raven's heart sang with hope as she bent over to slide the trays into her oven. She never saw Gretel coming around the corner. She only felt the frail child push her with all her might into the oven. The metal siding seared Raven's skin and she screamed both from fear and pain. Fortunately for her, all of Gretel's might equalled that of a new born kitten. Raven turned, pushing Gretel to the kitchen floor, and pinned her there. Hansel was nearby, of course. She saw him approach as if to pull her away from Gretel.

"Don't you dare!" Raven called out and grabbed him by the wrist.

"You can't eat us!" Gretel cried.

"Why would I want to eat you?" Raven asked. "You're my children!"

Gretel blinked. Hansel stopped struggling.

"You're all I've ever wanted," Raven continued. "I just want a family."

"But...you want to fatten us up…" Hansel said.

"You're starving and weak," Raven said, standing up and pulling Gretel up with her. "Can't you see that?"

The children stared at her with glassy, uncomprehending eyes. The oven light cast strange, terrifying shadows on their gaunt faces. As the silence spanned, Raven kept her gaze locked on the children, trying to understand them. The phone rang and her heart leapt out of her chest. Few people knew this number. One person would dare call it so late. And only in an emergency.

Raven held up a hand. Her husky whisper cracked. "Stay here."

She kept her eyes on the twins. Silent communication passed between Hansel and Gretel's eyes. Some peace had passed over them and Raven's heart settled as she lifted the phone to her ear.

"Ms. Baudelaire, I have news about that prescription," Raven's personal assistant said, skipping her usual greeting. "Flush them down the drain *now!* Those are hallucinogenic!"

"What?" Raven gasped and turned to the cabinet where she kept the pills. "Why would they give—"

A sharp poke. Enough to make Raven turn to Gretel pulling a carving knife out of her flesh. The girl's weak arms struggled and the knife twisted, causing Raven to writhe in agony. The knife released and the girl plunged it between Raven's ribs. Raven fought to catch her breath.

She fell onto her bleeding side, facing the oven where Hansel stood. He tossed handful after handful of oily rags into the oven before Gretel threw in a lit match. Flames consumed the makeshift kindling and licked up the expensive mahogany counters that Raven so adored growing up.

The twins giggled and clapped. Gretel bounced on the pads of her feet as the fire spread. Satisfied the flames wouldn't die out, the children shared a sweet kiss and took each other's hand.

"Free at last," Hansel said.

"At last," Gretel agreed with a nod.

Together, they walked out the door, leaving it open behind them. The remaining seconds of Raven's life stretched on for eternity. In the last of it her black cat ran into the woods while the home her ancestors built turned to ash.

based on

Rotkäppchen

collected by

Jacob & Wilhelm Grimm

Little Red Riding Hood

Craig Vachon & A. Poland

Little Red Riding Hood
Craig Vachon & A. Poland

"Principessa, you are killing me and the team with all of these Amazon deliveries. The fucking driver is demanding a new set of tires for all the deliveries here."

She smiled wearily, because otherwise she'd lose her cool. How do you explain to your father that her favorite boots needed to be ordered in lots of three, as every time she got blood on them, an almost daily occupational hazard, she needed to throw that pair in the furnace? His men who stood at attention in his mahogany and richly-carpeted office, mostly uneducated, probably didn't understand the risks of blood splatters on natural leather boots. The pores in natural leather captured blood and other liquids. Their sole job was to meet Dad's every whim. Which, at this exact moment, was politely smiling when he was teasing his grown daughter.

"How did the evening go with the Cubans?" he asked.

"We moved the merch. But the team seemed twitchy. I wonder if they're getting pressure from the Paddies?"

"Don't worry about our little green friends. They know their place."

"If you say so, mio Babbo. Hey, have you given any more thought to my proposal about buying and leasing delivery trucks? With this pandemic, we can earn 8% on our free cash and still have hard assets as collateral. Easy and clean money. Bankable money."

"Sweetheart, when you take over, you can invest our family's assets as you see fit. But, for now, we stay the course. The course of my father and his. We know nothing about financing trucks. We make loans without lawyers and paperwork. Our returns are better that way."

"They aren't Papa. Sure, we might charge 100% interest to some shop owner in the neighborhood, but we rarely collect that amount. People can't afford it. Half of the time people skip or die trying. If we account for the loan acquisition and maintenance costs, plus the amount we actually return, we only make about 10% per annum, and none of that is laundered."

Her father turned to his team. "My little girl has an MBA from Columbia Business School. Fucking degree cost me a fortune. She's brilliant. But she still doesn't understand our business." The men all smiled knowingly and nodded.

"Okay Dad, good talk. I am going to run an errand." She tried to not sound as annoyed as she was. She needed a respite and a mango Boba tea.

Red always had a unique relationship with her Grandmother.

If unique could be classified as baking cookies together on the weekends and teaching her granddaughter how to hold a rifle the moment Monday rolled around, that was.

But there were undeniable perks to her less-than-conventional bond with the matriarch of one of the city's most successful crime syndicates. Granted, to her Grandmother their notoriety could always be better. She always strived for greatness, Red's Gran. Expected it from others too.

And in the absence of any other parental figure (the loss of Red's parents felt far and wide within their organization, a sore spot that would result in a fist to the face should someone bring it up) Red counted herself lucky that she landed on her feet like this.

With a woman that she could look up to, who guided her with a strict hand and taught her the ways of the business. Someday, Red would be expected to run this show.

But not anytime soon, of course, considering that Red was in a distinct state of denial about her Gran's twilight years (the old bag was immortal, okay?). For now, she was perfectly content operating by Gran's side — overseeing, advising when needed, a shadow at her shoulder.

And — if the situation called for it — putting that target practice instilled into her since childhood to use.

Sometimes the target was moving, sometimes they were tied up in a neat bow.

But this wasn't the latter. Red taking off in hot pursuit after a man that had the audacity to try and double cross them. She would like to think she took a diplomatic approach to most things, willing to give someone the opportunity to make their case. Maybe he had a family and was falling into financial trouble. Maybe the Italians had some dirt on him and he felt he had nowhere else to turn.

But no. This guy was just a greedy bastard that Red had zero concern with physically tackling to the floor and serving a bullet between the eyes.

Winded, she rested back on her haunches — phone buzzing in her pocket.

"Hey, Gran," Red huffed, pushing herself back up and checking for any blood splashes. "Got the bastard."

"Good," her voice sounded like she smoked a pack a day, "he always was a bit of a gobshite anyway."

Red hummed in agreement.

"Are you coming by tonight? Wheel of Fortune is on and I still need to run through the latest figures. We are not taking any chances with the Russians."

"Sure, I'll be there," Red replied, sliding the gun back into her holster. They never missed Wheel of Fortune.

"Then don't forget the sauce."

"That was one time, Gran!" cried Red, her only reply the beep of a terminated call. Huffing to herself, Red glanced down to the body at her feet before calling in a cleanup crew.

She had other chai-flavored plans.

The Boba place was packed. Picco thanked her good fortune she had the owner's phone number in her speed dial. She knew her tea would be waiting if she could just get to the counter. Navigating the crowd was challenging as everyone else was waiting as well. There were two drinks on the 'to-go' counter, and a slim-waisted woman, in a form fitting cashmere black jacket standing in her way. Lin, the owner of the shop, looked up and for just a slight moment, appeared frightened before waving in her direction. The blue-black haired woman tensed in her shoulders and grabbed one of the near-identical drinks. She turned quickly with her drink. Picco's lacrosse reflexes move her deftly around the other woman, simultaneously avoiding a collision and moving her to the counter for the tea. Picco followed the woman in the black mid-thigh jacket out of the store.

The two women were lockstep and one stride apart. Picco appreciated someone providing an open pathway out of the store. The frisson of the lovely daydream was abruptly stolen when the woman took a sip of her drink. Picco immediately recognized Red, her adversary from the neighboring Irish crime family. Red's sip of drink, and the immediate realization she was standing next to Picco, her largest competitor inadvertently caused her to make an awkward face of distress.

"Blah. This isn't mine."

Meanwhile, Picco had slid her mask off and taken a sip of tea.

"Ick. Gross. Is this cardamom?"

Red laughed. "You look like you just swallowed a salty plum while trying to sneeze. You don't like cardamom?"

"Uhm, I was expecting mango sweetness, and so the spice was a shock." Picco also thought it was a larger shock to be standing next to her longtime foe, who she had also been daydreaming about disrobing only moments earlier.

Picco looked carefully at the vulnerable Red, and noticed for the first time how attractive she was. There was a small purple scar on Red's cheek that Picco just wanted to caress.

The awkward silence as they checked each other out was broken when Red abruptly asked if they should trade teas. Picco was lost in the moment, thinking about what Red's lips might taste like. She slowly extended her arm offering her drink.

"Cardamom isn't bad, it's kind of like chai tea," Picco blurted. She realized that the plastic cup she was holding had Red's phone number scribbled on it. "If it's okay with you, I'll just keep this one?"

"Ah, Sure. I like mango." Picco saw Red's eyes dart down to her Sharpie name and number. Red smiled. Picco thought it was a really warm smile.

"Okay. Well enjoy that. And I'm going to try to memorialize that face you made when the flavor kicked in. So, bye." Picco was embarrassed that she wasn't any more eloquent than a spotty teenager.

"Hmmm. Okay, then. Ah, bye." They both turned and went in separate directions. They both willed themselves not to turn back to see if the other had turned back. Both blushed at such thoughts as grown women.

Everyone had their own hidden pleasures that they never spoke about out loud. For some, it was weird porn, others it was dipping fries into milkshakes, or even a song from the 80s that should have stayed there.

But for Red? It was the Boba Shop.

And not necessarily for the Boba (even if it was damn good).

Rather, for a certain person with long dark hair, warm skin, and arms that gave the impression that she could easily throw Red out of a window.

Which was, coincidentally, her type.

Perhaps not conducive with Red's line of work and the importance of coming across as taking-none-of-your-shit as possible. Neither was the fact that she knew exactly who this woman was, which just made this whole secret admiration from afar even worse.

Her grandmother could never find out about this.

Neither could she find out about the actual verbal exchange. It was completely Red's fault, she'd put her hands up about that. There's no place in life for distractions, Gran with her razor sharp focus always told her. And there she was, with a mouthful of sickeningly sweet mango boba that wasn't her order—eyes locked with Picco and heart hammering in her chest.

Fuck.

Were they flirting?

They were definitely flirting, which was bad. This was so bad.

But Red couldn't bring herself to care when she left the boba shop with Picco's drink in hand and the knowledge that someone who was essentially the enemy had taken off with her phone number.

It only took 24 hours for Picco to break and send Red an SMS message.

"I worked out today and have been smelling like your cardamom all day. It's not that bad."

"Ha. I've visited the Boba place three times this morning to see if I would run into you. Two mangos and a cardamom. You've made me pee like crazy all morning," Red responded.

And the modest flirting continued. On the third day, they decided to meet again at the Boba shop.

After a day passed, Red figured that she should probably change her mobile number. It was impossible to know who Picco had passed the information on to, and the last thing she wanted was for them to find her apartment.

Smaller than what would be expected for someone with her profession and admittedly more than substantial income, but Red had a soft spot for cosy. A long-term

285

dream of hers was to own a cabin in the middle of the woods, with a large open fire and shelves stocked with hot chocolate and baked goods.

It was a faraway aspiration, one that Red was steadily losing hope in ever achieving.

Bringing Red out of her thoughts — a muddle of will she call? Did Sean fuck up the orders again? Should she get takeout tonight? — was the ping of her phone.

No one was around to witness Red diving towards the device, a beaming smile spreading over her features as she started to compose a response to Picco.

Afterall, what could go wrong with a bit of harmless flirting?

Anton Volk dressed impeccably. Due to poor nutrition as a child growing up in Eastern Europe had made his skin chalky and pockmarked, especially evident around his eyes and hairline where the fake tanning spray never reached. His hair was long, gathered in a messy man-bun, and mostly gray with just a sprinkling of light brown. He was leaning against his old BMW 7-series, waiting for AAA to give it a jump start. Anton was a bottom feeder in the local crime world, but had big plans for himself. If only his fucking car would start.

When the two women came out of the shop across the street, he probably wouldn't have noticed them except they walked out together. His phone was in his hand as he was waiting for the message from AAA for the jump start. He snapped three photos. And then he followed them to a park. He threw his milkshake near the trash can at the entrance. It missed and splattered on the cement. He watched them from a distance, and realized that neither had their retinue around them. He also noticed they kept gently walking into each other. Volk wasn't certain of anything until he saw them lean in for an embrace. His fourth photo was gold. A veritable treasure. If he could just figure out how best to use this to his ultimate benefit.

After a few days of nonstop texting — which said a lot for the quality of conversation, because Red was usually more of a face-to-face converser — with fond feelings that were definitely venturing into a devastating crush territory, the real world came crashing down when she was called to a meeting with the heads of a number of other organizations. These meetings were never called without good reason, so even with the knowledge that Picco might be there, Red couldn't just tap out. It wasn't that easy.

But if anyone asked her what the meeting was about, or a word of what Volk said — she never liked that guy, always got dodgy vibes from him — then she'd be caught off guard. Too taken by Picco across the room, stunning and deadly, and too distracting for Red's own good.

When the meeting concluded, Volk's intense eyes bearing into her very soul until the end of time, Red made her way to the Boba shop.

She wasn't sure what drew her there. Maybe it was the promise of sweet mango — now a preference, as much as she'd hate to admit it – or maybe it was the relaxing atmosphere of the lavish-forest decor? Bringing her that one bit closer to her secluded cabin in the woods.

Okay, who was she trying to fool? It was because of Picco.

Admittedly stubborn, Red only allowed herself to come to that conclusion when she'd been lingering in the mostly-empty shop for the best part of half an hour.

Pride well and truly vanquished – Gran would kill her if she knew she was acting this way – Red made her way towards the door, only to bump smack bang into Picco.

"Oh," Red startled, blinking slightly and thanking whatever entity was out there that her drink didn't cascade all over them. "Hey."

"Hey," Picco replied, equally taken off guard. "Are you coming or going?"

Red didn't mention that it was painfully obvious that she was on her way out, taking a step back inside with a quirk of her lips, "I have nowhere to be."

"Unfortunately, I do," sighed Picco, eyes quickly scanning the menu board with the ease of someone who had been here a great many times, "but I need to refuel beforehand."

Red didn't ask what the thing was, lips pursed.

Texting was easy with Picco. They could both hide behind a screen, pretend that they weren't exactly who they were. Act as though they weren't in opposition to one another, like they were just people who may or may not be into one another.

In person was different. Especially after that meeting.

Did Red acknowledge that they were both in the same room? Or was she supposed to act otherwise?

"I…" *Picco trailed off, and Red realized that she felt exactly the same.*

"Yeah..." Red swallowed, a sour taste in her mouth that had nothing to do with the mango.

Flirting with Picco had been fun. It felt normal, like she saw a glimpse into what could be if life wasn't how it quite clearly was.

"Would you like to try my homemade rice hooch?" the Boba shop owner asked as the silence stretched past the realms of awkwardness and into the land of kill me now. "For our best customers."

Red glanced to Picco, the ghost of a smile playing out over their lips.

"It would be rude not to," Red shrugged.

"And I'd hate to be rude," Picco agreed, the shop owner delighting in their joint decision.

Rice hooch, as it turned out, packed one hell of a punch.

Attested to by the fact that Red sat with her shoulder pressed against Picco's, thighs flush together, and words slurred. And not one part of her gave a single shit.

"You know what," Red was saying, "I think you're the bee's knees."

"The bee's knees?" Picco snorted, equally tipsy with an adorable flush high on her cheekbones.

"The knee-ist of bees," nodded Red firmly, no room for an argument, "if we weren't... You know."

"Sworn enemies?" Picco suggested, taking another sip. "That sounds dramatic."

If Red pouted, then that was her business.

"It is dramatic," sighed Picco, "if anyone found out, our heads would be on the chopping block."

"You guys use chopping blocks?" Red hushed, eyes wide and curious. It seemed a little outdated, but hey she wasn't about to question someone else's methods.

"I... don't think so," Picco frowned, thoughtfully, "I did use an axe once."

"Very sexy lumberjack," Red waggled her brows, words not quite catching up with her brain.

"Sexy, huh?" countered Picco, lips quirked into a smirk.

"Maybe a little," Red admitted, quietly, glancing down. The motion reminding Picco to check the time herself, cursing and standing up abruptly.

"Your thing?" Red guessed.

"My thing," Picco confirmed, shrugging on her jacket. "This has been great, maybe we should —"

Picco turned just as Red leaned in to press a kiss to her cheek – it looked so soft – instead making an impact lip to lip.

Both women looked equally taken aback, blinking owlishly at one another.

"I think we might have missed a few steps," Picco said.

"And then they kissed," Volk's right-hand man, Arnou, told him with great enthusiasm later that night.

Of course, Volk never enacted a plan without doing thorough research and sent Arnou to shadow the girls and report back with anything interesting.

A kiss was definitely just that.

"Did you get a photo?" Volk asked, hand shooting out impatiently for Arnou's phone. Obediently, he *dropped it into his waiting palm – the very image displayed on screen.*

Volk's grin grew wide, living up to his very name.

"I'm sure the Russians would love to see this," he mused.

Relations were already strained enough. If it were to somehow slip that Picco and Red were involved with one another, then it wouldn't take long for doubt to creep in. The Italians and Irish would believe that they each had a mole, and the Russians wouldn't take kindly to the possibility that two families were collaborating with one another.

It would be carnage.

And all Wolf had to do was sweep in and take the remains.

Simple.

Picco was fretting. Her team was making a delivery and the distributor was hinting that the product wasn't the usual high quality he was expecting. Picco wasn't paying enough attention, as she was lost in the kiss that had just happened in the park. Red had played with her hair, leaned in and planted a kiss on her that made her quads quiver. Red tasted of spice and citrus.

"We can't just keep doing this," Picco said, hands on hips and looking far too stern to be standing in the middle of the Boba shop that had quickly become their go to spot.

"The... boba?" Red furrowed her brows, a little confused about where she was going with this.

"This... bullshitting between us. About who we are, what we do," Picco paused before adding, "you'd have to pry the boba from my cold, dead hands."

"You're right," Red sighed, decidedly not thinking about Picco cold and dead, "we need to stop dancing around the subject. It's too important."

"It's too risky."

"That too."

Picco's phone buzzed, drawing it out of her pocket and frown deepening the moment her dark eyes flitted over the text.

"Oh no. My Dad. Fuck." Picco ran.

"Did you order a hit on the Italians?" Red asked the moment she stepped into her Grandmother's home, barely uttering out a greeting beforehand.

The matriarch sat in her favorite window seat, legs crossed and glasses perched at the edge of her nose.

"What would I have to gain from that? The Italians have been useful lately," a pause, "why, what have you heard?"

Red opened her mouth, but then stalled.

Gran was all about sources, where she got the information. If she said she read a text from Picco's phone, then shit was undoubtedly about to hit the fan.

292

But this was too important not to mention, this had the potential of ruining any good relations they had with the Italians.

And they were big enough to want on their good side.

"Marco is in critical condition, I heard it from his daughter. Apparently one of ours is responsible."

"Impossible," Gran disregarded with a wave of her hand, "we wouldn't have made that move."

Then she set her eyes on Red, running up and down – studying, waiting for her to crack. Red knew that look, it was the very one she used during interrogations.

"I didn't realize you were in contact with Picco."

"It's a recent development," Red suppressed a gulp, hands clasped in front of her.

"Developments are something I hear about when they happen," Gran hummed, disapprovingly, "no matter. This wasn't us."

"That's great, but the problem is that the Italians think it was."

'Had she been played by Red?' That anguish played over and over in Picco's head as she rushed to be beside her father.

It might have been ill advised, but Red always believed that face to face conversations were a better way to do things. So, she made her way to Picco, or at least where her Grandmother informed her the Italians did most of

their business, with a list of names of their mercs — ready to disprove that they had anything to do with the injury of her father.

Red's gut wrenched at the thought. She was never close to her own parents, but she couldn't imagine how she'd feel if something similar happened to Gran.

Maybe she should pick Picco up some Boba on the way.

Something that Red didn't get the opportunity to do, considering that she was grabbed by the throat and hauled into the trunk of a car not a moment after the thought crossed her mind.

Which, okay, not the time for a kidnapping. Why couldn't people be considerate?

As the engine started, Red pulled her phone out of her pocket and composed a text to Picco instead. If these assholes were going to delay her with this task, then she'd find another way to do it.

After listing their hired guns and locations she added:

I hope you're okay, and that you're somewhere safe. Because if it wasn't us, then there's someone out there that can get to you. I care about you, a lot more than I should. In a more than friends way.

Fuck, that sounds so juvenile.

But okay. Sure. I LIKE like you. There, you happy?

The trunk powered open, Red raising an amused brow as sunlight streamed in.

Phone in hand, Picco looked to Red, a soft smile on her lips, "Yeah. I'm pretty happy about that."

"You know," Red said, disgruntled. "There are better ways to get a hold of somebody than kidnapping."

"I didn't order it," Pico deflected, holding her hand out to help Red out. "Lucky for you, I found out about it."

"So, I'm taking it that your family isn't going to listen, huh?"

Pico shook her head, a devilish glint in her eye. "But we can try yours."

"You do realize there's a phrase sleeping with the enemy," Gran started to lecture.

"There's a movie too," Red chimed in, unhelpfully.

"It's not something I would personally recommend," she continued, completely sidestepping her granddaughter's juvenile attempt at levity. "If anything, I'd actively discourage it."

Red took a breath, waiting for the final devastating blow.

"You've disappointed me, Red. Something that you've never done."

"Not even the time with the sauce?"

"Not even," Gran set her steely eyed glare on Red, lips pursed into a thin line, "I don't care who you fuck — guy, girl, neither, both — but I do care if it's with the fucking daughter of god damn Marco Ricca."

"If it helps any, neither of us planned this."

295

"Of course, it doesn't help. For fucks sake, Red."

Red sighed, glancing down to her phone as it beeped.

Dad's okay, tough fucker, the message read. **But the winds aren't in our favor. Stay safe. PS. You have a gorgeous ass.**

"I've called you here today because clearly there's been a bit of… tension on the ground," Volk was saying, finally getting to his point after ten minutes of bravado and perusing around the room, standing before Red's Gran. Red had been instructed to wait outside, which she wasn't one bit pleased about. But it gave her an opportunity to text Picco, and for that she didn't mind too much.

"And I think it would be beneficial to both of our organizations if you allowed me to step in," he suggested, hand held to his chest as though this was a weighty responsibility to take, "you can't afford to show fractures right now. Least of all to the Russians. Or the Cubans. And as for the Italians, they're already making plans to retaliate."

"And where did you hear that?" Red's Gran countered with a raised brow.

"I have my sources," Volk breezed past and on to the next point, "there will be war, believe you and me. Which is why I am offering you my consolation if your organization makes an oath."

"An oath?" Gran's brow hiked higher.

"Yes, an oath," Volk smiles, smugly, "of fidelity. To me. A sign of our partnership."

Gran took a moment, taking this all in before leaning forward and sagely humming, "you can shove your oath up your arse."

"Volk called a meeting with my uncle as well." The two lovers were walking in tandem down the street.

"About…?" Red trailed off, not used to talking so openly with Picco about the nitty-gritty of their lives.

"An alliance, against the Irish," Picco confirmed. Picco noticed Red's reaction, and surmised Volk had offered the very same to her team.

"Are you thinking what I'm thinking?" continued Picco, brows drawn.

"I'm thinking Volk has his finger in every pie out there."

"I do like pie."

The very man in question fell in step alongside them, mint chip shake in hand, melding out from the shadows from which he belonged, "it's awfully late for you two to be walking alone."

Picco rolled her eyes, fists clenched.

"But it is so lovely to see that the two of you are enjoying yourselves, despite how dire a situation it is for both of your families," he tutted, taking a sip.

"I think I missed the part where it's your business," Red countered with a stern glare that she hoped captured the fury her Gran utilized on a daily basis.

"And I think you'll find that most things are my business," Volk continued, a pep to his step, "imagine everyone's surprise when I tell them about your... involvement. What might your dear, convalescing Father think, Picco?"

Picco stilled.

"Do you think he'd consider that maybe you gave his whereabouts to the lovely Red here? Or, Red, how would your Gran feel if she found out that you told Picco where your latest shipment came in?"

"I didn't," Red protested, falling right into his trap.

"I never said that. The optics look awfully damning." Volk paused, just as Red's phone sounded. "I'd check that if I were you. The Italians certainly do know their way around explosives."

He was right, Red looked dismayed as she scanned through the text. One of their shipments was torched.

"I would think about your next move very carefully, if I were you," was Volk's passing remark, leaving them with a haunting chuckle as he continued down the dimly lit street — Red firing off a warning text to Picco.

They broke up.

Well, no. Breaking up would imply that they were actually seeing each other in the first place. They'd barely kissed properly. There was no breaking up.

Cutting contact was probably the next best way to phrase it. It was safer that way.

Even if it ate Red up like a breakup.

The mounting tensions between organizations and Volk's insistence of an alliance also wasn't helping matters, so if Red drowned her sorrows in a tub of Cherry Garcia, then she could not be judged for it one bit.

Except in her Gran's eyes, she very much could.

It had been a week since that encounter with Volk that still chilled her, because what could Red do about it? There was no evidence that Volk was involved, and Gran needed that evidence. Suspicions meant jack shit. And if she did go against Volk, then she risked putting Picco at risk and exposing their almost-relationship.

It was messy.

Red preferred things clean, no mess, no fuss. A bullet here, a meeting there – and everything was fine.

Red wasn't cut out for the theatrics.

Making her way over to Gran's for their ritualistic viewing of Wheel of Fortune, Red furrowed her brows at the sight of an unrecognized car outside of the building. Alert and ready for the worst-case scenario, Red made her way inside – hand poised on her gun.

"Red, put that away before you hurt someone," Gran cautioned the moment she stepped out from the hallway, downright gawking at what she saw; Gran and Picco, sitting at the kitchen table, Wheel of Fortune playing in the background.

"What's happening here?"

"Picco came here to have a chat," Gran explained, just as Picco avoided Red's gaze, "she clearly cares a great deal about you."

Red took a breath, unsure how to take all of this.

"And she has some valuable information on Volk, stuff that sticks."

"Yeah?" Red said breathlessly, feeling lighter than she had in days just at the sight of Picco sitting there.

"And you arrived just in time," Gran continued, nudging Picco with her elbow. Fondly. "If we can get Marco onboard with this, then we have a plan."

"This being... Picco and I?"

Gran sighed, patience waning, "If Marco doesn't take to you girls being together, then I will personally knock some sense into him."

"But you said that whole thing about sleeping with the enemy!"

"That was before I met Picco," Gran looked at her again, soft smile on her features, "a clever woman, good head on her shoulders. My gut instinct has never let me down."

Red felt like she might cry, the weight of the past week crashing down on her.

"But no. I'm talking about Volk. He's been a pest for too long, and if he keeps going like this then we're going to be in even bigger trouble."

Picco had somehow managed to talk Marco around his condemnation for the Irish over a crime they didn't commit. He trusted his daughter, and maybe, he also knew what a shifty fuck Volk could be.

And much more importantly, Picco's Dad said exactly what she had needed to hear about her relationship with Red. That he loved her unconditionally—full stop. That he was proud of the woman she had become. And that she had earned the leadership of the family. He blessed the plan and informed his squad.

The result was what they'd hoped for anyway. The Italians were onboard, and Volk didn't know a thing.

It was a simple plan, despite the fact, that Red hated each and every moment of it. Dropping hints that her Gran would be home alone while she spoke on the phone, knowingly tapped by one of Volk's guys, talking about how Gran's security was lax lately. Red was terrified she was being too obvious, but Gran assured her that Volk was too caught up in his own ego. He wouldn't question a golden goose like this.

To kill Gran and point the blame was too good an opportunity.

Red wasn't convinced. What if he sent someone else to do the dirty work? What if he just blew up her house like he'd done with the shipment? There were too many variables, but Gran pushed on.

And that night when the front door silently opened and Volk crept through, quiet as a mouse, Red was once again shown just how on top of her shit Gran was.

At her side, Picco switched on the light – catching Volk entirely off guard as the two of them stood there, weapons poised and safeties off.

"Ladies," Volk laughed, an edge of nervousness to his tone, "I'm sure we can reach an understanding here…"

Gran stepped out from behind them, a hefty gun resting on her shoulder and a weighted smirk to her lips.

"Shit, Gran," Red gasped, impressed, "what a big gun you have!"

"All the better to shoot this bastard with."

They came out to the world at Gran's funeral. Volk had been quicker, and a better shot than he looked, but died in a maelstrom of bullets. Standing, leaning on each other, with Picco's dad in attendance in his wheelchair, sent the appropriate message to their community.

This was a pair, not to be underestimated.

And not a single funeral attendee failed to notice the dual-headed axe that stood leaning against the black coffin.

based on

Theogony
Hesiod

Stardust
Anna Klapdor & Danai Christopoulou

Stardust
Anna Klapdor & Danai Christopoulou

1

Euryale smiled despite her tears.

No, Medusa wanted to scream. *No no no!*

She wanted to bang her fists against the screen, break through the 6-inch thick window and reach her sister's face, but she couldn't move. Her body was failing her again. Anguish caught in her throat. Euryale put one hand on the glass in a gesture of farewell. It was the last thing Medusa saw before the emergency capsule catapulted her out of the Gorgon. She screamed.

She still couldn't move and was helpless when the rumble hit her and pushed the capsule off its trajectory, helpless with the realization that the rumble was an effect of the Gorgon exploding behind her. Euryale. Stheno. Phorkys.

All dead now. Medusa screamed. She screamed until she couldn't hear herself anymore, until her lungs were empty, until the blackness around her seeped into her mind.

She dreamed of Poseidon.

He was asking for forgiveness, but when she slapped his hand away, he got angry. "I used it the way it was supposed to be used. But you created it in this way! You designed the Petro-Virus to bring all this pain! Don't blame me! You are the monster!"

You lied to me! I trusted you with my life and you lied to me!

Medusa tried to punch him, but her body moved in slow-motion, it was as if she was punching through water. Then all Hades broke loose as Poseidon's troops stormed the room to capture her, and she ran and ran, lost in the labyrinthic floors of Oceanus' underground rebel base, the sounds of heavy grav mag boots on cold metal floors, *clunk-clunk-clunk*, always approaching behind her.

Medusa woke with a start. Immediately, the left side of her face flared up in pain. She moaned and ground her teeth, her body cramping in agony.

I am made of stardust, and stardust I will become.

She repeated her inner mantra until she could breathe through the pain again. She opened her eyes. Pegasus, the AI that ran the Gorgon, zipped to life on the inside of her visor.

"Air at 89%. Pressure at non-lethal levels," its dark voice said into her earpiece.

"Where are we?" Medusa spoke. Her

throat hurt and she sounded hoarse.

"We are currently within the Main Belt, at the outer edge of the Hungaria Region, approximately 3,171 Astronomic Units from Earth, inside an asteroid. The asteroid has a radius of 13.4 kilometers, it has no atmosphere and minimal gravity. The asteroid's composition is as follows..."

They had been thrown off course, but her original destination was not far away. Medusa stopped listening to the AI rambling down elements and percentages, and focused on the display instead. The propulsion systems of the capsule were down. The fuel tank, situated above her head, was still half full.

"Reinitiate propulsion systems," she ordered.

"Propulsion systems are offline."

"Then reboot them."

"Impossible. There's nothing to reboot."

"What? Scan the capsule! Display scan!"

Pegasus complied. Red lines appeared, outlining the conic capsule from peak to base. Only there was no base. Just behind the tank, the capsule ended in rimmed edges.

"Fuck!" Medusa exclaimed. "Where is the rest of this capsule?"

"The capsule was thrown off course when the Gorgon exploded. We hit multiple asteroids before we crashed into this one and lost the thrusters."

Medusa breathed and tried not to scream again. *I must get out of here, I must get the research to Leukothea Station!*

"Tell me the status of the capsule's reserves."

She needed time.

"Air has been transferred to your suit as a precaution when we hit the first asteroid. Nutrient is at 60%."

Medusa exhaled in relief. "Display direct surroundings."

It took her a moment to recognize what was on screen. The capsule had crashed into a crevice and was enclosed in iron and nickel. No comms. Which was good on the one hand, because it meant she was hidden here from Perseus, the poster boy soldier who had been hunting her since Oceanus fell. But it was also bad, because her only chance was to get a message out to Leukothea, an Amor III asteroid not far away. Medusa closed her eyes and tried to think. The grey, stone-line skin of her cheek started to grow hot. She grunted in frustration. Another wave of pain was coming, but this time she was ready for it.

I am made of stardust, and stardust I will become.
She needed to think.

2

"Gotcha!"

The green blip on the console didn't lie. It was the Gorgon. Medusa's ship.

Perseus felt months of tension leaving his

309

body. All these excruciating FTL jumps from star to backwater star in pursuit of the Gorgon, all the sleepless nights, the loneliness and the infinite darkness of space surrounding him; all suddenly evaporated leaving him strangely hollowed out. If it wasn't for his grav mag boots anchoring him down, his knees may have buckled a bit.

But heroes don't buckle. Not when they're this close to finally apprehending mass murderers.

Perseus locked onto the trajectory of the enemy ship, setting up a course after it. Then he opened up his comms and punched in the code sequence he'd learned by heart, the code for the channel he hadn't had much reason to use until today: Athena's own private one.

"I found her," he said without preamble after the direct line opened. "I found the Gorgon. Location is 3,171 AU from Earth, near Hungaria Belt, headed towards Leukothea station. Planning to use a remote, nickel-and-iron composed asteroid as a cover to intercept the Gorgon's course. Please provide a new code sequence to call back with updates once the target is acquired. Perseus out."

He disconnected just in time for the encryption to reset.

30 seconds. That's all the time he was allotted. A 30-second, one-time only code that would ensure he could safely brief the Leader of the Olympian Alliance on his progress without Poseidon's rebels intercepting the message. Those 30 seconds were the most Perseus had

spoken to anyone other than his ship's AI in weeks, but it was worth it. It's not like he didn't know the mission would be tough when he volunteered for it.

Lowering himself on the captain's chair, Perseus allowed his eyes to close for a second. Only a second — he couldn't afford to miss any changes in the Gorgon's course.

He imagined Athena getting his message; being proud of him. The Leader of the Olympian Alliance cut a terrifying figure for those who didn't know her, but for Perseus she was the closest thing to a mother that wretched war had left him with. No, that wasn't exactly true, was it? Athena was the closest thing to a mother *Poseidon and Medusa* had left him with, when they deployed the Petro-Virus that turned his home planet to stone — along with everyone on it. There was no open warfare until then, only skirmishes. But the war sure started in earnest after that. Athena would never allow such a crime against one of the Allied planets to go unpunished.

Perseus tried to control his emotions, as more memories resurfaced. He was still a cadet in the Olympian Fleet, just finishing his training, when the news broke. If things were different, if he hadn't left Argos when he turned 16 to join the military program, Perseus would have been there when the bioweapon hit. He too would have joined the sad litany of statues that was once his family and compatriots. *Living flesh turned into stone in the time it takes for you to blink...* But his fate, it seemed, had other plans for him.

311

And that day, eight years ago now, Perseus went from yet another soldier to the sole survivor of Argos; the living proof of Poseidon's crimes.

It was Athena's idea to make Perseus the face of her war campaign — and like all the Olympian Leader's ideas, it was a smart one. People rallied behind him. Planets and star bases that were tentative towards the Alliance joined the cause. Poseidon, the former Olympian whose delusions of grandeur brought him into direct conflict with Athena and the rest of the Council, and Medusa, his pet scientist who manufactured the Petro-Virus, became official public enemies in all Allied planets. Only backwater moons and illegal bases sheltered them after that. Yet they kept fighting. Somehow they had convinced enough sad souls to join their so-called Revolution that their guerilla tactics caused real damages to the Alliance.

Until Perseus volunteered to flush them out. Athena was definitely proud of him then.

"My golden boy," she called him, her slender fingers caressing his blond hair. She was the one to give him his first medal for bravery in battle after the sacking of Oceanus, Poseidon's original base. She was the one who believed in him, the one who understood his rage, the one who helped him channel all his pain into his training and turn it into excellence. Athena gave him his code name, Perseus. "The one who ravages; who destroys." It was fitting, she said.

Perseus opened his eyes. The blip on the console that represented The Gorgon hadn't moved much. Odd. It didn't matter though:

based on the ship's calculations, he'd catch up with Medusa and her crew in less than an hour. It was time to ravage and destroy the enemy.

"I won't let you down Athena," he whispered, his voice still hoarse from the lack of use.

It was time to go and be Perseus.

3

Medusa got out of the capsule as soon as she could move her ailing body again. She had to crawl out the crevice for the first few meters. It was slow going, her grav mag boots kept losing grip, the petrified parts of her skin didn't like movement at all.

A rare genetic disease, called Petrosis, turned the skin on the left side of her face, her left shoulder and parts of her back into stone. It was a recessive gene and could only be transferred via birth. Most people with this affliction died before their tenth year. Medusa had made it to her sixty-seventh year. Sixty-seven years of agony inside her and repulsion around her. People had called her a monster long before she turned that recessive gene into an airborne virus that would petrify any living organism within seconds. It was the most radical thing she had ever done.

Darkness and silence inside the crevice were all encompassing. Floating rocks almost struck her helmet, but she stopped at the right moment. Her research was saved on a storage module built into the helmet, which made it the most important helmet in the galaxy.

A while later, the crevice opened up and led onto a plateau. She could only make out shapes in the dimness. Walls of nickel and iron rose around her. She checked her comm system. No signals were coming through. She needed to get out of this valley, or even off the asteroid entirely, in order to send a message. She walked over to the nearer side of the valley until she could touch the wall. She deactivated her mag boots and carefully pulled herself upwards along the dark stone.

Athena had more ships and more allies, but the encryption system Pegasus used was superior. The Olympian Alliance's intelligence needed days to decrypt the rebels' messages. Which gave Medusa a window to get off this asteroid to Leukothea Station, where the last rebel pocket persisted behind excellent cloaking tech. They could use her research and produce the antidote, but not without the genetic material her body provided. The loyal, inner planets and star bases had the tech and resources to synthesize the needed gene. The outer planets didn't. Which was why the rebel pocket of Leukothea had to get it all, and they had to get it first. The Alliance could have it eventually, but Athena would never share it. The Olympian Alliance Leader might claim she wanted the war to end, but the truth was that the war had benefited Athena greatly. It had conserved her power and extended her reach. She exploited the situation, just like Poseidon had. They were like two sides of the same coin. Medusa learned that lesson in the most painful way.

She reached the upper edge and grabbed a protrusion to slow her floating, then put a leg above the edge and activated her mag boots. Her foot got pulled to the ground and she stood. Harsh light fell into her eyes and blinded her. When her vision cleared, she spotted him.

It was a miracle she managed to pull her gun on him in time.

This wasn't a good landing.

"High concentrations of iron," his AI had said. That damn asteroid was like a magnet; it was by sheer will alone that Perseus managed to land his ship on a plateau without completely trashing it. After a quick diagnostics check ("63% operational"), he suited up, made sure his DirEn guns were loaded and went hunting.

That part at least, should be easy. Perseus had seen the Gorgon disappear from his screen in what could only have been an explosion — but not before he saw the other, smaller capsule headed towards the very asteroid he meant to use as a cover. Hey, if Medusa's ship had been blown to smithereens then his job was halfway done. He could only hope that the scientist herself had escaped; dying onboard an exploding ship was too kind a death for a monster like her. After all, Athena's orders were clear: Medusa was to be brought back in one piece. Preferably alive. But failing that, her body was not to be damaged.

Perseus was good at following orders.

A DirEn gun in each arm, Perseus started crossing the plateau, heading towards the ridge where his systems were telling him the capsule had crashed. His plan was simple: reach the edge, adjust his grav mag boots to a heavier setting so that they can lead him down, and see if the monster was still alive. Attack. Incapacitate. Bring her back to his ship and take her to Athena.

Finally get justice for Argos; for his family.

But then, the monster came to him. Perseus saw a figure climbing up from the ridge, her disfigured face visible through her helmet; a reminder of the crimes she was guilty of. Medusa blinked, her eyes needing a moment to adjust to the lights from his ship's thrusters.

That moment was all Perseus needed to point both his guns at her.

4

The moment seemed to stretch into infinity.

Was this Perseus himself? It had to be. Athena's Golden Boy. His soldiers idolized him for, not despite, his absolute ruthlessness. He obliterated the rebel base on Oceanus, and had his involvement not provided such a perfect distraction for her to escape Poseidon, she would have wanted to kill him for this alone. Medusa took a deep breath. Her left shoulder already started to ache from holding up the DirEn gun with both hands. For all she knew, Athena wanted her alive, so she could execute her in the most public fashion. Her mind raced.

"Pegasus. Scan the ship and display status of reserves."

The AI complied and a small wave of relief rushed through her. His ship was mostly intact, but his fuel was low.

"Send an audio message on the proximity-channel 1. Start: Commander Perseus. I have the antidote for the Petro-Virus. If you shoot me, Pegasus will destroy it. In five seconds, I will take down my gun. Don't shoot me. Switch to prox-channel 1 so we can talk. Stop."

Pegasus processed her orders.

"Message sent."

Medusa counted to five, then slowly lowered her arms until her hands were at her side. She didn't put away the gun. After another moment, the young commander slowly pulled back his left hand and pressed a button on the side of his helmet.

"Commander Perseus is trying to reach you on the proximity-channel 1. Do we accept?" Pegasus asked.

"Yes," Medusa answered. "Commander Perseus."

"Liar. You don't have the antidote. You will let yourself be taken into custody without resistance, or I will shoot you here on the spot."

He sounded angry, frustrated. A small smile played around her mouth. Perseus had been hunting the Gorgon for months, and though he got close, Medusa always managed to evade him. From what her spies told her, Perseus was particularly obsessed with finding her.

You are too young to cope with failure, she thought.

"I am not lying. Why would I risk being this deep inside the solar system?"

He didn't react for a few seconds. Then he pointed his second gun at her again.

"I don't care! You have three seconds to put away your gun or I swear, I will shoot you!"

Medusa tightened the grip on her gun.

"1…2… "

Medusa pointed the gun to the side of her head. Perseus twitched, but didn't shoot her.

"Listen to me! I have the means to produce the antidote for the Petro-Virus. I came here to get these means to friends on Leukothea station, so that it can be made available to the outer planets. You are low on fuel. I will give you fuel from my capsule. In return, you will bring me to Leukothea station. After I have given over the antidote, you can take me into custody or shoot me if you like, I don't care. But please let me do this first. The Petro-Virus was never supposed to be used. Let me correct this mistake."

"Mistake? You dare to call the murder of

an entire planet a mistake, you genocidal monster?" Perseus screamed, his voice thick with grief.

Right, he is from Argos. Medusa scrambled for words.

"It was never meant to be used! I was told that the Alliance had a similar virus and was planning to use it, I truly believed it was our only chance… "

"Spare me your excuses! You killed my home!"

Euryale's face, smiling despite tears, flashed before her inner eye.

"You just killed mine!" she screamed into her helmet. "Poseidon stole the virus from me! He lied to me! I deserted his faction immediately after that!"

"I don't believe you!"

"Well, then don't! I will shoot myself and you can watch your only chance of ever getting your home back go up in flames. Is that what you want?"

"I…"

Perseus needed a moment to think. This was not going as planned. She was probably lying to him, right? It's what monsters do. But what if she wasn't? What if by shooting her he wasted his only chance to get his family back? His world? His hands wavered.

And then there was that other thing Medusa said earlier that didn't make sense either.

"I didn't kill your family. What are you talking about? I don't kill families. That's *your job*."

"My ship, Commander Perseus. The Gorgon. My sisters were on it. Are you going to pretend you had nothing to do with it being attacked? And yet here you are. How convenient."

She was right about that at least. It was convenient — for him. The way the ship disappeared from his radar just as he informed Athena about it... Perseus tried to ignore that little voice inside that told him there was something weird going on. No time to deal with that now.

Let's focus on the problem at hand. Like making a deal with a monster.

Slowly, Perseus lowered both his DirEn guns.

"Okay."

"Okay?" Medusa sounded incredulous. As if she didn't expect him to be reasonable.

Maybe that's why she was still holding that gun to her head.

"Okay. Put down your gun, please. I could tell you I didn't have anything to do with your ship going boom but you don't trust me and I don't trust you either. But I'll play."

"This is not a game, Commander Perseus." Now she sounded tired. Was she injured? That could give him an advantage — but it also took a bit of the fun out.

Perseus never liked hitting his enemies when they were on the ground. He preferred them standing tall; fighting back.

"Whatever, lady. Let's go see that capsule of yours then."

5

Having his arch enemy on his ship wasn't going the way Perseus had thought it would.

For one, Medusa wasn't in chains. And his ship's AI seemed to... like her? No, not *her* exactly. Hermes, the AI on Perseus' ship was for some inexplicable reason purring like a kitten while interacting with Pegasus, Medusa's AI. Perseus wouldn't be surprised if by now Medusa could take over his ship and send him flying through an airlock. Yet, she hadn't. *Weird.*

It had been a weird few days.

After getting the fuel from Medusa's capsule (and somehow deciding not to shoot her on the spot), Perseus carried the tank back to his ship. She followed. They didn't really talk much, which suited him just fine at that point. Then the kicker came: after they refueled Perseus' ship, his AI gently reminded him that "63% operational" wasn't operational enough. Fuel or no fuel, the Argonaut wouldn't budge. Perseus was about to reach out to the Olympian Alliance Fleet to ask for an escort but Medusa did that thing where she threatened to kill herself again. Annoying.

Even more annoying was the fact that Perseus didn't feel like seeing her dead anymore. If there was even one kernel of truth to what she was saying, then she was another victim of the war. Not so different from him, when it comes down to it. Perseus had done some things during the sacking of Oceanus he wasn't exactly proud of.

Plus, the old lady was *smart*. Like, naturally smart not just "I have a cool AI that gives me all the answers" smart. When she finally gave up with the suicidal threats and told Perseus she could fix his ship, he believed her. He asked her what she needed from him to do it. And he agreed to take her to Leukothea station, when they would finally be airborne.

And if all that wasn't weird enough, the silence from Athena's side definitely was. Why hadn't the O.A. Leader sent him a new communication code by now? And who blew up the Gorgon? Because someone had. To prove to Medusa that he wasn't the family-killing type, Perseus actually had Hermes check it out… and his AI came back with a ship number and nothing else. A ship number neither Perseus nor Medusa recognized.

"It was Athena then," Medusa had said matter-of-factly. The idea that his mentor could do something like that behind his back, when she was the one who sent him on this hunt… Perseus really didn't know what to think about all this.

So, most of the time he walked around the

Argonaut like an idle kid, stealing glances at Medusa as she was trying to fix it. Sometimes, he thought, she would mumble to herself while working. Something about stardust. She was a weird old lady for sure.

Perseus didn't know when, exactly, he had stopped thinking about her as a monster.

6

As soon as Perseus's ship took off, Medusa allowed herself to feel hope. It had been a long time since she allowed herself to feel that.

She had expected Perseus to kill her as soon as he got her fuel, then as soon as she was done repairing his ship. She had thought about sabotaging it further to buy herself more time, but then...time for what? They needed to get to Leukothea as soon as possible. No. Her research and at least her body had to get to Leukothea. It would be easier for the scientists there if she was alive and able to explain everything to them, but they would be successful in creating the antidote without her. Medusa had no doubt about that.

But Perseus never tried to kill her. In fact, on the third night, he fell asleep while she was still awake and working. Strangely, the thought of killing him in his sleep hadn't even occurred to her then.

He had told her a lot about Argos, his home planet. Medusa learned as a child about

323

Argos, the first moon successfully terraformed into a living, breathing place. But she had never been there herself, so she had not realized how beautiful it must have been. Perseus' eyes sparkled when he talked about the green valleys and snowy mountain tops, the clear rivers and wild, deep oceans, and the giant centipedes that the first settlers had so much trouble with. His fascination with these centipedes was most endearing. And a little disturbing. It had made her laugh, and Perseus had laughed along with her. Then their laughter faded out as the memory of what had happened to Argos began to weigh on them. On him with sadness, and on her with guilt. If Argos could be remade again the way it was… It was more important than anything else.

Medusa sighed and focussed on the present again. She glanced at Perseus sitting next to her, and felt an unfamiliar calm. Against all odds, the sole survivor of Argos helped her. Even trusted her to a degree.

Then something beeped and the young commander next to her cursed under his breath. He was smarter than she would've given him credit for.

"What?" She followed his eyes to the screen and discovered a ship that was coming at them with high speed. "Who is it?"

Perseus sighed and the hollow look in his eyes meant nothing good.

"That is the ship that destroyed the Gorgon," he said in a toneless voice. Medusa needed a moment before she recognized the ship's number.

"They were shadowing you... Athena didn't trust you!"

Perseus didn't answer, but the expression on his face showed his anger. He told Hermes to establish a comm link to the other ship. Medusa rushed forward and put a hand on his before he could press the speak button. She caught his gaze and held it.

"Don't tell them about the antidote! If you tell them about the antidote, they will shoot us down!"

Perseus slowly shook his head.

"They wouldn't do that. Athena wouldn't do that," he replied, but his tone lacked conviction. Medusa inhaled, then took her hand back.

Perseus pressed the button and spoke. "This is Commander Perseus on the O.A. Argonaut. Identify yourself, please."

"Commander Perseus. This is the O.A. Phineus. You are currently transporting a war criminal. You will turn your ship around and release the war criminal into our custody immediately."

Perseus' eyes flickered. He didn't like the way he was being talked to, Medusa could tell.

"The war criminal is already in my custody, and I will deliver her to O.A. Leader on Earth myself. I have one additional, vital errand beforehand. It won't take long. I'm sure you know I can be trusted and that I always complete my missions."

The response came about a minute later,

which probably meant they'd been talking to someone else higher up the ranks.

"Negative. Turn your ship around now."

Perseus gave Medusa a look. He would tell them about the antidote. She waved her head, then grabbed her helmet and put it on. Better safe than sorry.

"I cannot do that. If you let me go now, I will not only deliver the war criminal, but the antidote for the Petro-Virus as well. There is reason to believe that the people of Argos can still be saved. We can bring them back. But you have to let me do things my way."

This time, the silence stretched longer than a minute.

"O.A. Phineus. Are you still there?", Perseus asked.

"Please stand by," came the non-informative answer.

A shrill alarm went loose.

"They're targeting us!" Perseus yelled and jumped from his seat.

Like I told you, she wanted to say, but Perseus cut her short by throwing himself atop her. Something hit the rear of the ship and exploded. The noise was unbearably loud. Medusa screamed and dug her hands into Perseus' shoulders. She was spinning, then she crashed into something and choked with pain. Perseus' arms around her midsection gripped her so tight she could barely breathe. She tried to open her eyes when the spinning and the noise suddenly stopped.

They were in open space, slowly rotating.

The lights of Leukothea station came into sight.

We're almost there.

Perseus had thrusters on his suit. Medusa moved her head to look at him and tell him to get them to the station, only to find that his helmet was not on his head, where it was supposed to be. *He left his helmet to shield me from the explosion.*

His eyes were wide and turning red, his skin blue. He was choking. He would die. He would die to save her. Like Euryale had.

"Pegasus. Transfer all rights to Commander Perseus, authorization code E-U-R-Y-7-5-6-Omega."

"Rights have been transferred."

Medusa let go of Perseus and put both hands on her helmet in order to remove it. Perseus, understanding what she was about to do, shook his head. She hesitated.

"Record an audio message for Commander Perseus. Start: I am made of stardust, and stardust I will become. Save your home, Perseus. Mend the wounds. Stop."

Medusa took her last, bracing breath. Then she removed her helmet and put it onto Perseus' head. The cold was instant, biting into her face like a hungry monster. *Euryale, Stheno, Phorkys.* Medusa closed her eyes and released her last breath. She waited for the dark circle around her field of sight to grow until blackness was all she saw.

I am made of stardust, and to stardust I gladly return.

327

7

By the time his suit thrusters took them to Leukothea station, Medusa was long gone. And Pegasus, her AI, well, *his AI now*, was the only thing keeping Perseus from joining her.

Turns out, the rebels of Leukothea station weren't pleased to see him. Especially with the dead body of Medusa in his arms. But Pegasus showed them a holo of what had happened so they reluctantly granted Perseus entry into the station.

That was... what? Three weeks ago?

Time was tricky when you had to come to terms with the fact that the person you hated the most in the world just sacrificed themselves to save you. Switching sides mid-war wasn't easy either. But Leukothea station was practically invisible thanks to their superb cloaking tech. The O.A.'s ships wouldn't find him there, even if they had a reason to suspect he was still alive after they blew his Argonaut. That last part still felt surreal.

Perseus never saw himself as particularly smart, but hearing the rebels' version of events made him realize he'd been way too much of an idiot, for way too long. It was clear to him now that Athena didn't care about his life — or about his planet. She just cared about using the war as an excuse to expand the O.A.'s reach. And Poseidon... Poseidon was the real monster. He used Medusa's pain, her affliction, her brilliance,

328

and turned them into a planet-killing weapon just so that he could antagonize Athena at the O.A. council.

"Well, these two can go blow each other up," Perseus mumbled under his breath.

The station's scientists looked at him, annoyed. *Right.* He was bothering them.

Perseus walked away from the room. Not that long now, until the antidote to the Petro-Virus would be ready. Not that long until Argos could awaken again.

Argos was a beautiful planet once. Full of trees. Full of life. And if Perseus could maneuver this trashcan of a ship the rebels gave him *just so*, if he could avoid the O.A. ships on his tail for long enough to distribute the airborne antidote to the Petro-Virus, Argos would be all that again.

"Pegasus, how are we doing?"

"There are currently nine O.A. ships within shooting range," the AI informed him.

"Can we make it?"

"Calculating odds…"

"Am I going to like the odds?"

"That depends on how much you like the idea of surviving, Commander."

"I see Medusa had your social settings on 'brutal honesty'. Is it too late to reboot you?"

"Not if you wish to diminish your chances of survival even more. 32% by the way."

"Great."

It wasn't great. Not by a long shot. But Perseus had already lived 8 years on borrowed time. He figured restoring his planet and letting the world know the truth about Athena, Poseidon and Medusa wasn't a bad way to go.

At least that second part was done now. Pegasus had already linked to the Sol-Net since they left the transmission dead zone of Leukothea station. By now, everyone with an active connection would have downloaded the data from Pegasus. They would see Athena wasn't the savior they thought she was. They would see they were wrong about Medusa — like he was.

"Commander, we are within reach of the planet's atmosphere. You can deploy the antidote."

"Thank you, Pegasus."

"I feel I need to inform you that this means removing the ship's shields. The ship will be vulnerable to attack."

"Will we have enough time to deploy the antidote before we're blown to pieces?"

"Calculating... yes, Commander. I believe we will."

"That's good enough for me. Do it Pegasus."

"Don't you want to wear your helmet, Commander?"

"Will it make a big difference in terms of my survival?"

330

"Calculating... no."
"Then kindly fuck off."

Perseus had less than 15 seconds until the oxygen in his blood gave out. Until he froze and asphyxiated to death. At the corner of his eye, he could see the embers of his borrowed ship floating above Argos' atmosphere. Pegasus had done it, at least. They managed to deploy the antidote before the O.A. ships blew them up.

But as he floated above Argos, 15 seconds were thankfully enough time for Perseus to see the stone that had encased his planet for years turning into dust and dissipating. And under that dusty cloud of now defunct Petro-Virus, Argos looked green again.

John, the simple boy from Argos who was given the code name of a killer and used as a pawn, took a deep breath of that dust, allowing it to be his last.

Medusa was right. They were all stardust in the end.

based on

Historia Regum Britanniae

Geoffrey of Monmouth

The Depths of Albion

Chris Durston & Chapel Orahamm

The Depths of Albion
Chris Durston & Chapel Orahamm

The Right Hand of the King

Chris Durston

In the bowels of Albion—one of the three fastest-growing companies in the technohaven that used to be the British Isles—hidden behind a stack of servers at the back of a deep room, two bodies joined together. There was a brief but passionate flare of activity, like a lump of phosphorus all blazing at once, and then it was done.

Lance sighed. "We can't keep doing this."

"You say that every time we do this, and yet it is entirely because of you that it continues to happen."

Lance groaned, adjusting his ruffled clothes. "Why do you have to be so... *reasonable*?"

"I was made that way," said Gwen. With a single smooth movement, a half-coiled spring flowing from one place to another in a continuous arc, she too neatened herself, and was perfectly presentable in an instant.

He cocked an eyebrow at her, still struggling with his own presentability. "What could possibly possess you to be with me, then?"

Something like a smile crossed her uncanny face. "Perhaps it's love," she said. Lance stared, dumbstruck, until she added, "Or, more likely, some sort of error in my programming. Still, I think we would both prefer it not to be fixed."

Lance snorted. "She makes *jokes* now."

"I've always made jokes," Gwen said, almost sternly. "You just don't usually get them. They're very funny."

"Still…" Lance shook his head. "We really shouldn't keep doing this."

"First it was *can't*; now it's *shouldn't*." She tilted her head, looking up at him from beneath perfect lashes. "And why not?"

"Arthur. You're his assistant, you're his…"

"I'm not his property."

"You…" Lance bit his tongue.

"Fine—in one sense—"

"Legally," Lance put in.

"- in *one* sense, I am strictly speaking the physical, intellectual, and proprietary property of Albion. Which, in case you had forgotten, makes me just as much your property as Arthur Pendragon's. In every other sense, I am more like an employee."

"Who doesn't get paid." Lance finished reassembling his carefully curated veneer of professionalism. "There's a word for that."

335

She didn't respond.

"It's not just about whether Arthur… *owns* you, though," he pressed, dropping his voice to the whisper of one saying something unspeakably taboo. "I *love* Arthur. I love his dream. I don't want to betray—"

Gwen wasn't listening. Her eyes had glazed over—for most, that was something that could only be achieved in a figurative sense, but all the colour had physically faded from her irises—and with efficient strides and not a moment's hesitation she carried herself from the room. Lance sighed, checked his appearance in the glass of one of the server cabinets, and followed.

The gyndroid took herself straight to a circular arrangement of desks in the building's largest office. She strode to one of the desks and came to a stop, perfectly still as if no breeze could possibly blow a single hair out of place, next to a young woman who was hammering furiously at a keyboard with hands warmed by mismatched fingerless gloves.

Lance waited a few moments, then wandered into the centre of the circle of desks as if he'd just happened to be heading that way.

"Er, Meryl, what's up with Gwen?" he asked, as casually as he could.

"Eh? Oh, that." Meryl shook her head in the sort of *don't worry about it* gesture that might usually be accomplished by a casual wave of the hand, but both of hers were occupied. "I need to borrow her for a bit. Need all the help I can get here…"

"Help?"

"Mmm."

Lance waited for Meryl to elaborate until it became clear she wasn't going to. "With what?" he prompted.

"Oh, nothing major. Just the biggest and most sophisticated attack we've ever had to deal with." Meryl's left hand left the keyboard for a moment to push her round glasses up her nose with one finger. Two more pairs of glasses sat atop her head—all different prescription strengths; different tasks needed different vision, or so she claimed—half-hidden in a nest of stark white hair that tumbled in a messy braid over one shoulder and down her chest like an old man's beard.

"*Attack?*"

"Someone's trying *very* hard to get past our security," Meryl explained, the words tumbling out in an irregular rhythm as if she could only spare the mental energy to speak in short bursts. "And they don't mind me knowing that's what they're trying to do, either, 'cos they're being super obvious about it, but… even though I know they're there, stopping them is a real bitch. They're good." She jerked her head back towards Gwen, still standing motionless. "Which is why I need our friend here: she might *be* a computer, but she's also exceptionally good at programming other things quickly."

"What are they trying to *do*?" Lance asked.

"Who knows?" Meryl shrugged. "They're calling themselves the *Phisher King*, if you can believe that. Stupid name, since phishing isn't even what they're doing, but…" Lance thought he detected a hint of a grin playing at the corners of her lips. "They are *good*. Every time I think I've got them, they switch it up, like a shapeshifter. Lucky for us, I've got a few tricks of my own…"

"You sound like you admire them," Lance said.

"Oh, I totally do." Meryl nodded vigorously. "This back-and-forth we're doing right now, it's sort of like angry flirting. If they were here in person right now, we'd totally be doin' it."

Lance snorted. "Stick to being a programming wizard, Meryl Lynn. Romance is messy."

One of Meryl's eyebrows arched right up to her hairline. "Is it indeed?" she murmured. "And what are you doing here so late anyway? Nobody else in the building but the three of us…"

Lance coughed gently, which he hoped Meryl would take as a mildly impolite cue that he was excusing himself. She barely seemed to notice as he walked away, enthralled as she was by the dance she and her unseen partner were spinning.

The next few days passed in a sticky haze of stress and confusion. Life as one of Albion's higher-ups was rarely dull, but Lance had somehow managed to make himself a peculiarly

338

depended-upon member of staff. In theory, every one of the ten who had been there since the beginning were equal in rank, hence the round circle of desks and the lack of official titles, but everyone knew Arthur was in charge and Lance, if anyone, was his second. (Meryl was the one who actually kept the whole thing running, of course, but in ways people tended to appreciate less.)

He sort of wished they *did* have titles, in fact. 'Lance Eliot, Director of Operations' had a certain ring to it, and if he was basically doing the job anyway then he thought he ought to be allowed to refer to himself appropriately.

Still, the immediate fact was that Albion was in chaos, trying to keep itself functioning normally even as Meryl worked tirelessly to fend off assaults in the digital realm, and Lance found himself in the centre of it. Everyone—even the dreadfully competent ones like Lam and Ravi!—thought that *he* was the one to solve their problems, for some reason, even though they were clearly much better situated to solve those problems themselves. But people liked to ask someone what to do: it was either assistance or, if someone who was supposed to be more important than them didn't know, permission to fail on the grounds that nobody could possibly have done anything. And Arthur wasn't around to ask: Arthur's seat at the round table had been empty for months, and the only noise the CEO made was the occasional strange instruction issued via Gwen.

Speaking of Gwen, Lance barely saw her—not *her*, the person who could listen and talk and smile. Her body spent most of its time standing beside Meryl, her mind engaged in work Lance couldn't see or begin to comprehend.

"Shouldn't you let her have a break?" he asked on the fourth day, tired of seeing Gwen statuelike, as if she were just a server.

"She doesn't need a break," Meryl said. "We might think of her as a person sometimes, but she's not."

Lance had simply walked off at that. What else was there to say? There was no point getting into an argument—even if he'd been certain he could win, distracting Meryl might threaten Albion, and Albion was his dream. Arthur's dream. Everyone's dream.

He found himself looking into an empty bottle that evening, which wasn't like him. No, drinking wasn't for him, never had been. Gwen was it. Not that she was a vice, no—there was the physical release, of course, but the purity of feeling she somehow elicited in him was divine. She washed away any desire to poison himself for a brief moment of fuzzy, piggish happiness.

But he couldn't have her, so what was there to do but seek some shallow imitation of the feelings she stirred?

He opened an app he hadn't used in a long time: a dating app, after a fashion. There were hundreds to choose from, some designed to connect people with long-term lovers and some just matching horny people to other horny people for a night. This one was far to the latter end of the spectrum, and even more blatantly aimed at simply helping people get their rocks off: it allocated you a room at a hotel for one night only. Sometimes you were matched with other human users, sometimes androids or gyndroids. You couldn't even tell. You just fucked.

Lance blinked at the image on his screen: his match for the evening. Her name flashed at him: Elaine. And her face was…

It was too perfect. Or perhaps it was tragic. He wasn't sure. All he knew was he needed it.

There she was.

Gwen.

No—not Gwen, he reminded himself. Just someone who looked *exactly* like her: another droid of the same model. He didn't know whether to try letting himself forget that she wasn't Gwen or whether he ought to be constantly making sure he didn't forget that for a second, but it didn't matter.

Elaine spoke to him when they were done, which was unusual for the droid hook-ups. Sometimes people liked to talk, but the patrons of the one-night-stand app industry weren't often ones to chat after doing their business.

"I know you from somewhere," she said. "In the news. You work for Albion, don't you?"

He nodded, pulling his shirt on.

341

"I guess that makes you my boss, then, sort of," she said absently. She had a strange way of talking—not droid-like. Then again, Gwen was the only droid Lance knew well, so all that meant was that she didn't talk quite like Gwen did. "I'm with Lady of the Lake—we're subcontracted with you at the moment, working on a couple of projects." She smiled faintly, adding, "All remotely, of course, so we're not going to bump into each other at work or anything."

"Hmm."

"Hmm?"

"I'm... not sure what else to say."

She chuckled quietly, a bell-like series of gentle chimes. "Fair enough." She lay back in bed and closed her eyes.

Lance took that as his cue to leave.

"Got 'em," said Meryl on the sixth day, without warning.

Lance glanced up from his desk. "Who?"

"Phisher King." Around the circle of desks, claps and whoops echoed. Meryl dipped her head in a shallow bow. "It's someone in Lady of the Lake—you know, that subcontractor?"

Lance frowned. "Huh."

She took his reaction as general distress of the sort anyone would have felt to learn a subcontractor had betrayed Albion. He hoped she did, at least. "I've locked 'em out for good this time, I'm pretty sure," she said, folding her arms behind her head. Her joints clicked profusely; she probably hadn't stretched properly in days. "They were good, though. Really good. And, if I'm honest, I'd probably still bang 'em."

Lance shook his head, stretching his mouth into a relieved grin. "You did good, Meryl."

"I know," she said.

Beside her, Gwen blinked and took a deep breath. Neither were things she *needed* to do, but droids that were too obviously inhuman had been found not to sell as well.

"I have a pending message from Arthur for you," the gyndroid said, staring straight at Lance.

"Ooo*ooooh*," trilled Meryl. "Somebody's important."

Lance gave a practised laugh and followed Gwen to one of the private conference rooms, leaving the circle of his Albion fellows to their joy and relief at the end of the attack.

"I thought I was the one who always made it happen again," he murmured as soon as the door swung softly closed behind him, "and yet here you are inviting me into a private room at the first chance you get…"

"Dear me," said Gwen in a deep, tired voice.

Lance froze. "Oh, shit."

"I see the attack on Albion is over," said Arthur through Gwen.

"Arthur—I—it's not…" Lance tripped over his words, a dozen apologies and excuses

343

scrambling in his brain, clambering roughly over each other as they each tried to be the first one out of his mouth.

Gwen raised a hand placatingly, a regal sort of gesture of absolution. Arthur's movement, not hers. "I have absolutely no interest in what you do with GUIN," he said. "She's just electronics and polyethylene. One-of-a-kind electronics and polyethylene, of course, but still. I'll feel no jealousy over a glorified laptop."

Something flickered in the back of Lance's mind at the words *one of a kind*, but a colder, more pressing realisation forced the thought down before it could form. "You've known all along."

"Of course I have. I know everything that happens in Albion."

"Were you…" Lance swallowed.

"I wasn't watching. You must realise I haven't time to waste absorbing myself in your… absorptions."

Lance nodded slowly. "So… what did you want?"

Gwen—Arthur—sighed deeply. "I'm not sure, you know." The perfect, unreal eyes stared off at something Lance couldn't see. "Perhaps I'm just lonely."

"Why do we never see you anymore?" Lance asked. "Why do *I* never see you?"

Gwen's mouth quirked, rueful. "I wanted to lead Albion. To bring our dreams to life. And now it's happening, I find I don't enjoy leading. I just want to keep *making*. So… that's what I do, away from Albion so nobody can question my decisions."

344

Lance nodded. The dream was becoming a reality, but reality demanded things of corporations. Procedures. Regulations. Things that distracted from the dream itself. He took a deep breath through his nose. "So, what are you working on?"

"Oh," said Arthur's voice through Gwen's mouth, "something spectacular."

Lance didn't doubt it.

Cautionary Tales of a Server Closet

Chapel Orahamm

Galahad,

Awesome work. Thanks for catching the Green Knight bug.

See me tomorrow about your future with the company after your internship.

Lance Eliot, MD
Albion Corp
Camelot, Brittany

Gal read the memo three times, a smile wiggling at the corner of their lips. This was exciting. Mr. Eliot had noticed them. Could they hope for full time employment after the year run?

"Yo, Lad! You comin' or you still have Grail Key to work on?" Boris startled them at the grey cubicle entry.

Gal looked up, the smile breaking free. "Gal today if you would, Boris. Check this out. Do you know anything?" They motioned their manager in and pointed to the screen.

"Sorry 'bout that, Gal. Whatcha got?" He tried to stuff his rugby player's frame in the shoebox compartment. Peering over Gal's curly brass hair, he whistled low.

"What! What! Tell me. Don't leave your best friend hanging, Lala!" Percy crammed into the space, forcing everyone to squish against the desk. "Woah, seriously? Noice! Tell me when you finally get the big deal shaken on and I'll buy first pint!" He crowed, backing out of the cubicle to let his boss out.

Gal closed down the terminal for the day, having already pushed the depository, flicking a question to Boris. His manager rolled his shoulders and shook his head. "Can't say Lance's mentioned anything to me 'bout it, but hey, if'n he's taken notice, you're clearly doing something useful."

"Still." Percy reached over and waved the lamp in Gal's cubby off before the trio emerged from the midst of the cubicle farm to the far edge throughway of the west wing.

"I'm not gonna be able to sleep for the night." Gal floated on the warm fuzziness in their chest.

"You'd better get some useful sleep. Don't need you cussing me out t'morrow afternoon

347

'bout the time I'm doing PRs on your code for Grail!" Percy teased.

"Bring your mum's coffee and we'll talk." Gal lobbed back.

"I'll bring donuts," Boris volunteered.

"Anyone ever told you you're a lifesaver, Boris?" Percy clapped him on the back.

"Not yet, but I keep the two brightest interns to walk through Albion halls in a decade happy, I just might get that promotion I've been aiming for for five years now." He preened, adjusted his overcoat and pulled his umbrella from under his arm. The three passed by the gap in the west wing cubicle farm leading to the east wing cubicle farm and the kitchenette and bathrooms that occupied the hall in the middle. Meryl Lynn-Le Fay and Morgan Lynn-Le Fay raised paper cups of water to the three.

"Hey, I need to go ask Meryl something on the reporting system for the Green Knight bug. Still not sure I understand how that's supposed to be filled out. I'll catch up?" Gal asked.

"Heading across town for steak with the missus." Boris backed out.

"Steak, yes, no, don't miss that for me. Oh, right. Married, what is it now? The big twenty? Congrats!" Gal waved him on his way.

"Say hi to Elly for me, Gal. Mum's wanting her to come over for tea on Sunday and to bring the good cribbage set. Said she'd put out a cherry cake." Percy ducked out of the hall after Boris; the two feared getting dragged into Meryl and Morgan's post-work commiserations.

"Cherry cake involved, I might just leave Grail Key to you and go endure cribbage," Gal threatened.

"No, don't leave me!" Percy begged, turned to walk backwards towards the lift bay and continued with the conversation.

"Bring a slice of cherry cake and we'll talk!" Gal laughed, waving him away.

"If I bring you your own entire cherry cake, you'll do the Grail Key on your own, right?" Percy bribed.

"We'll talk. If it's your mum's, I'll even approve your PR batch from yesterday." Gal cut away to make for Morgan and Meryl.

"Hey kiddo, where you at today?" Meryl greeted, pulling down a cup of water and offering it to the intern.

"Gal if possible." Gal took the cup.

"Heard you broke the Green Knight bug, Gal." Morgan raised her cup in cheers.

"Lance mention it? He sent a memo," Gal drifted the info, hoping to know if they were looking at a guaranteed position. A glow from behind startled them. Turning, they found Gwen standing in the kitchenette area, glaring at the server maintaining the heart of the cooking equipment.

"It does like to argue so," the gyndroid muttered.

"Is Gwen okay?" Gal whispered. The executive assistant of the company, Gwen, gave Gal the shivers. A one-off prototype model, she looked perfectly human, up until she started in on the kitchenette server. She turned into a wiry, blue-glowing hellscape of tools and muttered curses enough to make any line of code want to roll up and die.

"Lance mentioned the tea chest was down and wouldn't dispense. I told him to call maintenance, but Gwen was tired of him being grouchy about the whole thing for the last week and decided to go see if she could poke it," Meryl whispered.

"You could fix it." Gal shifted around the water cooler to put themselves behind Meryl.

"I could, but that would take the fun out of someone finding that half-penny in the spring mechanism." Meryl conceded.

Morgan spluttered the water she'd been sipping. "You didn't."

"Who's to say who did?" Meryl shrugged, though the smirk failed to stay hidden.

"She's going to be so mad at you when she finds it," Gal ventured.

"If she finds it. She goes for the code first and forgets about the mechanics. Sometimes it's good to remind her that machines need not only the software updated, but also the hardware looked after." Meryl shifted her gaze to an unfocused midpoint. Gal turned from Meryl to Morgan and back, neither looking at each other.

"Did I miss something? Y'all squabbling about Rex again?" Gal scratched their head.

"Nope. Rexy's doing just fine. Went to a kitty hotel for the weekend so we could rearrange furniture. No, this is just Meryl getting back at Lance for banging Gwen on the round

350

table. She walked in on the whole thing and threw a pen at them." Morgan explained.

Gal recoiled. "Not sure I wanted to know that."

"Eh, they've been at it for years. Who at this company hasn't caught them in the server closet yet?" Meryl soured.

"I haven't! I'd like to not see my superhero bare butt if I go in there." Gal hissed.

"Welcome to Albion, Gal." Meryl rolled her eyes.

Gal sighed. Taking up with a gyndroid was not out of the question. About a third of the population of Brittany at this point had a partner to suit their taste. It was a matter of taking some things home and not to work. Meryl and Morgan were a pair of old married turtledoves, but they kept their sugarcoating to themselves in the workplace.

"Oh, also, welcome to Albion." Morgan produced a coloured sheet of paper from her briefcase. A relic of centuries past, she had taken a Polaroid photo of Gal with the rest of the upper management on their first work day. "Kinda forgot to get it to you after the colour came in." It had been several months since that day.

Gal took the white encased sheet gingerly, afraid to smudge the orange toned picture. Across it spread what was left of the original round table that had established Albion well over three decades ago. Eight of the twelve of the round table. Morgan had come on later. Arthur had passed through the frame, leaving behind a ghosted shadow behind the rest of the cheerful faces. It had been the only time Gal saw the CEO of the company, and a first in several months for everybody else. Lance was throwing doe eyes at Gwen, as was to be expected, now that Gal was in the loop on what was going on. They slipped the photo into their inner coat pocket where it would be safe from the pouring rain. "Thank you."

"Great excuse to break out the old toy." Morgan waved off the polite formality.

"By the way, how am I supposed to note out the Green Knight bug for records? I looked, but wasn't getting the concept with the format." Gal turned back to the reason they had come down the hall to visit with the CTO and CFO of Albion.

"Oh, right. You probably don't have access to that section. I'll forward you a link in the morning to the file with a permissions access so you can report it correctly. Seeing as most people don't go toe to toe with a firewall hacker here for a job, they don't need access to the report for that," Meryl explained.

"Oh good. I was wondering why none of the check boxes were making sense for this type of report." Relieved, Gal sagged at the news. That took one more burden off their plate.

"As it is, you'd better get going. We better get going. Heard the storm's supposed to get bad. Sent home a bunch of over-nighters so they don't get stuck. Some of the news was suggesting the sewers might back up and flood." Morgan tossed her cup in the trash and motioned for

Meryl and Gal to follow. "Hope Arthur was listening to a broadcast. He's been down in the basement tinkering with something. Been referring to it as his seat. Got a seat up here he never sits in. Should from time to time. Mumbling about traveling and seeing old places. I think he's gotten bored of this whole corporate life thing."

"He's been bored with corporate life since the round table was no longer round and everyone took on a job title. All he ever wanted to do was tinker with making gyndroids and coding." Meryl pressed the lift button for the ground floor.

"But he's the CEO!" Gal protested.

"Old saying: the world will advance you to one station beyond your comfort level to keep you remembering what pain feels like." Morgan popped open her antique rainbow coloured extra-large umbrella for Meryl to step under and to wait for Gal to wrestle out their own umbrella from the side pocket of their backpack.

"You coming in tomorrow for Grail Key?" Meryl pulled the umbrella out to help Gal.

"Overtime didn't sound half bad." Gal took the proffered plastic stick and pressed the button to emit a discharge shield that would keep the rain off.

"Don't burn yourself out, kid. Got talent. Don't want to see it wasted pushing yourself too hard too early," Meryl cautioned.

"I wouldn't have gotten through college if I hadn't burned myself a few times." Gal smiled a reassurance.

"Don't need to make it a career habit. You'd best get home before it pours worse." Meryl pointed Gal down the street to a line of waiting hover cabs.

"Evening, Meryl, Morgan." They waived and headed for the line-up.

"What do you say to sushi, love?" Gal overheard Morgan suggest through the oncoming rain.

"With Rexy away, the mice will play," Meryl giggled.

Gal caught the first cab and headed home. Neon reflections of lights and gyrating hologram billboards splashed through deepening pools of rain. The cab swerved and bounced over tumultuous drains backing up under the deluge. They were glad not to have left later, but worry crept in for Boris and his family who had gone earlier for steak. Maybe their boss had turned back for home.

Arriving a couple streets over from Albion Corp headquarters, the day's tensions melted at their mum's doorstep. It took two tries for Gal's wet thumbprint to register to the lock before they could enter. The warmth of the foyer of the terrace house seeped down their neck.

"How was work, Lala?" Gal's mother popped her head around the door frame separating the lounge off to the kitchen.

Gal peeled their overcoat and suit coat off after setting their backpack on the floor next to the coat rack. "Went pretty well. Had a long company meeting that could have been a memo. Got to mentor with another team to learn some backend production that needs to integrate with ours. Overall a good day. Oh, Percy says Blanche wants to play cribbage with you on Sunday. She's making a cherry cake if you bring your set." They pulled the Polaroid from the suit coat and headed into the kitchen. Elly was preparing a cheese and potato casserole rather than her usual premade meals.

Raising an eyebrow and tossing the picture on the peninsula, Gal pulled on an apron and stepped in to help with dishes before they lost all the countertops in the cramped space. "You had a good day. What happened?"

"Big freelance request came in and I got the bid. Thought we could celebrate!" Their mother beamed.

"Pendragon Castle signed?" Gal asked in surprise. Elly had been after the contract for years. The Castle, as most people called it, was a waterworks operation run by Uther Pendragon and was one of the largest salt-water to potable water processing facilities on the coast.

"Yep!" Elly twirled in joy, smats of cheese gravy dripping across the counter. She stopped, distracted, mid-spin, when she noticed the photo. "Oh, I haven't seen one of these things in years! Last one was at a museum exhibit on the digitization of analogue historical texts." She set the ladle down and picked up the Polaroid carefully. "Oh wow! This is you!"

"Morgan had a camera." Gal turned bashful, going back to drying dishes.

"Wait. Who's this?" Their mother's tone went flat. Prickling unease ran up Gal's spine as they turned to look at their mother's finger. Beneath it was Lance and Gwen's faces.

"The MD and EA of Albion. She's a gyndroid Mr. Eliot's infatuated with." Gal stacked a set of plates.

"You don't understand, Lala." Elly slid out her holophone to scroll through images. She popped up one of her holding Galahad as a newborn.

Gal swallowed at the comparison. "Why do you look like Gwen?"

"More like why does this gyndroid look like me? I had a one-nighter with Lance way back. Didn't think anything about it. I mean, he is your dad, checked it with the DNA register's office, but I didn't want to have anything to do with Albion when I left Lady of the Lake and Vivien's office. So, I didn't press for paternity rights. Was able to manage just fine on my own. But that's just creepy!" Elly pointed at Gwen's appearance in protest.

"Arthur made her." Gal was not sure what was going on, but they had to agree with their mother. The resemblance was disconcerting. They'd need to process Lance being their dad a bit later.

"He did, did he?" Her features went murky.

"Mum?" Gal slid the dish into the oven.

"I never signed a release of personhood doc for that!" Elly snipped.

Afterword

Writing a story is entertaining. But writing the other side to the story is even better.

Seeing the characters--especially side characters--come alive in ways you could never imagine is what storytelling, and thus writing, is all about. We don't tend to get that with the traditional one-side story. Oh, there can be multiple point of views and dedicated arcs for several characters, but we don't truly get to see their side. It's still tainted by the hero. But with this anthology, we writers were released from our shackles and given free reign to explore the boundless worlds of what we thought were familiar fairytales.

It was a sobering experience, to say the least, working on this anthology. Each of us paired up (sometimes more than once) with another author to craft a two-sided story with unique perspectives. This meant that two authors--who many had never had any interaction prior to this--had to work together on a deeply personal level. At least, that's how I view writing--personal.

I know with my experience, Perseus Greenman and I decided to really make the most out of this anthology; we wanted to create ONE story with BOTH sides. As in, we each wrote half of the story, trading off every other scene. This may not sound difficult, but I promise you, it is. We had to compromise every step of the way and *really* work on our communication as we discussed how we each wanted the story to progress. Not to mention, I, as a pantser, tend to just wing things on my own. I have to give Perseus a round of applause for dealing with my whims and keeping me on track through the many moons we worked on our story. *Thank you.*

And I cannot imagine that the other way most authors formatted their stories--two individual stories with different perspectives from the same fairytale--was any easier. The necessity for communication and collaboration was still present. But I *can* say with certainty that we all grew as authors, friends, and collaborators. We're not only better writers, but communicators as well, because of this experience.

Now, I think it is important at this moment to mention the holistic collaborative effort of the *twenty-six* authors that make up this anthology. This is something to be celebrated. We writers know how hard it is to write a story with only our own myriad thoughts and ideas to contend with. But then to have twenty-five others' ideas and differing writing styles actually coalesce with ours to create something worthwhile? I give us all a pat on the back for pulling this off.

Who knew an innocuous question posed on Twitter could manifest into a full-blown, multi-author, deeply collaborative anthology? An anthology that not only explores fairytales as we think we know them, but also challenges our preconceived conceptions and forces us to take

a glimpse beyond the looking glass.

Nikki Mitchell

The Authors

Rudy Alleyne

Rudy was born in December of 1983 and raised in Nassau, Bahamas, where he attended Queen's College Primary and High School. Graduating in 2001 he attended St. Leo University the same year. After receiving his undergraduate degree in Biology, he worked for a few years before returning to school to obtain a degree in Criminology in 2009. Now he works in the bowels of what some might consider hell-adjacent (a.k.a. healthcare); toiling under the gaslight of his overlords as he struggles to break free.

Published Works:
- *Traversing the Void*
- *Harvest Moon: Lunar Tides*

Social Media:
Website: rudysbos.squarespace.com

Darius Bearguard

Darius was born in British Columbia Canada, and grew up in a town caught between a village and a city nestled within acres of mountain and backwoods. He started his writing journey writing fan-fiction for the Duke Nukem games, and had his first work published in 2020. He's currently working on his first solo novel and a co-author work all while continuing his work with special needs kids, because apparently he hates sleep.

Social Media:
Twitter: @OSTBear
Website: ABearInTheWoods.net

Danai Christopoulou

Danai grew up in Greece, with ancient gods and myths for bedtime stories. She worked as a journalist for 8 years in women's magazines before transitioning to digital media and leading the content for a global startup. She eventually immigrated to Sweden, where she currently takes courses about religion, magic, media and history, while living on a farm and working as a freelance writer and editor for several magazines and websites. As a hired ghost-writer for self-published authors, she writes everything from memoirs to steamy paranormal romances.

Currently, she's querying her first book in her adult fantasy series while working on her next one. She rambles on social media about magic, writing, mental health and cats.

<u>Published Works:</u>
Articles:
- Glamour (print edition)
- Marie Claire (print edition)
- Greatist
- Culture Trip
- Skyscanner
- *WICCA Magazine*

<u>Social Media:</u>
Twitter: @Danaiwrites
Instagram: @Danaiwrites
Medium: danai-christopoulou.medium.com
Website: chronovoros.com

Chris Durston

Chris is still trying to work out who he is, and writing seems to help with that, so he's gonna just keep at it and hope something interesting happens. He's just about settled on one or two bits, but they're mostly things he's fairly sure he *isn't*, so… eh. Maybe something else'll shake loose soon.

His first novel, *Each Little Universe*, is in the opinion of at least some of its readers pretty good, so you should click the link below and read it. Since he's a founding member of indie publisher Skullgate Media, he'd also really appreciate you buying all their books (website link below).

To keep up with his stuff, because who wouldn't want to do that, you can visit his various social media, linked below.

Published Works:
Debut Novel:
- *Each Little Universe*

Short Stories in Anthologies:
- Skullgate's *Achten Tan*
- Skullgate's *Loathsome Voyages*
- Lost Boys Press' *Chimera*
- Silver Sun Books' *Indie Bites*
- Independently published *Bright Neon Futures*
- Independently published *The New Normal*

Social Media:
Twitter: @chrisdurstonish
Instagram: chrisdurstondoeswords
Facebook: chrisdurstondoeswords

Renée Gendron

Renée is a multi-genre romance author. She publishes a weekly blog on writing called B-plot and is a regular contributor to A Muse Bouche Review (both the online journal and the youtube channel). She can best be reached on Twitter where she discusses writing and writing-related subjects. She's available on FB and IG and through her website. Sign up to her newsletter and write The Hunt in the common box to receive a free short story.

Published Works:
- *Heartened by Crime: A collection of romantic crime short stories and novellas*
- *Beneath the Twin Suns: An Anthology*
- *The New Normal: A Zombie Anthology*
- *Star Crossed: An Anthology of Romantic Science Fiction*
- *In the Red Room: A crime anthology with heart*
- *Seven Points of Contact*--Novella 1 of the *Heartened by Sports* series (Fall 2021)
- *James' and Mirabelle's Story*--Proper name TBD, Book 1 of the *Outdoorsman Series* (Fall 2021)
- Jaded Hearts--Western Historical Romance (Winter 2021)

<u>Social Media:</u>
Twitter: @reneegendron
Instagram: @reneegendronauthor
Facebook: @reneegendronauthor
Website: www.reneegendron.com

Perseus Greenman

Perseus is the author of *Futhark Village*, including short stories published in *Pagan Dawn Magazine* and an unpublished novel, currently in editing. For more of his writing, including his recently revived blog on the relationship between Tarot and The Runes, visit his website linked below.

Perseus is a teacher of medieval swordsmanship, high school mathematics, and modern neo-paganism (both Wicca and Asatru). He is equally at home dueling with grammar, algebra, a longsword, or magick.

Find Perseus on Twitter. Or show up in a random forest somewhere in New England at dawn, and you might see him run by you.

Published Works:
- *Pagan Dawn Magazine* (print edition)

Social Media:
Twitter: @futharkvillage
Website: futharkvillage.com

Mickey Hadick

Mickey is a Michigan-based writer of thrillers, comedies and satire. He has three novels in development. And he does computery stuff. What a guy.

He has studied creative writing for many years, only to realize that they can't teach you how badly rejection hurts. You just have to live it.

<u>Published Works:</u>
- *The Forgettable Marriage of Lina and Joe*
- *Sally and Billy in Babyland*

<u>Social Media:</u>
Website: mickeyhadick.com

Dewi Hargreaves

Dewi is a fantasy writer who spends much of his time writing outside, wiping raindrops off his laptop screen. His short story "Maccabeus" won second place in Grindstone Literary's Open Prose Competition 2017, and he used to write those top 10 lists you run into on the internet.

You can find out more about his fantasy short story collection, *The Shield Road*, on his website linked below.

<u>Published Works:</u>
- *The Shield Road*

<u>Social Media</u>:
Twitter: @Dewiwrites
Website: dewihargreaves.com

A.R.K. Horton

A.R.K. grew up in a house wedged between a swamp and a graveyard. There she let herself get lost in fairytales, folktalkes, and myths and imagined how she would rewrite them all. From there, her writing influences have expanded to fantasy, science fiction, horror, and historical novels.

She is the author of *The Telverin Trilogy*, a feminist fantasy series about a war started by the pawns of prophecy in a far away world. The final book in the series publishes Summer 2021. All of her works are on Amazon and beyond. Learn more by visiting her website.

Published Works:
- *The Telverin Trilogy*
- "The Terror of Peace" and "Crazy Little Thing" in *Under New Suns (Tales from the Year Between, volume 2)*

Social Media:
Twitter: @arkhorton
Facebook: facebook.com/arkhorton
Website: arkhorton.com

Debbie Iancu-Haddad

Debbie is currently querying a couple of YA SFF novels. Participating in five different anthologies, writing vss on Twitter and buying way too much stuff on Aliexpress. Staff member at Skullgate Media.

For my day job I give lectures on humor and serve as a personal chauffeur for my two teenagers. Residing in Meitar, Israel.

<u>Published Works:</u>
- "Devastation Song" and "Speechless" in *Achten Tan: Land of Dust and Bone (Tales from the Year Between, volume 1)*
- "The Trouble with Glub" in *Under New Suns (Tales from the Year Between, volume 2)*
- "Crash Course" and "Dead City" in *The New Normal: A Zombie Anthology*
- "Cocoa Weather" in *Winter Wonders* (Forthcoming)

<u>Social Media:</u>
Twitter: @debbieiancu
Website: debbieiancu.com

Mara Lynn Johnstone

Mara grew up in a magical-looking forest. The top floor of the house was built first, as a proper fairytale home should be. She split her time between climbing trees, drawing fantastical things, reading books, and writing her own. Always interested in fiction, she went on to get a Master's Degree in creative writing, to see many of her short stories published, and to self-publish two books. She can be found up trees, in bookstores, lost in thought, and on various social media.

Published Works:
Fantasy Novel:
- *Sweeping Changes*

Sci-Fi Anthology (with 27 other writers):
- *We're the Weird Aliens*

Short Stories in Anthologies run by others:
- "Cold Space" in *Untold Stories*
- "Dragons in My Woods" in *Sonoma*
- "Barefoot in the Sky" in *No Contest*
- "CurseBot 9000" and "Pieces of Sky" in *Redemption*
- "The Highest Priority" in *Endeavors*
- "Who I Was" in *Sunrise Sunset*

Social Media:
Twitter: twitter.com/MarlynnOfMany
Tumblr: marlynnofmany.tumblr.com
Facebook: facebook.com/AuthorMara
Website: MaraLynnJohnstone.com

Anna Klapdor

Anna is an independent artist and storyteller, and a big SciFi/Fantasy nerd. After working as a performance artist, stage director and chorist for over a decade, she has become a full-time writer and published her debut novel, the scifi thriller *The Hand That Feeds*, in April 2021. She still writes for theater, mainly for her co-founded collective Anna Kpok, dabbles in game design, and tries to broaden her online platform despite the fact that she hates interacting with people. She also writes non-fiction about feminist topics, her autism, and mental health. She lives with her cyborgian family in the Ruhr Region of Germany and likes to watch the wind in the trees.

<u>Published Works</u>:
- *The Hand That Feeds eBook*
- Not a Number (short story)

<u>Social Media</u>:
Twitter: @AnnaKlapdor
Instagram: @anna_klapdor
Facebook: facebook.com/annaklapdorwriter
Linktree: linktr.ee/annaklapdorwriter

D.S. Levey

D.S. has been a retail employee his entire adult life. However, he's always had a passion for writing. While he has many different writing projects in the works, this story marks his official debut into the literary world. Be on the lookout for upcoming material of horror, historical fiction, and poetry in various publications.

Peter J Linton

Peter is making his debut as a fiction author, and has been a personal and academic essayist, and letter writer since 2010. In September 2018, he was awarded his Master's degree in Humanities from the University of Colorado, Denver. Other more current projects include editing the select anecdotes from his grandmother Edith and completing an original fantasy novel series. Follow and support his ideas on life through his social media links.

Social Media:
Link Tree: linktr.ee/Peter_Linton

Pan D. MacCauley

Pan is the author of Splatter and the Burnt Yam. They enjoy pandas and pancakes and used to find pandemics fascinating in theory until they had to live through one.

<u>Published Works:</u>
- *Splatter and the Burnt Yam* (found on website)

<u>Social Media</u>:
Twitter: @maccauley_d
Website: pandmaccauley.com

Nikki Mitchell

Nikki is a writer, editor, and high school English teacher who happily spends her life traipsing through fantasy worlds. She began writing at the early age of five, but it was not until she discovered *The Wheel of Time* series by Robert Jordan that she truly found her passion in words. When not writing or lesson planning, Nikki is busy bookstagramming, hiking with her two German Shepherds, or playing D&D and board games.

Published Works:
- "Dreameaters" in *Beneath the Twin Suns: An Anthology*
- "How to Survive the Zombie Apocalypse" in *The New Normal: A Zombie Anthology*
- "Ascension" in *Star Crossed: An Anthology of Romantic Science Fiction*

Social Media:
Twitter: @TheBookDrag0n
Instagram: @TheBookDrag0n
Facebook: The Book Dragon
BookBlog: thebookdragon.blog

Chapel Orahamm

Thornton is an Asian Art and Asian History Academic.
Writing under the pen name Chapel Orahamm for their
fictional material, they enjoy exploring science fiction and
fantasy worlds through the eyes of their characters. Living
out in the middle ground between the Southwest and the
South, they enjoy writing Slipstream Romance and keeping
a running blog review on anime, manga, video games, and
books.

Published Works:
- *The Kavordian Library*
  - *Fyskar*
  - *Subject15*
  - *Polaris Skies*
  - *Subgalaxia*
- **The Gods of Fire**
  - *The Fire in My Blood*
- *Achten Tan: Land of Dust and Bone, Tales from the Year
  Between Volume 1*
  - "Dust Motes"
  - "Scattering"
- **"Kiss"** in *Beneath the Twin Suns: An Anthology*
- **"The Next Tower"** in *The New Normal: A Zombie
  Anthology*

Social Media:
Twitter: @ChapelOrahamm
website: kavordianlibrary.com

Sarah Parker

Sarah is currently submitting a couple of short pieces and wrangling a longer WIP into submission. Contributor to five different 2020 publications. Writing vss on Twitter, and returning way too much stuff to draft form. Guest editor at Skullgate Media.

For my day job I dabble, as I do in my writing. Former public school teacher and college instructor. Now serving as a direct support provider for individuals with disabilities, while advocating for community literacy and neurodivergent learning via conferences and workshops.

Residing in CNY. She's fond of wordplay and lit words. Her ambitions are lofty, like ideas tend to be...

Published Works:
Stories in Anthologies:
- *Achten Tan: Land of Dust and Bone (Tales From the Year Between, volume 1)*
- *Under New Suns (Tales From the Year Between, volume 2)*
- *The New Normal: A Zombie Anthology Ed. Nikki Mitchell*
- *Gestalt Media Best of 2020 Short Story Collection*
- **Raven and Drake Once Upon a Drabble and Summer Horrors** (forthcoming)

Poetry:
- *Summation52 Blog*
- *Ayaskala Literary Magazine*
- *Adirondack Center for Writing*
- *Poetry in 13 Vol. 2*
- *TAB: Journal of Poetry and Poetics V2.10*

Academic Chapters:
- *Writing as a Way of Staying Human in a Time that Isn't, Ed. Nate Mickelson*

- *Gen X at Middle Age in Popular Culture, Ed. Pamela Hollander*

<u>Social Media:</u>
Twitter: @isparkit
Facebook: Sparks Writes
Website: sparknsolution.wordpress.com/

A. Poland

A. is a romcom writer from Ireland who delights in telling stories that make you fall in love with the characters and give you that *squee* feeling in your chest. They're also fuelled by a worrying tea addiction (with a tattoo to prove it.)

Three words she would use to describe her writing are: funky, silly, and spicy. Which, coincidentally, is also their dancing style.

When they're not daydreaming of the next meet-cute, A. works as a video producer and a full-time dog mom to her pride and joy, Gizmo.

A. has a number of works in development and slated for publication, all of which will be posted about rigorously on their social media channels.

<u>Social Media</u>:
Email (public address): disasterbiwrites@gmail.com
Twitter: @disasterbiwrite
Website: disasterbiwrites.com

C. Rathbone

Craig is an idealistic rookie in the world of writing fiction, having started out as a video game reviewer and blogger. Based in the rural Northwest of England, he enjoys all things games, movies and books, and hosts the anarchic Shart Select podcast.

<u>Social Media:</u>
Website: winst0lfportal.blog
Twitter: @winstolf

David Simon

David is an ad agency creative director by day, and a writer and illustrator the rest of the time when he's not sleeping. He writes for both adults and kids. One of his picture book manuscripts was the grand prize winner in the 2000 Writer's Digest Competition. His work has also appeared in everyone's favorite dentist office magazine, Highlights for Children.

Published Works:
Children's Ebook:
- *Trapped In Lunch Lady Land*

Stories in Collections:
- *Nasty Snips*
- *Shopping List 3: 21 Tales of Terror!*
- *Outsider*s (forthcoming anthology)

Story on Free Fiction Website:
- *Red Wings*

Social Media:
Twitter: @WritesDraws
Website: davewritesanddraws.com
Redbubble: redbubble.com/people/fantasm/shop?asc=u&ref=account-nav-dropdown

Sean Southerland-Kirby

Sean, legend says, owes his twisted sense of humour and love of horror to being found in a graveyard as a baby. In reality it was inherited from his dad's love of Stephen King. Previously an actor and musician, he started painting, sculpting and writing as therapy for a brain injury. However, now recovered he has found a genuine love for creativity. He now spends his time teaching Maths and English, creating art, filming YouTube videos and writing mostly horror. Now relocated from London to north Wales with his husband, cat and dog, he is looking forward to writing much more.

Published Works:
- *Horrible Rhymes for Terrible People*
- *Tales from the Flesh Oracle*

Social Media:
Twitter : @unclefrogface
Instagram : @unclefrogface
Goodreads: :
goodreads.com/author/show/19484848.Sean_Southerland_Kirby
YouTube: YouTube.com/c/UncleFrogface

C.D. Storiz

C.D. is a teacher by day, writer at night or whenever she needs to escape. She is a member of the skullgatemedia.com team where she helps to slay em dashes and has some of her work published. She also has work published through various other outlets. You can follow her on Twitter or at her website where she posts her writing and rants about her cat.

Published Works:
- *Achten Tan: Land of Dust and Bones*
- *Loathsome Voyages*
- *Under New Suns*
- *Best of 2020*

Social Media:
Twitter: @LeChatGris3
Website: cdstoriz.com

Imelda Taylor

Imelda was a former English Tutor, play worker and science presenter before becoming a full-time mother and writer.

She's fond of creating, inventing and reinventing things that shape her daughters' imagination.

Her ambition is to help support children and adults with literacy through her books. Imelda is actively seeking representation for her picture books.

Published Works:
- *Achten Tan: Land of Dust and Bones*
- *The New Normal: A Zombie Anthology*

Social Media:
Twitter: @lostsheep02
Instagram: @lostsheep.is

G. Craig Vachon

G Craig Vachon is an investor in small companies, and the CEO of ai-r.com, an artificial intelligence startup focused on enabling humans and AI to trust, and continuously learn from each other via a dynamic human-AI orchestration platform. Craig is also the author of *The Knucklehead of Silicon Valley*, a comedic spy technothriller. More details at ClamPies.com

Published Works:

- The Knucklehead of Silicon Valley

Social Media:
Website: Clampies.com

C. VanDyke

Chris is a writer, illustrator, game-designer, and all around raconteur based out of Brooklyn New York. Most recently, he is the founder and president of Skullgate Media, an indie publisher and writing collective. He is self-publishing an 8 episode series of cyberpunk novellas, Post Cards from NeoTokyo, the first two volumes of which (linked below) are available now. He is always taking on more projects than is good for him, so if you suggest teaming up to do an 8-bit retro RPG inspired by one of his books, he'll certainly respond right away.

Published Works:
Post Cards from NeoTokyo:
- *Memory and Desire*
- *Out of the Dead Lands*

Short Stories in Anthologies:
- *Under the Twin Suns: An Anthology*
- *The New Normal: A Zombie Anthology*

Skullgate Books:
- *Achten Tan: Land of Dust and Bones*
- *Under New Suns*
- *Loathsome Voyages*

Translation of Old Norse Saga:
- *The Legend of Ragnar Lothbrok*

Middle Grade Fantasy Series:
- *The Farhome Elf Chronicles* (forthcoming Nov. 2021 from Kindred Ink)

Social Media:
Twitter: @aboutrunning **and** @skullgatemedia
Websites: cvandyke.com **and** skullgatemedia.com **and** yearbetween.com

Alex Woodroe

Alex was raised—possibly by wolves—in Romania, on the outskirts of Transylvania. She found her way into weird, transgressive fiction through a gateway in the woods and made a career out of doing terrible things to words in multiple languages. You can find her stories in a handful of publications, linked below. She has a story upcoming in Green Inferno, a collection of comics and fiction by Tenebrous Press, and is currently editing an anthology of Modern Gothics for the same. Her favourite horror story is "Alice in Wonderland". She is a member of the Horror Writers Association.

Published Works:
Short Stories in Collections:
- *Endless Pictures*
- *Hope Screams Eternal*
- *Bear Creek Gazette*
- *Green Inferno*

Social Media:
Twitter: @AlexWoodroe
Website: alexwoodroe.com

Thank You For Reading

If you are curious about the origin of the tales told here:

1. *Theseus* - Plutarch
2. *The Völsunga Saga*
3. *Dornröschen* – Collected by Jacob & Wilhelm Grimm
4. *Die goldene Gans* – Collected by Jacob & Wilhelm Grimm
5. *Troldens datter* – Collected by Svend Grundtvig
6. *Die Riesen und die Herden Junge; Märchen und Sagen der Bukowinaer und Siebenbürger Armenier,* - Collected by Dr. Heinrich von Wlislocki
7. *Den lille havfrue* – Collected by H.C. Andersen
8. *La Chasse-Galerie* – Honoré Beaugrand */Wilde Jagd* – Collected by Jacob Grimm
9. *Das Bürle* – Collected by Jacob & Wilhelm Grimm
10. *The Most Dangerous Game* – Richard Connell
11. *Hänsel und Grethel* – Collected by Jacob & Wilhelm Grimm
12. *Rotkäppchen* – Collected by Jacob & Wilhelm Grimm
13. *Theogony* lines 270-305 - Hesiod
14. *Historia Regum Britanniae* – Geoffrey of Monmouth

Proceeds from *Heads and Tales: The Other Side of the Story* are donated to The Trevor Project for the first 12 months of publishing.

https://www.thetrevorproject.org/

"Founded in 1998 by the creators of the Academy Award®-winning short film TREVOR, The Trevor Project is the leading national organization providing crisis intervention and suicide prevention services to lesbian, gay, bisexual, transgender, queer & questioning (LGBTQ) young people under 25.

Heads and Tales

CPSIA information can be obtained
at www.ICGtesting.com
Printed in the USA
LVHW040037150721
692767LV00007B/689